SUNSET BEACH

SUNSET BEACH

A SPIRITED LOVE STORY

TRIP PURCELL

RTP

Research Triangle Publishing, Inc.

This novel is a fiction. Any reference to historical events; to real people, living or dead; or to real locales are intended only to give the fiction a sense of reality and authenticity. Names, characters, places, and incidents either are the product of the author's imagination or are used fictitiously, and their resemblance, if any, to real-life counterparts is entirely coincidental.

Published by
Research Triangle Publishing, Inc.
PO Box 1223
Fuquay-Varina, NC 27526

Cover design by Micah Sanger

Library of Congress Catalog Card Number: 96-67868

ISBN 1-884570-47-X

Printed in the United States of America
10 9 8 7 6 5 4 3

FOR JACKIE

ACKNOWLEDGMENTS

MANY THANKS TO MANY for much, especially Ann Rouse, Marti Simmons, Kathy and Gary Davis, Lisa and Sean Naber, Jean and David Hollowell, Shari and Hank Stewart, and Lynda and Keith Stewart. It's nice to have friends and family.

And speaking of friends and family, thanks for everything to my very best friends: Jackie, Skip and Laine.

PROLOGUE

Saturday, August 7

LAURA BABSON QUIETLY OPENED the sliding glass door leading to the cottage's back porch. She was careful not to wake Jacob, her eight-year-old, who rather than sleep in the same room with his ten-year-old sister often chose the den couch near the TV. It was just past six in the morning, the last day of the vacation.

Laura had been up around sunrise — or before — most mornings since coming to Sunset Beach seven weeks earlier. It had been her second trip there. She wondered if it would be her last.

She settled into a rocking chair, coffee mug in hand. As she gazed across the salt marsh separating the small barrier island from the Intracoastal Waterway, she rocked methodically, as if to evenly distribute the caffeine before beginning her morning walk. From the back porch of the Laughing Gull (3 BR, 2 BA, AC, DW, W/D, cable, screened porch, sundeck, dock, excellent views, $625/week in season), she could see, though barely, the one-lane pontoon swing bridge that crossed the waterway and led to the mainland. The bridge—which brought traffic to a halt by opening on the hour for pleasure craft, on demand for commercial vessels—was a nuisance at times, depending on one's perspective. Some wanted to replace it with, of all things, a real bridge. But for many, construction of a towering mass of steel, concrete and asphalt at Sunset was unthinkable.

"It's not a bridge—it's a passageway," Laura would say. "So you have to wait a few extra minutes. Or even thirty. Big deal. It gives you a chance to slow down, clear your head, and get ready for what's next—coming or going."

It was still dark enough for Laura to see the bridge lights. The distinct aroma of the marsh at low tide engulfed the calm humid air. Despite an early morning shower—the seventh day in a row with rain—it would be another sultry summer day on Sunset. But by the time the sun was at its hottest, Laura would have embarked on the three-hour drive to Farmington. Up U.S. 17 to Wilmington, then I-40 and finally the winding country roads that led to home.

It will seem odd to be back, she thought. It occurred to her she had not been away from the small town this long since she and Jay moved there ten years earlier.

She wondered what had changed and then laughed at herself. It took longer than seven weeks for things to change in Farmington, North Carolina. She and her friend Noell—who like Laura was not a native but married one—often joked about erecting signs on either side of town that read: "You are now entering Farmington Standard Time Zone. Please turn your clock back twenty-five years."

But Laura had changed in seven weeks.

Some of the changes were superficial. Her skin had turned several shades darker, the deepest tan she'd ever had. And her hair, brown to an almost brilliant auburn with golden highlights. "You look fine," Jay—the rational one, the one she married seventeen years earlier—had told her when asked. "Of course, you'll probably get skin cancer."

But there were other changes. She had a different look about her even without the sun-induced cosmetics. The look was evident at least to Bonnie, her mother-in-law, whose idea it was to spend seven weeks on Sunset in the first place.

"I do declare, Laura, I think this vacation has been good for you," Bonnie had said last week at dinner. "And the kids, too. They seem to be enjoying it. We just might have to do this again next year. The lady at the agency said we have until next Thursday to be assured of these same weeks. What do you think?"

Laura shrugged. She didn't tell Bonnie she had quit thinking, just started reacting, about six weeks earlier.

She was doing so much without thinking that after finishing her coffee she slipped out the screen door, descended the wooden steps and started walking on Bay Street toward 40th without even realizing it. She noticed the empty mug in her hand and decided to set it on Neal's fence when she passed, hoping she would remember it on the way back from the beach.

After she turned right on 40th, she soon reached the row of cottages that backed up to Mad Inlet on her right. By now she knew the names by heart: Serenity, Tranquillity, Salubrious View, Mauna Kea, Calypso and finally the Bullish Outlook. From the back of any, one could watch the sun descend over water while still keeping an eye on the ocean, not something possible in many beach homes on the East Coast. But Sunset Beach—like the other Brunswick County, North Carolina beaches, on that portion of the Atlantic Ocean called Long Bay—enjoyed an unusual proximity. The beaches faced more south than east. At Sunset Beach, the sun appeared over the Atlantic in the morning but set over Mad Inlet on the western side of the island. It had been while watching a sunset from Neal's back deck some weeks earlier that Laura had fallen. No, not off the deck. But in something—and maybe from something, too, she reasoned.

She reached Neal's cottage. Not his, really, though in some ways it always would be, Laura thought. Someone else held title to it for now—the husband of Neal's ex-wife. "My best friend and hero," Neal called him. "Took her off my hands while asking nothing in return."

It was strange not seeing Neal's old Cutlass convertible parked beneath the cottage, which like the others on the island rested on ten-foot stilts. Even worse was not seeing him sitting on the railing of the long wooden walkway on the 40th Street beach access. For many of the mornings over the past seven weeks, he had been waiting there for her.

"Good morning, Starshine," was his standard greeting, generally delivered with great enthusiasm. She once asked him why he called her that. He merely shrugged and said, "Just seems to fit."

Together they would walk the beach. In retrospect, she would decide, it was the walks she most liked — just walking and talking. Sometimes they headed east, past the fishing pier and all the way to Tubbs Inlet, which separates Sunset from Ocean Isle Beach. But most days they would go west. That was the direction Laura went.

She had checked the tide chart, as had become her habit. Low had been at 5:39 A.M. The hard-packed sand near the surf was nearly dry. She wore nylon shorts over a two-piece bathing suit. The top was strapless. Laura avoided tan lines when possible.

"I know a few beaches in the Caribbean where they've found a cure for tan lines," Neal had told her. "Maybe we'll go one day."

But no, they wouldn't, Laura thought.

Twenty minutes later she reached the narrow inlet between Sunset and Bird Island, the southernmost barrier island in North Carolina, which lay partially in South Carolina. Undeveloped and uninhabited — at least for now — Bird Island was a pristine playground for pelicans, herons, egrets, seagulls and osprey as well as the home of some mystical being known only as Kindred Spirit. No one had ever seen the Spirit. Many had felt it. For some it embodied the mile-long island, was its conscience, its guardian. It even had its own mailbox, located atop a dune on the state line beside a driftwood bench. Inside the mailbox were steno pads on which visitors wrote to Kindred Spirit, telling it things they perhaps wouldn't tell even a close friend or relative.

With the tide out, Mad Inlet was less than a foot deep in most places and not more than thirty feet wide. Laura waded through, the salt water bathing the sand from her bare feet. She walked about fifty yards and sat on the beach, facing the ocean. The sun was beginning to appear, its beams having found a path through the lingering clouds.

She had a picture of herself in almost this very spot, this very pose. Neal had taken it last week with her camera. The one-hour photo shop in Shallotte processed the film, double prints. Laura generally deplored pictures of herself. But she liked this particular one—though the photographer had failed to hold the camera perfectly straight. The early morning sunlight cast a warm glow on her tanned skin, blending nicely with the beige sand. The wind blew her hair just right. She sat with her knees under her chin, arms wrapped in front. Laura was looking in the direction of the camera but not at it. Instead she seemed to look through the lens, the film and the eye of the photographer.

Confident, content, hopeful.

What was it? she wondered. Love? Lust? Lack of complete sensibility and common decency? She knew, but it hardly mattered now. For at this particular moment, she felt beyond analysis, even beyond emotions. Over the past seven weeks she had dealt with them all, growing weary of the ride. She had laughed a lot, cried some and even prayed a time or two. And finally, just three days ago, she made the long trek to the mailbox on Bird Island and had the final word on it with Kindred Spirit.

So on this morning she just sat and looked. The ocean, the sand, the gulls, the sea oats. She wondered why she couldn't just stay in that spot, right there, forever. She knew there were countless reasons why but at the time couldn't—wouldn't— think of any.

Laura studied a V-formation of pelicans on breakfast patrol. My last walk on the beach for the summer, she thought. If the kids really wanted to go later in the morning, Jay would have to take them. To her left, the sunlight glistened across a gray flat surf. She could see the silhouette of an old couple heading down the beach. The man was wearing long pants rolled to the knees, his hands in his pockets, his companion holding her hands together behind her back. Ahead a shirtless young man was jogging, earphone cords bouncing off his chest and shoulders. To his left a young woman walked briskly with her dog, a yellow lab. Several gulls came near, hovering in hope Laura might offer food. Seeing none, they quickly glided away.

A minute later, she stood up and started back across the inlet. There were suitcases to pack. Carpets to vacuum. Cars to load. And, as always, choices to make.

Twenty minutes later, she reached the wooden walkway and started up the steps toward the street. She twice considered turning for another look at the beach but didn't.

WEEK ONE

CHAPTER ONE

Saturday, June 19

IT'S HOTTER'N FORTY-SEVEN HELLS down here," Jay Babson, MD, said as he trudged up the wooden steps leading to the front porch of the Laughing Gull for what seemed to him the forty-seventh time. He carried the last of the luggage from his wife's Chevy Suburban, his mother's Buick LeSabre and his Mazda 929.

Meagan, his daughter, already had changed into a swimsuit, surfed the cable channels twice and whined at least three times, "Mom, when are we gonna go to the beach?"

"We're at the beach, Meagan," Jay said. "This is it. Seven weeks of packing, unpacking, sunburns, spending money and generally worrying the crap out of each other. Better you guys than me. And that damn bridge. I thought we'd never get across. Don't these people pay taxes down here?"

"My, my, Jay, aren't you the happy beach bum," replied Bonnie Babson, the woman who brought him into the world thirty-nine years earlier and down to Sunset Beach on a beautiful but sweltering Saturday. "It's that 'damn bridge,' as you call it, that just makes Sunset."

"Makes it a pain in my butt," he said. "If that bridge goes out and I need to get back for an emergency—"

"Jay, will you please take a chill!" Laura yelled from the back bedroom on the left side of the cottage. "Tell Meagan to put her clothes away . . . neatly. And where is Jacob?"

"Visiting the facilities," Meagan said. "Can I go roller-bladin' now?"

"My god, that boy can take a dump anywhere," Jay said. "I haven't been here thirty minutes and already I'm consti-pated."

"You're not constipated, Jay, just anal retentive," Laura said. "And no, Meagan, not yet. Explain to your father how to hook up the VCR. I've almost got the bedrooms straight."

One thing about Laura, Jay thought, she knew how to put things in their place, including some people when the occa-sion called for it. But she could never get the best of the good doctor, who always knew how to treat the wife.

No more than thirty minutes later, it was done. The Babson brigade had laid claim to the Laughing Gull, home the next seven weeks for all but Jay, who promised to visit nearly ev-ery weekend and spend at least two full weeks. As usual, he had lied.

"I do love this back porch," Bonnie told Laura. "I plan to rock until I'm seasick."

Bonnie had visited the cottage two years earlier with her cousin Louise, whose son, a developer in Cary, owned it. It was the fifth on the right on Bay Street and one of about six hundred homes on the three-mile-long, one-mile-wide island. The summer before, Bonnie had treated Laura and the chil-dren to two weeks at the cottage. This summer it had gotten out of hand. At first it was going to be four weeks and then went to six and finally seven when Louise's daughter-in-law called, said they had a cancellation the first week in August and would throw in that week for free — which was good, Laura rationalized, since the children had a week of church camp in July and this way they would still have six weeks at the beach.

Though seven weeks away from home did seem like a lot, Laura didn't argue. Friends and other family could come to visit during the summer. After all, Bonnie was paying, the kids loved the beach and it wasn't like they would really miss Jay.

"It'll be just like at home," she told Meagan. "We'll never see your father."

The summer before, Jay had planned to spend both weekends at Sunset and one full week. He ended up staying one night the first weekend and didn't show until Thursday night the second week, which ended on Saturday. "Just too much going on," he had claimed. "I think half the damn town is sick."

The Laughing Gull was not a short distance from the beach, just over a half mile away. But the back porch offered an unencumbered view of the marshes and the waterway. And the rent was about a third of that of the oceanfront homes.

Laura did not mind the walk. A sand chair, a decent book, a few light beers and a bag of pretzels were all she needed for a day on the beach.

But the kids' beach arsenal was nearly endless — including boogie boards. So she usually drove, hoping to land one of the precious spaces at the parking area on 40th and West Main streets. If none were available, she'd drop the kids off, drive back to the cottage and walk. It was a hassle at times but always worth it once she got on the beach.

Laura had always loved the beach. As a child growing up in Charlotte, she would vacation with her family in Myrtle Beach, just a few miles south of Sunset, in South Carolina. But getting Jay to the beach had always been an ordeal. He didn't like the sand, the taste of the drinking water, the heat, the humidity and so on.

"Just like his father," Bonnie would say with a knowing expression. "But don't tell him I said so. I hate seeing that look on his face."

"It's still low tide," Laura said, studying the tide chart taped to the refrigerator door. "Come on, Jay. Come with us."

"I'll go tomorrow, babe," he said. "But I'll drive you guys down there and pick you up whenever. I'll even go to the grocery store. How 'bout steaks on the grill tonight? Mom and I will take care of everything."

"Can't we go to Sharky's for pizza?" Meagan asked.

"Yeah, Sharky's!" Jacob said, holding his hands above his head to mimic a fin.

"You know I don't like pizza," Jay replied firmly. "Your mother will take you when I'm not here."

Thanks, hon, Laura thought. She wasn't surprised Jay didn't want to go with them to the beach—or out for pizza or anywhere much for that matter. But she didn't argue— they had done enough of that lately.

Ten minutes later they stored the gear in the back of the Suburban. Jay let them off at the 40th Street beach access. It was 4:36 P.M. Low tide had been at 2:12. He'd return at six, he promised, while dialing the hospital from the cellular phone. "Need to check on Mr. Minshew and Miss Pauline."

Laura, Meagan and Jacob started down the narrow sandy path between two oceanfront homes toward the wooden walkway that crossed the last set of sand dunes before the beach. The hike was more than a hundred yards.

Laura had never seen a beach quite like Sunset. But who had? she thought. The oceanfront homes rested well back from the beach, an immense area of sand dunes and sea oats standing guard between the homes and the surf. Not that the ocean ever posed much of a threat at Sunset. Unlike those beaches that constantly battled erosion, the beachfront at Sunset was actually growing. "It grows at about the same rate as your fingernails," a local would later tell her.

As they reached the end of the walkway and began their descent of the final set of steps, Laura quickly realized why she had consented to seven weeks. "It's as gorgeous as I remember," she said to her children, who were already bounding down the steps onto the white sand.

The beach was flat, the high dunes to the rear providing isolation as well as insulation from traffic noise. Once down the steps, only the tops of the houses were visible. No highrise hotels or condos. A beach-lover's beach. The kind of place poems are written about, Laura thought. She would insist Meagan, the family's self-proclaimed poet laureate, write one.

Laura and company staked out a spot to the left of the walkway and headed for the surf. Jacob ran a zigzag course through the tidal pools. Meagan was much more restrained and dignified, blowing it only by nonchalantly tugging her bathing suit out of her crack. They walked into the calm surf. Thirty yards out and the water was only knee deep—an ideal saltwater playground. Even at high tide it usually was calm. Surfboards were a rare sight at Sunset.

To their left, out beyond the end of the island's only fishing pier, a catamaran zipped across the ocean, a slight southwest wind catching the blue, yellow and orange sails. Two shrimp boats cruised the ocean, heading back to Little River Inlet with the day's catch.

Meagan and Jacob soon opted for the boogie boards, while Laura retired to her sand chair. She situated it east-to-west, facing the sun. She opened the small cooler and removed a Bud Light.

"Cheers to me," she said, cracking the can and taking a long sip, which was more like a gulp. A beer, a beach and a book—a trashy adventure-romance Bonnie had recommended. The heroine ruled a vast broadcasting empire. Wealth, fame, power and, of course, much misery spawned by a series of foiled relationships and chronicled in great detail for more than five hundred pages. Laura vowed to find another book. She could take a mindless read on occasion, but the sex scenes weren't even sexy in this one. A good courtroom drama was more to her liking.

It wasn't until she sat down she realized how tired she was. The packing had started early in the week, the planning weeks earlier. The kids had finished school Tuesday, Meagan graduating fifth grade, Jacob third—both, of course, with high honors. The annual awards day at Farmington Elementary produced a bounty of hardware for the Babsons. Jay heard all about it—and then some—that night when he got home at his usual time of nine. He had promised to attend awards day if possible.

"I really wanted to go, but I just couldn't get away," he had said. "We were swamped. It's not like I can arrange for people to get sick at convenient times."

Nevertheless, Laura considered Jay a good father and a good husband. But not really a great father and certainly not a great husband.

"I know I shouldn't complain, and I sometimes feel guilty when I do it," she recently told Noell, the closest thing she had to a best friend. "I guess I have everything you could ask for, or at least expect. But he really needs to get away from that damn office once in a while. It's not like he's the only doctor in eastern North Carolina."

But to many in Farmington he was, just as before him there had been only one: his late father, most often called Doc Babson. Thus when Jay finished his residency and returned home to join the practice of his ailing father, relief swept through the town, home to about 3,500. There was only one other doctor in Farmington, a Korean named Lim Tu. The Babsons knew him to be a wonderful physician. But apart from the blacks and other minorities, Lim—the local rednecks called him Hopsing—didn't have many patients. The few times Jay would close his office, Tu would take his calls. But most whites in Farmington and the surrounding farming communities in the small county of less than 10,000 residents would just suffer until Doc Jr. could see them. Or if it got bad enough, they'd drive twenty-plus miles to the emergency room at one of the hospitals in the surrounding small cities of Greenville, Kinston, Goldsboro or Wilson.

Shutting down his office for even a few hours was an ordeal. As such, Jay would leave Sunset Sunday night and open as usual at eight Monday morning. Just listening to all the messages on the answering machine Sunday night would take nearly an hour.

Since his father's death, Jay talked repeatedly about hiring a young doctor to join his practice. But thus far none had opted for the life of a small-town physician.

"I guess the problem is," Laura once said, "if you ever found one who was dumb enough to come to Farmington, you wouldn't want him."

The one big hope was Ted Parker, a Farmington native who just that month was completing a general practice residency in Lynchburg, Virginia. He was the first graduate of Farmington County High School since Jay to attend medical school. He and his wife, also a local, were considering coming back. Jay and Laura had entertained them a few times in the spring, once at the country club outside Goldsboro. Laura talked incessantly of the joys and simple pleasures of a small-town doctor's wife.

"I felt like a sleazy used-car salesman," she later told Jay.

Tuesday night, after Meagan and Jacob had gone to bed, Laura asked Jay the question he had been dreading for over a week.

"When do you think you'll hear something from Ted? I really hope he takes the offer. Maybe then you could even get away for three weeks this summer."

"I meant to tell you," Jay said. "Ted turned me down."

"When?" Laura demanded, her eyes stinging. "And you didn't even tell me. What happened?"

"He wanted too much money," Jay said. "He'll probably join an ER practice up there. He loves all that trauma stuff. Grew up riding around in an ambulance."

"How much more did he want?" Laura asked.

"I don't know, ten grand or so. Hell, if I paid him that much he'd be making almost as much as I do."

"Jay! Ten thousand dollars. You mean for just ten more he'd come. Jay, when are you going to get another chance like that?"

"Yeah, Laura, but that's money right out of our pocket."

"Look, I'll go back to work. You know I could get a teaching job. The kids are both in school now and we'd have the same hours. Call Ted back. Now. Jay, you're going to wind up killing yourself."

"No, Laura, you worked enough while I was in med school. And it just wouldn't look . . . well, you know, right."

"Wouldn't look right! What's that supposed to mean?" Laura asked, knowing exactly what it meant. The doctor's wife in Farmington simply wasn't supposed to work.

"You've got a job," he said. "You work all the time now just hauling Jacob and Meagan around. Besides, you hated teaching. I'll find somebody and we'll get through this. I've got a few more prospects, one good one for next year."

He was lying and Laura knew it.

"The problem here isn't just money, Jay, and you know it," she said. "The problem is you think you're the only damn doctor who can look after the people in this crappy little town. When are you going to let it go? You're going to look around one day and your kids are going to be grown and . . . shit, I might as well be talking to the moon. Good night!"

They hadn't spoken again until the next night when Jay tried to make up by coming home early with a bottle of Asti Spumante and a solemn promise he would do all he could to find a doctor to join the practice. "I'm just trying to do the best I can for us, our family," he told Laura. "I know I work too much. But I just don't want to do something that doesn't make good economic sense. There's so much uncertainty. Hell, I never know if I'm going to wake up one morning and find out I'm working for the damn federal government. And we're going to have college to pay for soon. But it'll get better . . . soon. I promise."

They made up — to some extent — and even made love for the first time in nearly a month. As was usually the case when they got around to it, the sex was good, though not great.

For Laura, however — on that first afternoon at Sunset — things were about as great as they had been in some time. The late-afternoon sun still had some punch. Her skin felt warm, her senses soothed by a one-beer buzz. She realized she had eaten very little all day when the alcohol went straight to work. She glanced over her shoulder. Meagan and Jacob were actually playing together in the sand, building something resembling a fort. They finally were old enough she didn't feel compelled to keep a constant eye on them.

For the next seven weeks, she promised herself, she was going to set aside the things that so often seemed to nag at her: the kids' homework and teachers, little league softball and baseball, church work, housework, volunteer work. And Jay. She couldn't influence him, let alone control him. Being away from each other would probably be a blessing, she thought. And when Jay did come to the beach on weekends,

Laura speculated, they would go out, just the two of them —
or perhaps with Noell and Jim.

She hoped to go to some of the many beach-music clubs
in the Ocean Drive section of North Myrtle Beach, commonly
called "OD." And there were the scores of restaurants they
planned to try. Bonnie never minded the baby-sitting. Maybe
Jay and I will even sneak out one night and take a tumble in
the sand dunes, she thought.

Laura considered drinking another beer. Just as when she
ate, Laura always thought twice before indulging. Not since
she was fourteen years old had she been overweight. Even
when the children were born she left the hospital weighing
only a few pounds more than when she became pregnant.
And now, with her thirty-ninth birthday less than a month
away, she wasn't about to fold. She went to For Women Only,
a fitness center in Goldsboro, at least three times a week and
in the last month had dropped a few pounds in preparation
for the beach, as if she even needed to.

Laura was tall, nearly five-eight and was quite pleased the
scales had read two pounds less than her ideal weight that
morning. She knew how to keep herself in shape, even if Jay
didn't. Laura estimated he had gained approximately two
pounds for each of their seventeen years of marriage.

"What the heck," Laura said, cracking open another can,
"beer's fat free and I'm at Sunset Beach."

As LAURA SAT AND drank the second beer, Neal Nickelsen saw
her for the first time in nearly twenty years. He didn't recog-
nize her but did think she looked familiar.

"I know I've seen those legs before," he said to himself as he sat on the railing of the wooden walkway looking down at his self-proclaimed domain. Though the beach was fairly crowded for late afternoon, Laura stood out, as if in a spotlight. She wore a pair of gold Ray Bans—her brown shoulder-length hair pulled back in a ponytail—and a bright blue two-piece swimsuit.

He guessed her to be in her early thirties. "My, my. What have we here? Ms. Yup-Mom America, herself. Man, I bet she's making some guy miserable," Neal said to himself.

Neal had never been—as his mother often put it in detailed explanations to inquisitive friends and relatives—lucky at love. He had been quite adept at falling in love over his forty-three years, but it usually didn't take long for things to take a nasty turn.

"I guess the thing is with me," he would later tell Laura, "is that I love women. I mean that. I love 'em. And to be good at this you're supposed to love one woman."

"No, Neal," she would reply, "my guess is that women don't love you. At least not for long."

Neal and three of his golf buddies had just finished eighteen holes at The Pearl, one of the many courses in the area. He was feeling pretty good, especially about that birdie on the last hole. He had knocked it stiff with an eight-iron from a fairway trap 143 yards out and made the five-footer. He and his partner, Larry, had taken their arch-rivals, Fred and Mark, for at least sixty bucks.

The guys were at the cottage across the street at the corner of 40th and West Main, still figuring the bets and arguing this hole or that. Neal never liked that part of the game, even though he usually won money. It was the game of golf he loved and he was good at it—a handicap that ranged from one to three at his home course, Carolina Country Club in Raleigh. Those who knew him usually required Neal to spot a few strokes.

He sat on the railing watching the beach, replaying the key shot—and that look on Mark's fat face. He was sipping his first drink of the day. He rarely drank when he was playing golf, though he often got drunk afterwards. He knew this would be a long night. The guys would hit Myrtle—a steak place and then probably one of the topless clubs. Ten bucks bought a table dance and an up-close, personal examination of the wonders of silicon.

Neal already had tired of it. He was glad it was Saturday. The clubs in Myrtle would close at midnight. But it was a stupid law, he thought. Did a majority of the South Carolina legislature really think if guys got home from a strip club a little early on Saturday night they would be more inclined to go to church Sunday morning and repent? What would you say during the silent prayer: Father, forgive me, for I looked until my eyes crossed? But for tonight it was acceptable in Neal's sight. Maybe they would get back to Sunset at a decent hour in preparation for a nine o'clock tee time at Oyster Bay Sunday morning.

Neal's drink of choice that afternoon was a double—he may have legged it into a triple—Absolut Citron and grapefruit juice. At times he liked to start his beach drinking with a Salty Dog—potato juice makes for a good base, he would say—before switching to beer. As long as he stayed away from the brown stuff, he managed to avoid hangovers. Three ibuprofen and a Pepsi before bedtime, followed by three more in the morning with another Pepsi, and his back and head would be good for at least eighteen holes. The other guys were heading back to Raleigh Sunday afternoon. They had stopped at a Wings and bought their wives and kids tacky T-shirts to present along with stories of how much they missed them during their golfing hiatus.

It was just past six.

"How's it going?" Jay asked casually as he passed Neal on the walkway.

"Great," Neal replied. "And you?"

"Just fine."

Like most eastern North Carolinians, Jay greeted anyone who made even slight eye contact. The folks in Farmington loved him for it.

Jay had managed to find a parking space on Main, right beside the corner cottage—Bullish Outlook—that had been Neal's residence for the past two weeks. Neal had another six weeks to go on a cleverly negotiated sabbatical that had been months in the planning.

"Look, if I find out all you're doing down there for two months is screwin' off, your ass is mine," his editor had warned. "That book needs to be finished by August one and I still expect at least two decent columns a week."

No problem for Neal Nickelsen, featured sports columnist for the Raleigh newspaper, the most widely read daily in eastern North Carolina. He planned at least three columns a week, which he would send by modem from his PC. And maybe a few golf features on some of the new courses in the area. And the book, a collection of his columns, was about

finished, though he hadn't told his boss. He was even tink-
ering with another book or two. But it was his golf game that
interested Neal most. I'll be scratch, at least, by the end of
the summer, he thought, and then if I can just keep my back
in one piece over the next eight years. . . .

He knew his chances of making the PGA Senior Tour
were, at best, remote. Every decent forty-something golfer
had that dream. "But what would I be if I didn't even try?"
he'd say to himself. "I'm tired of writing about other people.
I want someone to write about me."

Neal noticed Jay helping Laura pack up. So that's the poor
slob. "How does a damn guy like that get such a good-looking wife?" he mumbled. "I guess he's rich and she's a bitch."

The Babsons soon passed Neal on the walkway.

"Have a good one," Jay said.

"And you folks also," Neal replied, glad Laura was bringing up the rear of the recessional. He watched her all the way
to the street. She had an athletic gait, long legs that took grace-
ful yet meaningful strides. Over the two-piece she wore a
white sleeveless cotton blouse, unbuttoned but tied at the
waist. She had put on one of Jay's Carolina Tar Heel hats,
her ponytail threaded through the opening in the back.

"Whoa," Neal said as he hopped off the railing. "Now
that's what I like about the South."

Once Laura was out of sight, he took a moment to admire
the ocean again. He glanced to the right toward Bird Island.
He'd spent a lot of time on Sunset but had never made the
mile-long walk to the secluded beach.

"Maybe I'll get over and practice some sand shots," he told
himself. But for now it was time for a cold beer.

Chapter Two

Tuesday, June 22

By early afternoon of their fourth day on Sunset, Laura decided Meagan and Jacob needed a break from the sun. Though Laura had applied and re-applied the sunscreen, Jacob appeared burned slightly. He and Meagan got into a tiff just as boredom was beginning to set in on Laura.

"That's it," she said. "Come on, kids. Pack it up."

Later that week she would take them to the water park in Myrtle Beach, she decided. She would love to wait until the weekend and go with Jay. But it would be more crowded and he'd squawk about it anyway.

They loaded the Suburban, which was parallel-parked right beside the Bullish Outlook. She had taken note of the spacious modern house. It looked deserted, though she had seen an old yellow convertible parked underneath in the mornings. It was ninety-one degrees on Sunset. As had been the case for the last two days, there was a slight chance of afternoon thunderstorms. But thus far it had been dry.

Laura decided to make the short drive into Calabash and visit a few shops. She had meant to buy a gift before she left home for the Murray girl in their church who was getting married the following weekend. And she thought she might hit the beachwear boutique she had liked so much the summer before. She'd bought four new swimsuits that spring. But when you were going to wear a bathing suit practically every day for seven weeks, another one wouldn't hurt.

Bonnie consented to keeping the kids. After all, it was the first time Laura had been away from them except for the early mornings when she would get her daily exercise with a brisk walk on the beach.

Laura showered and dressed in a pair of white denim shorts and a light blue denim sleeveless shirt that buttoned up the front. At first she tucked it in, but then decided to pull it out and wear it tied at the waist. Hey, I'm not forty yet and I'm not going to dress like I am, she thought.

She checked herself carefully in the mirror. Her stomach was still flat. Just like my chest, she thought. She even applied a bit of makeup and some perfume. Laura always felt under some pressure to try to look her best, even when she went to the grocery store. She knew it was self-imposed. And Jay didn't help either. She often would ask him after she got ready to go out, "How do I look?"

"Fine," he always would answer. Never good, beautiful, great, terrific or ravishing. Always just fine.

The stoplight was green for mainland-bound traffic when Laura reached the bridge. She slowly drove the big Suburban over the wooden planks, turning left onto Highway 179 at the intersection.

Neal's was the first car at the light for island-bound traffic. He saw Laura as she passed. It had been that afternoon, on the practice tee at Sea Trail, that he thought he remembered who she was.

"Laura Regan," he said right in the middle of his swing. "I know damn well that's her." He almost shanked the shot but delighted in having solved the mystery that had been running through his head since Saturday afternoon.

As the bridge light turned green, Neal floored his prized 1968 Olds Cutlass convertible. But rather than crossing the bridge, he did a U-turn. He saw the white Suburban turn left onto the road to Calabash. How could you miss it? he thought. The woman's driving a semi.

Neal was a half-mile down the road when he asked himself why he was following her. He didn't know. He just drove — past the stylish homes that overlooked the waterway and finally around the bend in the road.

He had seen Laura a few times since Saturday. After golf on Sunday he went to the beach walkway and saw her digging in the sand with the two children. Waldo, as he called Jay, wasn't around. He'd also seen her Tuesday morning, just after seven. Neal had gotten up to take a leak, a hit of Pepsi and some ibuprofen. He'd stayed up late the night before writing. Or at least trying to write. But a six-pack had gotten in the way and he kept hitting all the wrong keys. Then a horror movie came on HBO and — like a fool, he thought — he sat there and watched it. It was nearly three when he staggered to bed. He awoke with a full bladder, a dry mouth and a headache. Got to find another hobby other than drinking, he thought. The sun was just beginning to peak through the glass doors leading to the deck on the ocean side of the house. Neal went to the window to close the blinds when he saw

Laura at the access, returning from the beach. She was alone. She had on a black tank suit, a pair of gray knit shorts over it. She walked straight past the Bullish Outlook, up 40th Street. Neal stumbled to the other side of the house, bumping his shin on an end table. He watched her until she turned left on Bay Street—or, he wondered, was it Inlet?

It took him over an hour to get back to sleep. The book. A column due by four that afternoon. That stupid double bogey on sixteen Monday at Oyster Bay. He couldn't believe he had blocked that swing so badly. Hit it right in the damn water. And now her. Some vacation.

Neal followed Laura across the bridge over Calabash Creek and into the small town that billed itself as the seafood capital of the world. Calabash was home to more than forty seafood restaurants and numerous gift and beach shops.

Laura drove past Callahan's, the big gift and golf shop on the left, eventually turning left into a bank parking lot. Neal drove past and parked at a convenience store across the street. Laura got out of the Suburban, went to the automated teller machine and withdrew a hundred dollars from Jay's checking account. She knew she'd get in trouble for it. She was to use his account for emergencies only. She always hoped he wouldn't notice—he always did. But Laura had decided not to use any of her "allowance" to buy a wedding present for somebody she hardly knew.

She turned left out of the bank lot and went to a small shopping center on the right. She headed straight for the beachwear boutique. Neal soon pulled into the parking lot. He watched her walk into the store. He debated going in. Bump into her and ask her if she's Laura Regan, he thought.

But what if she wasn't? He'd feel stupid. The store looked fairly crowded, hardly a place to carry on much of a conversation. Finally he decided to go in. Laura had picked out three suits and was entering a dressing room at the rear of the store when Neal spotted her. He casually walked through the displays of T-shirts, shorts and swimsuits. He glanced at her dressing room. The bottom of the door was nearly two feet off the floor. He could see her feet. She kicked off her flip-flops. Seconds later Neal saw the white denim shorts hit the floor around her ankles. Laura stepped out and slid them with one foot to the back of the dressing room.

I'm gonna have a stroke, Neal thought just as a teenage clerk asked him, "Can I help you find something, sir?" A respirator, he thought. "No, thanks. Just looking."

In a minute Laura emerged, wearing a red two-piece. She wanted to check the fit in the three-way mirror. "Don't worry, it's perfect," Neal said under his breath.

When Laura went back into the dressing room, Neal suddenly chuckled at himself. This is crazy, he thought. I'm stalking this woman. What a sicko.

He left the store and walked to his car. He then turned and took note of the license plate on the Suburban. He scribbled the letters and numbers down on a scrap of paper.

Neal drove back to the Bullish Outlook. It was almost four-thirty. He wanted a Salty Dog but had promised himself not to drink before five. What a dumb thing to promise yourself at the beach, he thought. After all, he had knocked out the column by eleven that morning. A not-so-good piece on the Atlanta Braves' early season slump. He mixed the drink and called the newspaper's newsroom and asked to speak to

Charley O'Briant, one of the crime reporters, who sometimes played golf with Neal. He could hit it a mile, in most any direction. He also tended to be a bit on the eccentric side at times. But in my business, Neal thought, who isn't?

"Charley, need a favor," Neal said.

"I don't know, man. I'm having a bad tune day."

"Bad tune day? What in the hell does that mean?"

"You know how it is, Neal, when you get this tune running around your head and you can't get it out and in this case it's a particularly bad tune. I just can't shake it."

"Oh, yeah. Well, I'm sure you'll shake it eventually."

"Don't you even want to know what tune it is?"

"Sure, Charley. Name it."

"In one note I could name it. It's the theme song from *Petticoat Junction*. And the thing is I hated that show. And I hate the theme song even worse."

"I'm sorry. But look, I really need a favor here."

"Only if you'll sing something."

"Sing something?"

"Yeah, like another TV theme song. Maybe if I hear you sing it I'll get this one out of my head. Try *Gilligan's Island*. That's not such a bad tune."

"Sorry, Charley, but I don't remember it."

"Sure you do. About the castaways. Come on."

Why does he do crap like this to me, Neal thought as he sang a few bars. He really needed this favor.

"That did it," Charley finally said. "Thanks."

"Now about this favor: If I give you a license plate number, can't you call over to DMV or somewhere and find out whose car it is?"

"Not really supposed to, I guess, but we do it from time to time."

"North Carolina tags, DDX-48. Can you do it today?"

"No problem, Skipper. Give me your number and Little Buddy here will be right back. Got a hot scoop going down there?"

"I don't know. It's a long story. Here. Let me give you the number."

Within ten minutes Charley had called back.

"That one is co-owned by a Jacob Willard Babson Jr. and a Laura Regan Babson. It's a Farmington address, wherever the hell that is," Charley said. "Does this mean I get an invitation to the beach?"

"Sure. We'll play Tidewater. It's great."

"Now those of us in the fourth estate do get complimentary green fees down there, don't we?"

"Yeah, but I always pay," Neal joked.

"Right."

"Come this weekend if you like. Lou will be here."

"Got to work. But I'll hold you to this one. Can we go to one of those titty palaces?"

"Sure, Chuck. I'll buy you a table dance."

Neal hung up and went onto the screened-in porch at the rear of the house, overlooking Mad Inlet. The roof of the porch was a sun deck. Great view of the sunset but a hot spot until very late in the afternoon. He gulped the Salty Dog. He was sweating. He went inside and changed into the only bathing suit he had, a blue nylon that went nearly to his knees. It had a wide, lime-green stripe down one leg. He put on a T-shirt and a pair of old Top-Siders.

Neal left his cottage, walked across the street to the beach access and started toward the ocean. He kicked off his shoes and dropped the T-shirt in the sand beside his shoes. And then he did something he hadn't done in many summers, something he enjoyed so much as a child the few times his mother—and once even his father—brought him and his brother to the beach. He wasn't sure why, except he just felt like it.

He went swimming in the Atlantic Ocean.

Chapter Three

Thursday, June 24

Neal began his watch right around sunrise. He considered it a long shot. But after having seen her return from a walk early Tuesday morning, it was worth a try. He sat in a wooden rocker on the deck overlooking the beach access. He was just about to doze off when he saw her. She didn't look his way, but he pretended to read a newspaper just in case.

It was a cloudy morning, remnants of a minor storm front that passed through during the night still lingering.

Neal watched Laura out of the corner of his eye until she reached the wooden walkway. He got up and walked down the steps to the driveway. Laura had almost reached the beach. He started down the path toward the steps. By the time he could see the beach, Laura was walking toward Bird Island.

Should he follow? No. Walk to the pier, turn around and meet her on the way back. He wondered how far she would walk. He knew it was nearly low tide. Neal had heard it was an easy walk through the inlet to Bird Island at low tide. Would she walk that far?

This is silly, he thought. But he really wanted to see her — see if she remembered him. He was sure she wouldn't. But what if she did? Did she know he had become so famous? Did she see his picture in the newspaper with his column — Neal guessed at least some people in Farmington got the Raleigh paper — and say to her friends, "I knew this guy. He used to ask me out. But I always turned him down."

And then did she say, "What a fool I was." Or instead, "He was a dweeb."

He knew she was married — or at least assumed she was — to Jacob Willard Babson Jr. But he hadn't seen wide Willard since Saturday.

Several hundred yards down the beach, Laura walked at a steady pace toward Bird Island. Others headed in that direction, too, the shallow inlet beckoning. Laura looked forward to the weekend. Jay would come late Friday night, bringing Noell and her husband, Jim. Noell was one of only two attorneys in Farmington. She and Laura had much in common, it seemed, though they were very different. The main bond was a general disdain for some of Farmington's provincial ways. But like Laura, Noell had to keep it low key — Jim Beaman worked in his father's insurance agency.

"These guys around here have some weird thing about their fathers," Noell often said.

"Yeah, but doesn't everyone," Laura would reply.

Jim and Noell had met in college, at Campbell University. Jim was a sixth-year undergrad, finally graduating in seven, and Noell was in her second year of law school. Though she and Jim now were approaching their late thirties, they didn't have children.

Plumbing problems, Noell called them. "But once Jim found out it was my fault, that he wasn't 'shooting blanks,' he was OK with it," she once said. "Like that makes sense."

They often considered adopting. "Or kidnapping your two," Noell would say to Laura. "I'm not sure which of the two people in Farmington would find more acceptable."

Noell went to high school in Fayetteville, an army brat who was born in Germany. She had a smart mouth at times. More and more Laura found herself emulating it.

"Noell is such a neat woman," Laura once said to Jay.

"I don't trust her," he responded. "And she'll talk your damn ears off."

But Jay got along well with Jim. Though he did not attend Carolina, Jim also was a big Tar Heel sports fan. When the two couples went out together, it was not unusual for the guys to sit together up front and talk sports, leaving the back seat for the women. Jim once joked, "This is the low-class way to sit, you know. The middle class sits with husbands and wives together. And the high class with each husband sitting with the other one's wife."

"No way," Noell retorted. "My idea of high class would be for me and Laura to go out with our gigolos and you guys stay at home and dust the blinds or something."

Laura hoped the four of them would go to Ocean Drive or Myrtle Saturday night. It would be too late Friday. They probably wouldn't arrive before midnight, knowing Jay.

She finally reached the inlet and crossed to Bird Island. The water in the inlet felt warm, though the air was a bit cooler than the other mornings that week. Laura wore a T-shirt and shorts over a bathing suit. Soon she turned and went back across to Sunset. Back to the cottage, where she and Bonnie would start breakfast.

She was about halfway to the beach access, looking across the surf at nothing in particular, when she heard a friendly voice bellow, "Good morning!"

It was Neal. "Hi," she replied. He's sure in a good mood, she thought. And then didn't give him another thought.

Neal returned to the Bullish Outlook around three-thirty that afternoon after a match at Sea Trail. He and one of the assistant pros, who had played at Clemson, had taken on a couple of high rollers from Michigan. They should have killed the jerks, but Neal had played terrible. His partner had saved him with a thirty-four on the back. Still they lost forty bucks. At Neal's insistence, he paid off the entire bet.

"I hope you'll give me another chance," he told the young pro. "I don't know where my head was today."

Actually he did know. It was on Bird Island, Sunset Beach, a women's dressing room and the varsity tennis courts at the University of North Carolina at Chapel Hill, where twenty years earlier he had seen Laura for the first time. She was a freshman and played number six in the Tar Heels' varsity lineup. She wasn't the most beautiful girl he had ever seen, but the combination of her petite face, long hair, smooth complexion and athletic body was, well, just about too much.

It was his first year out of journalism school at UNC. He had landed a sportswriting job with the daily in Chapel Hill. It had taken him over two months to get up the nerve to ask Laura for a date.

Neal parked the convertible under the cottage and walked to the beach access. At first he couldn't find her. But then he looked again and saw her in the ocean, helping Jacob with a boogie board. She was wearing the red two-piece. Yes!

Neal walked quickly back to the cottage. He changed into his bathing suit and a T-shirt. He even combed his hair, brushed his teeth and splashed on some after shave. He considered taking a shower, but stuck a deodorant can under each arm instead.

Neal tossed a six-pack into a cooler—the same brand he had seen Laura drinking on the beach the Saturday before. Though he seldom drank light beer—a reg'lar ole St. Louie Red was hard to beat—he had bought a case for her at the grocery store. "A guy's gotta dream," he told himself.

He looked around for a book, settling on a couple of magazines—one on boating, the other an old *New Yorker*. Maybe she'll think I'm an intellectual yachtsman, he thought. He grabbed a sand chair from the storage room under the cottage and headed for the beach.

Laura had set up camp to the right of the walkway, about thirty yards down. She had just come out of the water and was drying off when Neal plopped into his chair, between Laura and the walkway, a few yards behind her. Got her boxed out, he thought.

Neal opened a magazine and stared at the words, glancing occasionally at Laura. After a few minutes, he got up and walked to the surf, washing his feet in the saltwater. He turned to go back to the chair and noticed Laura look in his direction. The children were still in the water. Now! he thought.

"Excuse me," Neal said as he casually approached her. "I may be way off base here, but aren't you Laura Regan?" He was relieved he hadn't said Laura Babson.

"Well, yes, I am," she replied. "Well, used to be, I guess. That was my maiden name." Laura studied Neal with what seemed to him to be suspicion.

"Gosh, I guess you don't remember me, but I'm Neal Nickelsen," he said, crouching in the sand five feet away from her. "I remember when you played tennis at Carolina."

That one stunned Laura.

"Wow. That was a long time ago. Did we know each other?"

"Sort of, I guess," he said. "I was a sportswriter for the Chapel Hill paper your freshman year. I covered some of your matches. We used to talk."

"Oh, sure," Laura said, but the memory was fuzzy.

"I even asked you for a date one time — well, three times actually, but hey, who's counting. Finally you said you were going with some guy or something." Neal felt a sense of pride about getting right to the point.

"Oh, sure, I remember that. And yes, I was going with some guy. In fact, I'm married to him."

"Must have been serious."

Laura laughed. "Yeah, I guess so."

Talking to Neal made Laura feel slightly uncomfortable. Men in Farmington seldom talked to her, except for a few of the old ones. Neal was a good-looking man, she thought. Probably mid-forties. He was over six feet tall — just a tad shy of six-two, he would have told her if she had asked — and in what appeared to be good shape. Nice legs, good tan. His hair, parted on the side, had streaks of gray. But his face had a boyish look. He wore his sunglasses on top of his head. His eyes were a bluish-gray.

"So what brings you to Sunset?" Neal asked.

"Vacation . . . gee, I guess that's obvious," she said. "My mother-in-law actually. She's rented a place down here for seven weeks."

"Nice to have in-laws like that. Isn't it a great beach?"

"Yes, it is. We're enjoying it."

"Hey, I was just getting ready to grab a beer," Neal said. "Got some cold ones in the cooler there. Would you like one?"

Sure, Laura thought but said, "No, thanks. I guess not."

"Oh, come on. You can tell me all about your tennis career. I left the Chapel Hill paper after your freshman year and kind of lost track."

"Not much to tell after that year."

"Hang on. I'll get us a beer."

Laura didn't protest. Neal brought over the cooler and took out two cans.

"I've got a cup if you want one," he said.

"No, the can's fine."

He put the top back on the cooler and sat on it.

"Cheers," he said.

They sat on the beach and talked.

"Blew out this knee the summer after my freshman year," she said, pointing to the side of her left one. "See, I've still got the scar." Neal examined it intently. " I tried it the next season, but just couldn't get it back. Finally gave up. All the better, I guess. School was hard enough without practicing tennis four hours a day."

She gave a quick synopsis of the resulting life. Married Jay the summer after they finished undergraduate school at Chapel Hill. He was premed. They had met at a mixer the second weekend of her freshman year.

Jay went to UNC med school, just like his father. Then to a residency at Bowman-Gray. Laura taught elementary school, first in Chatham County, then in Forsyth. During the final year of his residency, Jay was considering a job in Charlotte, much to Laura's elation. She gave birth to Meagan the March before he finished his residency in June. But instead Jay returned home to Farmington to join his father's practice. The old man suffered a mild stroke and needed help. They were now going on ten years. Jay's father had died six years ago.

Soon they were well into a second beer and a quick Neal bio. Divorced, fourteen years now. A sixteen-year-old daughter who lived with her mother and stepfather but was spending the summer in Europe. Sports columnist for the Raleigh paper. Thought about giving it up many times.

Good sense of humor, Laura thought. Easy to talk to.

"So what brings you to Sunset Beach?" Laura asked, finally feeling relaxed. Maybe it was the beer, she thought.

"That's something I don't tell many people," Neal said, "but I'll make an exception in your case."

"I'm honored."

"You see, I'm the governor of Sunset Beach," he said. "Not many people know that. For the record, thus far only you and a couple of mermaids I met the other night out here."

"I didn't even know Sunset was a state," Laura said, playing along.

"A recent phenomenon. Just happened a couple of nights ago. We were out howling at the moon, called a vote and sure enough we seceded from North Carolina and declared statehood."

"And they elected you governor," she said.

"Close vote, two-one. I voted for one of the mermaids, they both voted for me. The governor's mansion is just across the street there. First house on the left on 40th."

"Oh, I've seen that house. It's very nice."

"I'll be flying the new state flag from the sun deck as soon as I can get one made. You don't sew, do you?"

"Hardly. But tell me something, Governor," Laura said, thinking how Noell might handle this, "are all sportswriters bullshit artists, or are you unique to the species?"

"No, I only babble on like this when I'm in the company of a lovely woman," Neal said, opening a third beer and tipping it in her direction.

"Well, thank you. I'm very flattered. But you still haven't told me what you're doing here. Do you own that house?"

"No. It's sort of in the family — long story," Neal said. "I'm there through July. Working on a book."

"Sounds exciting. I guess this is a great place to write."

"Some very inspiring scenery."

"Well, this has been fun," Laura said, "but I really think I need to round up my bambinos before they fry."

"It is hot. But really, Laura, you look terrific. I mean that. You must be playing a lot of tennis."

"Thanks. But no. I haven't played tennis five times in the past ten years. I don't exactly live in the tennis Mecca of the Carolinas. It's kind of hard to get up for it when the people on the next court are wearing tank tops, cut-off jeans and high-top sneakers."

"No, you don't see that at Wimbledon very often. But I do hear you folks have some good football teams. A couple of state championships?"

"The whole county closes for football games. It's like a religion."

Laura called the children.

"Can I help you with anything?" Neal asked.

"Thanks, but we can get it. We're getting to be experts."

Neal settled back into his chair, staring at a magazine.

"Thanks again for the beer," Laura said as she walked past, arms full.

"Sure. Maybe I'll see you around."

"Yeah, probably so."

Probably so, Neal repeated in his head, glancing over his shoulder to watch her walk up the steps. Probably so.

WHEN LAURA GOT BACK to the Laughing Gull, she studied herself in the mirror for a minute before getting into the shower.

"I can't believe he recognized me," she said to herself. "I can't believe he said I look terrific—good thing I was wearing sunglasses and he couldn't see these crow's feet. Can't believe he asked me for a date and I said no. Three times!"

But she could believe that. Guys asked her out numerous times in college, but she'd always said no. Four years in Chapel Hill and I dated one person, she thought. What kind of hold did Jay have on me then? What was I thinking? Was I thinking?

About ten hours later, around three in the morning, Laura knew what she was thinking. "I am about to roast," she said slowly, kicking off the sheet and getting up. Earlier in the evening, while watching a video with Bonnie and the kids, the cottage had gotten chilly. She had turned up the thermostat, evidently a bit too much.

She walked into the den. The TV hummed, Jacob asleep but, like Laura, sweating. She turned it off and then moved the thermostat to seventy-two. She was wearing one of Jay's T-shirts, which stuck to her back.

Laura poured a small glass of orange juice and decided to go out on the porch for a minute. She'd had a restless night. She'd be glad when Jay got there. She didn't like sleeping by herself. Laura moved to the edge of the porch and looked through the screen. It was quiet, but a slight breeze stirred, cooling her off.

Laura finished the juice, went back inside and placed the glass in the kitchen sink. In her mind she saw the yellow ball scream down the line, just out of her reach. Another went cross court. She pivoted, a bolt of pain shooting through the knee, but she couldn't get a racquet on it.

Why, she wondered, after all these years, would she dream about tennis?

WEEK TWO

CHAPTER FOUR

Saturday, June 26

J AY, JIM AND NOELL had arrived just before midnight Friday. The kids tried to hold out but didn't make it. It had been a busy day. Laura took them to the water park and then finally to Sharky's on Ocean Isle for pizza. She wasn't sure who enjoyed it most but knew she was a contender.

Even Laura had dozed before they arrived. But she awoke when she heard car doors shutting underneath the cottage. They stayed up past two, talking on the porch. Noell had consumed more than her share on the way down. "Where the hell is the head?" were her first words. "And where are my children? I'm sleeping with Jacob."

Jay was in a good mood. He and Jim talked sailboats. Noell and Laura talked talk. "At least they've gotten off football," Noell said. "I heard it for three friggin' hours."

Laura enjoyed sleeping in the same bed with Jay again, though his snoring woke her twice. She even skipped her morning walk.

Bonnie was the first to rise. With company in the house, she did what most decent Southern women would do—

cooked a huge breakfast and made sure she banged enough pots and pans around to wake everyone earlier than they would have preferred.

"If I look at that sausage gravy one more time I'm gonna ralph," Noell—who had knocked back a few Black Russians just before going to bed—whispered to Laura.

During breakfast, they worked on the day's plan. It was obvious Jay and Jim didn't want to spend much time on the beach but were going to be accommodating. Jim would have preferred golf, but Jay was not a golfer.

"Don't have the time or the temperament for it," he'd say.

He had taken up golf during his residency and played fairly regularly when he first moved back to Farmington. But he gave up the game abruptly one Saturday afternoon. He'd never told Laura about it. But she had heard the story, though she had never mentioned it to him.

Jay and three others were on the twelfth hole at Willow Springs, a course in Wilson. He'd been playing lousy. The hole was a 155-yard par three over water. Jay had topped three consecutive balls into the water.

"Excuse me, but I'm hitting one damn more," Jay told the others. "And if I hit this ball in the water, I'm gonna . . ."

"You're gonna what?" demanded Larry Carson, a local gentleman farmer Jay never really liked. "Just what are you going to do, Doc Jr.?"

Jay hated being called Doc Jr. He teed up another ball and said, "I'm going to quit. Forever. I'm gonna throw my goddam bag and clubs in that pond and I'm quitting."

Jay swung his six-iron. He pulled the shot left toward some trees, but it cleared the water easily, only to hit a large pine fifteen yards on the other side and ricochet into the pond. Larry and the others roared.

"Just like it had eyes," Larry said.

Jay was furious. He removed his golf bag from the cart and headed for the water.

"C'mon, Jay, don't do that," Russ Johnston said. "It's just a game."

"But he promised," Larry said loudly. "Do it, Junior."

Jay hurled the bag into the pond and left the three of them without saying a word. He walked across the course toward the clubhouse when the stupidity of the whole thing hit him. No, he would never, ever play golf again—no endeavor that would cause him to lose control like that was worth undertaking. Then the reality of the whole thing hit him: His car keys and wallet were in the golf bag.

He returned to the pond, where Russ already had fished the bag out of two feet of water. They talked Jay into finishing the round and then all laughed about it in the clubhouse afterward.

Jay even said he would not quit. And they all promised not to mention the incident again—to anyone. But by late Sunday just about everyone in town had heard the story in some fashion or the other. One version had Russ jumping in the pond to save Jay from drowning.

"Yeah, tried to drown himself," Larry would recount. "But I wasn't worried. He never could keep his head down on a golf course."

Jay seemed to take all the kidding well, but inside it was a different story. He took his clubs to the county landfill on Wednesday after work.

"I've got a great idea," Jim said, spooning out another serving of Bonnie's scrambled eggs. "Why don't you ladies take our credit cards and go shopping in Myrtle Beach for the day. Jay and I will keep the kids."

"You're kidding," Noell said.

"Damn right I'm kidding."

"I've got a real idea," Noell said. "We are at the beach, right? So why don't we go to the beach."

Jay and Jim could think of a hundred reasons not to but consented. By ten-thirty they were in the sun. The men took the children swimming. Laura and Noell read.

"*In vitro* fertilization," Noell soon said. She was reading an article about it in a magazine. "Jay says it might work."

"You ought to give it a try," Laura said. "You'd make a good mother."

"I was planning on letting you raise it," Noell replied. "Especially if it's a boy."

"Sorry, but I'm out of the diaper-changing business," Laura said.

"Speaking of boys," Noell said, changing the subject. "Why don't we go blow in our husbands' ears and get them to make us a pitcher of Bloody Marys?"

"Yuck," Laura said. "I can't drink in the mornings."

"Yeah, but as slow as they are it'll be late afternoon before they get back."

The women joined the men in the surf while Meagan and Jacob took a break. Laura crept up on Jay, who was standing in about three feet of water. She pounced on his back, wrapping her arms around his neck. He lost his balance and they tumbled into the surf. Laura came up laughing.

"Dammit, Laura," said Jay, coughing up sea water. "You're worse than the children."

"Sorry," she said. "I'll keep my distance from now on."

"Aw, kids, let's not fight," said Noell, always the peacemaker when tempers flared. "I came begging a favor. Bloody Marys. Gotta do something about this hangover."

"Noell, have you ever had your liver examined?" Jay asked seriously.

"No, Doc, but if you get me a Bloody Mary I might let you take me up into those dunes over there and give me a complete physical. You got your tools on you, don't you?"

Laura and Jim laughed. Jay just shook his head. The comment seemed to embarrass him.

"C'mon, Doc," Jim said. "Let's get these wenches a drink. We might end up getting lucky tonight."

The men left. They would have to cross the bridge to the liquor store since Noell had drained the vodka the night before. Then to the Sunset Beach Island Market for some Bloody Mary mix. It didn't take all day, but it would be nearly noon before they got back.

"I swear that woman gets on my nerves sometimes," Jay said to Jim as they waited for the bridge light to change.

"Noell's just that way," Jim said.

"I didn't mean her."

"Oh."

"I mean, it's like she has no concept of reality. I don't know."

"Wish I didn't sometimes," said Jim, not really sure what to say. "Maybe she's worried about turning forty. This summer, right?"

Jay thought a few seconds. "No, next year. She'll be thirty-nine this July. The eighth, I think. Or ninth. Hell, I can't ever remember."

Back on the beach, Laura and Noell played with the children. Laura had hardly spoken since the men had left.

"I think Doc needs to take a drink," Noell finally said, "or maybe some Prozac."

"I'll say," Laura said. "Worse than the children. Jesus! And this morning, I asked him if he liked my new bathing suit, and he says, 'Oh, is that new? It's fine, I guess. A little skimpy, but OK.' Jesus, I could just scream."

THEY STAYED ON THE beach until past one. Bonnie greeted them at the cottage, saying lunch had been ready since lunch time, which to her meant noon. It was one of her light specialties: ham, at least five vegetables and biscuits.

During lunch, Meagan and Jacob somehow talked Jay and Jim into taking them to a miniature golf course in North Myrtle that afternoon.

"I'll keep score," Jay said.

A few hours on the beach was more than enough for the men. And they also wanted to visit a few marinas on Little River. They always were on the lookout for a deal on a sailboat. They had been shopping for over two years, ever since Darrell Lane, the dentist in Farmington, had taken them sailing. He had a thirty-five-foot Catalina at a marina in Oriental. Jay and Jim vowed that day coming home they would buy a boat together. Jim had found plenty he thought were acceptable, but Jay had been a picky shopper.

"Look, I'm giving you until August," Jim warned one day. "My butt's gonna be on my boat come Labor Day."

"I wish they would buy a boat and get it over with," Laura told Noell later that afternoon as they sat on the beach. The two couples had been sailing with Darrell and his wife a few times in the Neuse River and Pamlico Sound. The summer before they had taken Darrell's boat down Adams Creek to Beaufort and spent the weekend. It had been a fun time.

"Bermuda," Noell said. "I want them to get a boat and we'll sail to Bermuda. It's beautiful over there."

"Never been," Laura said. "But if they've got a beach, I'm in favor of it."

It was relaxing to Laura to be on the beach without the children. And fun to have someone to talk to. Not that Bonnie made for bad company. But Laura's conversations with her always tended to be somewhat superficial. Bonnie seemed to have a reluctance to express herself fully and at times could be very withdrawn, almost to the point that Laura would forget she was in the same room. Laura always wondered why, but attributed it to generational differences.

Noell, on the other hand, was all together different. She always had something to talk about, most of it fairly interesting—this case, that lawyer or some place she once lived. She knew everybody and everybody knew her. But only in the past year or so had Laura really become close to her.

"You're not going to believe what happened to me this week," Noell said.

"What?"

"I got propositioned . . . by a judge."

"You're kidding."

"Hell, no. Right there in his chambers. I was furious."

"What happened?"

"I'm defending this guy on a drug charge. And they've got Horace Applewhite—you know that drunk I'm always representing—up there as a witness. The DA asks Applewhite if he's ever been convicted of a crime. And he says, 'Nope. Got charged with drunk driving four times but Miz Beaman there got me off every time.' The courtroom cracked up.

"Anyway, after the session, the judge motions for me. It was that slimy one with the bad teeth. I go back there and he says, 'I see you're quite adept at getting people off, Miz Beaman. Maybe you could demonstrate your technique for me sometime.'"

"What did you say?" Laura asked.

"I just made a joke. What could I say? He's a damn judge."

"You should have kicked him in the groin or something."

"It's hopeless. They all think I'm a slut after that deal with Dan Harvey," Noell said. "And I guess I am."

Laura didn't respond. She knew about the Dan Harvey deal—at least some things—but never knew what was true or just rumor. It had been a major gossip item in Farmington.

"If it's true," Laura remembered hearing one of those old biddies who hung out at the beauty shop say, "she ought to have to leave and take up practice in another county. Or maybe she should be disbarred."

Laura had wanted to respond to that remark but pretended not to hear. Disbarred. For having an affair. What kind of person thinks that way? For that matter, what kind of person am I to live in a place where people think that way. Hey, she screwed up. Give her a break.

"You know, you never mentioned that to me," Noell said. "I've always appreciated that."

"Didn't think it was any of my business," Laura responded, relieved she had restrained herself the many times she had started to ask. "I figured if you wanted to talk to me about it, you would."

"Well, I did want to talk to you about it, but it just seemed like we never got the chance," Noell said. "I won't bore you with the details. It's been nearly two years now. But I will tell you this . . ."

And with that Noell launched into the story:

Her relationship with Dan began on a professional basis. The grandson of a former state legislator and lieutenant governor, Dan became a high-powered litigator at a young age, specializing in civil suits. Noell was representing a young black mother from Farmington County whose daughter was born blind and retarded because of complications during delivery.

Initially, Noell didn't think she had a case. But she mentioned it to a nurse who worked at the hospital. She confided in Noell that she remembered hearing about the birth and a few rumors that the doctor and the hospital may have been at fault.

Noell quickly realized the case was beyond her and called Dan to seek his assistance.

Dan knew Noell, who was well known in most area courthouses, if for nothing else her looks. Most men described her as perky. Perky strawberry blond hair, perky nose and cheeks, perky breasts and butt. Noell knew men found her attractive and tried to make the most of it. She always wore business suits in court, but the skirts always stopped well above her knees.

It took well over a year, but Dan and Noell eventually won the case, settling out of court with the hospital and the doctor. Despite splitting the till with another lawyer, Noell earned her biggest paycheck ever. The day of the settlement, Dan and Noell went to the bar at a Hilton late in the afternoon to celebrate. Two bottles of champagne and an hour later, they were in a hotel room in bed.

"How long did this go on?" Laura asked. "Did Jim ever know?"

"Almost a year. And yes, I told Jim. Felt like I had to. Word was getting around."

"What did he do?"

"Nothing. Just sulked for a few weeks and put it behind us more or less. It's not like he's got a clean record himself."

Laura figured as much but didn't ask for details.

"It was fun while it lasted," Noell said. "But then . . ."

"Then what?"

"Dan told his wife. I couldn't believe it. Told her he was in love with me and was going to leave her. What a dumbass. And of course she had to blab to some of her country club friends."

"Were you in love with him?"

"No way. We hadn't even mentioned the word love—it was sex. Just a little sport-fucking. That's all it was supposed to be. And next thing I know he wants me to leave Jim. What a wimp. That one put an end to my running-around days."

Noell's outlook amused Laura. Nothing seemed to bother her.

"Well, I'm very honored that you would tell me . . . I guess," Laura said. "If I ever have an affair, I'll tell you."

Noell laughed.

"What's so funny?" Laura asked.

"You . . . having an affair."

"What's that supposed to mean? I think some men still find me attractive."

"I didn't mean that," Noell said. "You're a knockout and you know it. It's just you're not the type."

"Not the type? Why do you say that?"

"Look, Laura, I grew up reading *Cosmo* and you probably grew up reading *Good Housekeeping* or some of that crap. It was your lot in life. I'll bet Jay's the only guy you've ever made love to. Am I right?"

"I'm not answering that."

"Like I said," Noell countered, "you're just not the type. But I respect that and have never held it against you."

Laura couldn't help laughing, then added, "I guess you're right. I'm not the type. And please don't take this the wrong way — I'm not trying to judge you — but I just don't think it's right."

"I know you don't," Noell said. "You're a good little Catholic girl and all that, and I'm not. But I hope when I grow up I'll be just like you."

They didn't speak for several minutes. Laura finally started to say something when she noticed Noell had drifted off to sleep.

Good little Catholic girl, Laura thought. She guessed at heart she was, even though she had left the church soon after the move to Farmington. There was no Catholic church in Farmington. And it didn't take Laura long to figure out that people in Farmington regarded Catholics with some degree of suspicion. And little did she know some in Farmington still referred to her as "Doc Jr.'s purty little Jew wife from Charlotte."

"She ain't no Jew, she's calf-lick," Charlie Simpkins, who operates a country store outside Farmington that is a popular gathering place for farmers, once corrected Henry Ray Lancaster.

"So?" Henry Ray shot back just before spitting a glob of chewing tobacco juice in a cup.

Laura eventually joined Jay's Episcopal church. She and Jay seldom went to church when they were first married. But with the birth of Meagan and the move to the small town, it seemed, no, it was, the right thing to do.

Her father was furious.

"They're almost like Catholics," she told him.

"Mother Mary in heaven," he declared. "I'm not listening to this. Not from my own daughter."

He took pride in his faith but even more in that the Regans were one of the first Catholic families accepted for membership in a prestigious Charlotte country club. Laura still found it amazing the club did not accept Catholics until after Kennedy was elected president.

"I really don't want to join his church, but I'm just trying to do the best thing for everybody," Laura had told her mother. "Jay just doesn't think it will look right if I don't go to his church."

"The important thing is that you raise your children in a church," her mother had reassured her. "Don't worry about your father. I can't even get him to mass except at Christmas and Easter."

Laura had never felt strongly about religion anyway. But she always had followed the rules, because . . . well, they were the rules.

The guys should be getting back soon, Laura thought. It was nearly five. She would let Noell sleep only a few more minutes.

What she had started to tell Noell, but now in retrospect was glad she didn't, was that she once almost had an affair — sort of. But not really. Just the chance. With Bill Sanford, the city executive with the bank in Farmington. It had been over five years now. Bill and his wife, Janet, had since moved away.

Laura had always liked Bill, who also was a Charlotte native adjusting to the culture shock of living in Farmington. Several couples had thrown a large bash at Walnut Creek Country Club, about seventeen miles away. Some in Farmington were members, the closest decent country club in the area. Jay left early, called away by his beeper. He insisted Laura stay and have a good time. She could catch a ride home with Jim and Noell.

Laura ended up spending most of the evening with Bill, whose wife was at home with a cold. Bill was there, he explained, because he considered it his duty to attend all social functions, especially those with free food and drink.

"Like somebody here may need a loan tonight?" Laura joked. They talked for nearly two hours, mostly about Charlotte. He asked her to dance, but she declined. Laura felt she was drinking too much. She seldom, if ever, had more than two drinks in an evening. But it seemed Bill was refilling her wine glass every fifteen minutes. When he offered to take her home just past eleven, she accepted, knowing Noell would be closing the place down well past midnight.

As they cruised the country highway back to Farmington, Bill and Laura chatted. He had filled up a plastic cup with wine for her before they left and she was having trouble keeping up with how close to town they were. Laura was wearing a new shorts outfit. At one point Bill dropped his right hand in the seat beside her leg, and then placed it on her knee. Laura kept talking, not acknowledging the advance.

In a couple of minutes, Bill turned off the main road onto a side country road. He went about half a mile before pulling off the road under a grove of trees. He put the car in park and slid across the seat towards Laura and kissed her. She kissed back, which she always attributed to the wine.

It was a real kiss. But when Bill began sliding his hand up Laura's leg, inside the leg of her shorts, it was as if something snapped in her. She grabbed his hand.

"No!" she said firmly. "We can't do this. I just can't."

They drove home in silence. Laura poured the wine out the window of the car.

"You won't say anything to anyone about this, will you?" Bill asked when they reached her driveway.

Yeah, like I'm gonna put it in the church newsletter, Laura thought. "No, it'll just be between us," she said politely, thinking, what a jerk — won't say anything to anyone about this.

Laura rose from the beach chair and stretched. She and Noell had been sitting a good while. She was glad she had resisted the Bloody Marys earlier. Too salty. Made her retain water. Besides, drinking during the day just made her sleepy. But it was getting about time for a beer, she thought, checking the position of the sun. Laura turned toward the cooler and opened it. It was a mess. A few empty soft-drink cans, two paper cups floating in what was mostly water.

Laura found a paper bag to put the trash in and then headed toward the garbage barrel at the bottom of the steps of the wooden walkway. She was almost to the barrel when she glanced up and saw Neal sitting on the railing. He was looking toward the fishing pier. He turned his head and looked directly at Laura.

"Beautiful day for the beach," he said. They were less than twenty feet apart.

"Yes, it is," she replied.

"Where are the kids?"

"They're off with my husband and my friend's husband," she said, pointing at Noell, "playing Putt-Putt."

"I think that's what I should have done today rather than play golf."

"Not a good day, huh?"

"I've had better."

Neal wore a white golf shirt, tan shorts and Top-Siders.

"Good to see you again," Laura said politely after putting the trash away.

As she walked off, Neal called her name. "Does your husband play golf? I've got a friend down and we're trying to get up a foursome."

"No, afraid not," Laura said, thinking Neal probably would find Jay's golfing escapade amusing.

"Thanks anyway."

Laura returned to Noell, who had awakened in time to keep a watchful eye on the short conversation at the walkway.

"New friend?" Noell asked teasingly.

"Old one, actually," Laura said. "He asked me out in college. And of course I was going with Jay and never dated him."

"And you remembered him?"

"Not really. But he recognized me. On the beach Thursday. I couldn't believe it. That was twenty years ago."

"You must have left quite an impression on him. How did you meet?" Noell asked.

"To tell you the truth, I don't really remember. But he called me a few times. He was a sportswriter for the Chapel Hill paper and had covered some of our matches my freshman year."

"What's his name?"

"Neal Nichols, or something like that. No, Nickelsen. He writes for the Raleigh paper. He's staying down here this summer. Writing a book."

"So that's Neal Nickelsen," Noell said. "Talk about your basic drop-dead-good-looking. Even better than he looks in the paper."

"I didn't know you read the sports pages."

"I just look at the pictures. I can't wait to tell Jim. Did you tell Jay?"

"Tell him what?"

"That Neal Nickelsen asked you for a date one time."

"What's the big deal about that?"

"The guy's almost famous, Laura," Noell said. "He's even on TV sometimes. He's real controversial. Jim hates him. Says he's a Duke fan."

"He went to Carolina," Laura said, almost defensively. "What were y'all talking about?"

"Nothing . . . he wanted to know if Jay played golf. Said he was looking for somebody to play with tomorrow."

"I wish he'd play with me," Noell said.

"I thought you said you were through playing around."

"Hey, for Neal Nickelsen, I'd make an exception."

WHEN LAURA AND NOELL got back to the Laughing Gull around six, the men had returned. They were fishing with the children off the short pier at the back the house. At low tide the marsh was almost dry, but at high covered with water.

Jay's playing Daddy, Laura thought. At first she wasn't going to bother him, but then changed her mind.

"Hey, Doc," she called. "Need your help a minute with the shower."

Like most of the houses on Sunset, the cottage had an outdoor shower underneath. This one was particularly nice — a small dressing room, the whole thing enclosed by wood siding.

"What do you need?" Jay asked.

"You, inside," Laura said pointing to the shower.

She locked the door, pulled back the shower curtain and turned on the water.

"Take your clothes off," she said.

"What?"

"You heard me."

"You first," Jay countered, the first time all day he had sounded pleasant.

Laura stripped off her suit and entered the shower. Jay followed in turn.

When they were first married, they often took showers together—washed each other's hair, scrubbed each other's back. And so on. But neither could even remember the last time.

Laura kissed Jay's neck. It tasted salty. "I'm sorry about this morning," she said, knowing full well it wasn't her fault but not willing to let it ruin the weekend.

"It was my fault," Jay said. "I've just been uptight lately."

He started to say something else, but Laura cut him off with a kiss—a long kiss.

"Let's make love," she said.

"In here? What if the kids hear. They're right outside." Jay was taken aback. Laura was seldom the aggressor.

"We'll just have to keep the screaming to a minimum," she said.

Which they did.

NEAL AND LOU MINTOS, the sports editor at the paper, left the topless club in Myrtle Beach around ten.

"Ten o'clock and I'm already broke," Lou lamented. "Was she something or what? Now that'll put some lead in the ole pencil."

Neal didn't have many close friends, but Lou—in addition to being his boss—was one. Lou was in his early fifties. He and his wife, Betsy, had three children. They often invited

Neal over for dinner. He had even spent a few Christmases at their house. Plus Lou was a decent golfer and had taught Neal more about writing than anyone.

"If Betsy could have seen you drooling over that little girl like that she'd probably choke you," Neal told Lou.

"You know, if you could sneak a video camera in one of those places," Lou said, "that would be one heckuva note. Tape the guys and then make 'em buy the tape for about a grand. Or else. Be a good way to make some money."

"Be a good way to get your ass whipped," Neal said.

Lou, with two children still in college, was always trying to think of good ways to make extra money. About the best he'd come up with was being Neal's partner on the golf course. They had easily taken a couple of Yankees for nearly a hundred earlier that day at The Pearl even though Neal had an off day. One of the pros had set up the match. Neal and Lou decided one of their opponents was a sexual theologian, because after most shots he'd say, "Jeeeezus fuckin' Christ."

"You wanna hit 2001 or is it time for the ump to call this one?" Neal asked as they got into the Olds.

"It's thirty for me, unless you really want to," Lou said, using an old newspaper term, meaning "the end."

"Not really."

The ride back to Sunset was a quiet one. Neal kept wanting to ask Lou the question. He had been waiting for several months. Maybe tomorrow on the course, Neal thought. But as they turned onto 40th, it just came out.

"Lou, need your help on something," Neal said.

"Sure, big guy. What is it?"

"I hear Fred Hayworth is going to retire next year."

"Aw, Neal, you can't be serious."

But Neal was. After twenty years of sports, he was ready for a change. Fred was the paper's prized columnist/humorist. He would be sixty-two the next May.

"I am serious. I feel like I'm at a crossroads in my life."

"Cliché," Lou said. He had the same disdain for clichés in conversations as he did in print.

"OK," Neal said. "Like putting lead in the ole pencil isn't?"

"True, sex is a cliché."

"Not for me," Neal said.

"You single guys make me sick."

"Hey, don't change the subject on me. You could get me that job."

"I got no pull."

"Bullshit. You're the most respected man on the staff. Can't you talk to someone about it?"

"That would be a step down for you. You'd be miserable."

"I am miserable. That's the problem," Neal said.

"Middle-age crisis."

"I don't consider forty-three to be middle-aged. Come on."

"Neal, I'll be honest with you," Lou said. "You don't need a new job. You need a wife."

"Not that again."

"You're not getting any younger, pal. Why did you break it off with Julie? She's a wonderful woman."

"You're changing the subject."

"Neal, you're the best writer on our staff. News or sports. I think you're the best writer in the state. And I know you're not happy. That's why I let you come down here for two months. But it's not the job you're unhappy with. What you need to do is get over this thing about marriage. Just because you got burned once doesn't mean —"

"Cliché," Neal said.

"What?"

"Just because you got burned once. Sounds like a cliché to me."

"Now you're changing the subject."

"Damn right I am," Neal said as he turned the car into the driveway of the Bullish Outlook. "Lou, I love ya', but you don't have a clue as to what you're talking about here. Let's drop it, OK?"

CHAPTER FIVE

Sunday, June 27

LAURA, NOELL, MEAGAN AND Jacob drove to the beach access parking area around nine-thirty Sunday morning. Jay and Jim had driven back to Myrtle to take another look at a boat they had seen Saturday afternoon. The dockmaster at the marina had said the owner would probably be there. The men were hoping for a possible sail.

"We'll be back by eleven," Jay had said.

Eleven tonight, Laura thought.

There was one open parking space among the seven on Main beside the Bullish Outlook. Laura had become moderately adept at parallel-parking the huge Suburban, but it was never a lot of fun. It hadn't been her idea to buy something so big. Jay had surprised her with it.

"The four-wheel drive will come in good when it snows," Jay had said, even though it snowed in Farmington only about once a year.

But Laura knew the truth. The Suburban was a socially acceptable vehicle for a doctor's wife, plus its purchase meant the Babsons weren't about the only folks in Farmington

County without either a pickup truck or some kind of four-wheel drive vehicle.

"You're going to hit that car!" Noell screamed from the passenger's side as Laura tried to wedge into the space. The car in front was about a foot over the yellow line in Laura's space.

"You better get out and direct me in," Laura told Noell.

At just that moment she heard a tap on her window. It was Neal, who had been watching while putting his golf bag in his trunk. Laura rolled down the window.

"Do you have to get a special license to drive one of these rigs?" Neal asked.

"Yeah, but obviously I flunked the test," Laura replied.

"I think I got a better idea," Neal countered. "Since my house is right here and it's got a three-car driveway and there's never more than two cars here, why don't you just park in my driveway? You can use it all summer, or at least until August when I leave."

"Good idea," Noell said.

"Why . . . well, I wouldn't want to inconvenience you," Laura said. "I can manage."

"Laura, you'll have a dozen dents in this thing if you keep trying to park here," Noell said.

"It won't inconvenience me," Neal said. "Consider it my pleasure, one Carolina alum to another. Just pull around here. It's really no problem."

Neal walked behind the Suburban toward the driveway, motioning.

"I can't park in his driveway," Laura said to Noell.

"Why?"

"It wouldn't look right."

"To whom?"

"Well . . . Jay, especially after what you said last night about Neal," Laura said.

"Grow up, Laura," Noell said. "The man's making you a great offer. Maybe you wouldn't date him, but the least you could do is park in his driveway."

Laura wheeled the Suburban around, turned left onto 40th and then left into the open space in Neal's driveway.

"Pull underneath the cottage," Neal said. "Might as well keep it in the shade."

"This is fine," Laura said.

"It'll keep your dash from cracking," Neal said.

"Do what the man says, Laura," Noell insisted. She was really starting to grate on Laura.

"OK, dammit," Laura said to her. "As usual I'll just do what everybody tells me to do."

"I'm just trying to help," Noell said.

Laura drove underneath. Neal opened the door for her.

"Like I said, I'll be here until August and I never use this space. Please feel free. It's a shame to let it go to waste."

"That's very kind of you," Laura said. "The parking thing is a pain sometimes."

"Well, no more. Consider this your space," Neal said. "And you and the kids — feel free to use the hose or shower here. Make yourself at home." He added quietly, "It's not everybody who gets to park at the Governor's Mansion."

"Hi, you must be Neal Nickelsen," Noell said, walking around the front of the Suburban, hand stuck out. "I'm Noell Beaman, Laura's attorney. She's told me all about you."

Noell noticed the look Laura gave her. I love it, she thought.

"Nice to meet you, Noell," Neal said, shaking her hand. "Tough client?"

"The worst—always on the wrong side of the law, especially when it comes to driving," Noell said. "How many speeding tickets is it I've gotten you out of now. Four?"

"One," Laura said.

"I love your columns," Noell said.

"Thanks."

"My husband says you're a Duke fan."

Laura considered bopping Noell on the head with Meagan's boogie board.

"He must be a Carolina fan," Neal said. "The State fans say I'm a Carolina fan, the Carolina fans say I'm a Duke fan and the Duke fans say I'm illiterate. Comes with the job."

"What's it really like inside those locker rooms?" Noell asked.

"They smell like locker rooms," he said.

"Thanks again," Laura said loudly, ready for the encounter to conclude. "Let's go, Noell."

Just then Lou came down the steps. "Just a second, let me introduce my boss," Neal said.

"Lou, this is Laura Babson and her friend, Noell Beaman. and Laura's kids. Meagan and Jacob, right?"

Laura nodded.

"Lou Mintos. Pleasure to meet you ladies," Lou said.

"Lou's our sports editor."

"I don't remember seeing any of your articles," Noell said.

"I'm the behind-the-scenes guy," Lou said.

"He tells us what to do and then criticizes us when we do it," Neal said. "Just kidding. He's really a great editor . . . and a great friend."

"So you're the tennis player," Lou said to Laura. Neal winced. He couldn't believe Lou was saying this. "Neal told me all about you."

"Time to go," Neal said. "Don't want to miss our tee time."

"That Neal, always did have a thing about women tennis players," Lou said. "You remember that time you got to interview Chris Evert when she played an exhibition in Raleigh? And then Gabriela Sabatini that other time. Now she's a looker. I thought the poor guy was going to have a cardiac."

Neal considered clubbing Lou with a driver. "This has sure been fun. But we gotta go," he said.

"We do, too," Laura quickly said. "Thanks again."

"If you ever get arrested in Farmington," Noell added, "give me a call. Number's in the book."

After the women had crossed the street, Neal said to Lou, "Told you all about her. Why in the hell did you say that?"

"Because you told me all about her. Last night, remember? And you were right. She's very easy on the eyes."

"I just mentioned her. You shouldn't have said that."

"Why?"

"I don't know. Never mind. Let's go."

LAURA WAS UNUSUALLY quiet on the beach. "What's wrong with you, Chrissie?" Noell teased.

"Bite me," Laura said.

"Bite yourself."

"Why did you say I had told you all about him?" Laura asked. "I don't know anything about him."

"Maybe you should get to know him."

"Oh, Noell, really."

"At least you got yourself a parking spot. Pays to keep yourself looking good."

Laura felt uncomfortable about the parking thing. It was great, of course. Keeping the Suburban in the shade, a hose to wash the sand off the kids before they got in.

"Don't tell Jay about the parking," Laura said.

"Why?"

"You know, he might get the wrong impression. Impressions are everything to Jay."

"Whatever you say, Gabbie," Noell said. "But if I were you, I'd start working on the ole backhand again. You might get interviewed — up close and personal."

About the only use for a tennis ball Laura could think of was to plug Noell's mouth. The two couples had gone out to dinner Saturday night, at which time Noell described how Neal had spotted Laura and remembered her. Laura cringed at the thought of what Jay might think.

But then Jim asked Jay, "Did you read what he wrote about our secondary after spring practice?"

"Oh yeah, the guy's lost," Jay said.

The men then launched into a twenty-minute discussion of the many virtues of the Tar Heels' defensive backs and, to Laura's relief, Neal's name didn't come up again.

Jay and Jim finally showed up on the beach around noon Sunday. Only an hour late, Laura thought. The boat must have been a dog.

"Did we buy a boat?" Noell asked.

"It was a dog," Jay said.

"I liked it," Jim said. "Just needed a little TLC."

"I don't want a boat that's been kept in this much salt water," Jay said. Then why did you go look at it? Laura thought.

"Let's go swimming," Laura said. "I'm baked."

"You're using sunscreen, aren't you?" Jay asked.

"Yes, Doc, fifteen. We're wrapped up in it."

"You better get some twenty-eight for Jacob."

"Will do. Ready to swim?"

Jay decided to do as Laura asked. He couldn't believe he had put off telling her about next weekend. He knew she'd be furious. He'd have to find some way to make it up to her. He'd let her get some money out of his checking account. Tell her to buy something new to wear. And something for Meagan, too. She liked shopping for Meagan.

"We'll miss you this week," she told Jay once they were in the water. "You think you can get away early on Friday?"

"Laura, I really hate to tell you this, but Tu and I've had a little mix-up. I guess it was my fault."

"Oh, shit!" Laura said to herself. "You damn right it's your fault." But she didn't let her face show her feelings.

Dr. Tu would be leaving Farmington Friday, July 2, Jay explained, to attend the wedding of a nephew in New York. It was a big family deal for him. Jay had promised to work but had forgotten to tell her about it. But Tu would return Saturday, July 11, and Jay would go to Sunset that afternoon and then take the whole next week off.

"Jay, you'll miss my birthday. And the Fourth," Laura said. "Can't you at least get away for the weekend."

"I wish I could, babe, you know that. But I just can't leave the county without a doctor. Dad would roll over." That was dumb, he thought.

"Look, I'll try to drive down for the day on the Fourth," he said. "and then the next Saturday we'll just celebrate your birthday a little late. We'll go to that club in OD you talked about. I should be here by early afternoon."

Laura started to suggest—again—that Jay simply put a message on his answering machine saying he was on vacation and that in the event of an emergency go to one of the emergency rooms or urgent-care centers in another county. But he would simply rebut by saying that's a good way to ruin your practice. It wouldn't look right, not in Farmington. Either he or Tu just had to be on duty at all times. That's the way it was. Instructions from on high. No questions.

Laura knew she had two choices. Bitch at Jay about it and end a somewhat pleasant weekend on a bummer. Or smile and accept it gracefully. She nearly always chose the latter. Conflict management had never been her forte.

"I'm stuck down here for two weeks with just Bonnie and the kids," Laura later told Noell before she, Jim and Jay left. "Can't you get away? I thought Jay was going to be here, but I thought wrong. And I haven't invited anybody."

"I wish I could," Noell said. "But I'm jammed this week. Then we're going to Richmond for the Fourth with my sister and then court the next week. It's gonna be a bear."

Laura thought about her brother and his wife—Bobby and Jan. But she remembered they would be at Nags Head with some friends. And her parents would do the usual thing at Lake Norman. And Bonnie had invited her sister Frances from Whiteville for the weekend of the Fourth. She wondered if she could talk Darrell's wife, Anna, into it. Meagan liked their daughter, Jennifer. But no, they would be at the regatta at Oriental.

Dammit, Laura thought, I might as well go home to Farmington. But she knew she wouldn't see Jay much more than she would at Sunset.

It was about one o'clock in the afternoon. The men had been kind enough to pack a lunch — with Bonnie's help. And a cooler of beer. The ham sandwiches looked good, Laura thought. The beer looked better.

She decided to drink lunch.

Chapter Six

Monday, June 28

Laura woke up around five in the morning. Too early to walk, she thought. But after about five restless minutes, she got up and went to the kitchen to fix coffee. She thought about banging a few dishes around but then considered herself cruel for thinking such a thing. Bonnie had a proclivity for getting on one's nerves occasionally, but all factors considered, she was a wonderful woman and mother-in-law.

Laura enjoyed talking with Bonnie, even though in the last few years her hearing had slipped. Jay once suggested a hearing aid.

"I don't need a hearing aid," she roared. "You people just need to talk louder."

At times, Laura thought Bonnie was faking. But at other times, no. The woman really was losing her hearing, which suited Meagan and Jacob just fine. They loved staying with Granny B, who unlike their parents never told them to get quiet. Jay's change in schedule also disappointed Bonnie. "But you do what you have to do," she told her son. "We'll manage just fine on our own."

Then she mumbled something Jay didn't hear, but Laura thought sounded like, "I've got fifty years of practice at it."

Laura left the cottage for her morning walk just before six. She was well down the beach access path, almost to wooden steps before she saw Neal sitting on the railing, looking toward the ocean. He turned his head toward her and their eyes met as her left foot hit the second step.

"Well . . . good morning, Starshine," he said.

He hadn't planned to say it, had not planned anything at all, except to sit and wait for her on the off-chance she would take another early morning walk. He just wanted to see her. That was all.

Usually a late sleeper, Neal had been up since four, blaming his restlessness on a sore back. He had hit down hard on a buried lie in a sand trap and felt an unpleasant twinge on the left side, just above his butt. But he didn't mention it to Lou, who had left around four o'clock Sunday afternoon. Neal then cooked on the grill for just himself and finally worked on the book a little. He later started on a column but didn't get far.

"Good morning," Laura replied. She felt slightly embarrassed, thinking back to the conversation under Neal's cottage. She started to say something about the governor but decided not to. When she got beside Neal she stopped to admire the beach.

"You always up this early?" Neal asked, fearing she would walk away.

"Usually. Best time to walk. It's so peaceful. Just gets my day off to a good start. So, I see you're an early riser, too."

"Oh, yeah," Neal lied. "I love the mornings."

"Well, have a nice day," Laura said, beginning to walk away.

"Laura," he called. She stopped and turned. He had said her name louder than he had wanted to. She looked almost startled. "Which way are you walking?"

She pointed west. "To Bird Island," she said.

"Does it take long? I've never been."

"You've never been to Bird Island," Laura said. "And you call yourself the governor of Sunset Beach. I think you should be impeached."

"I guess I have been derelict in my duties. Mind if I tag along?"

Laura shrugged. Free beach, she thought.

"You won't be able to get over to Bird this morning," she said, "unless you want to swim. Tide's too high. But it's still a nice walk. The beach is beautiful down that way."

"So does this mean you do mind if I tag along or you don't mind?" Neal asked.

"Oh, sorry . . . I mean, sure, no, I mean . . . I don't mind. As long as you walk fast."

"I'll try to keep up," Neal said, hopping off the railing. He winced when he straightened up his back.

"You OK?" she asked.

"Sure, just a little sore. Swung wrong yesterday."

They descended the steps, walking through the powdery white sand, eventually reaching the darker hard-packed variety. They walked close to the surf, Laura on the right. She noticed Neal was still several inches taller than she was even though she took the high side of the slope. He noticed her earrings, gold hoops, and the way the wind blew her hair, occasionally covering the corner of one eye. They walked for nearly three minutes before Neal broke the silence. Laura had started to speak just before but stopped the words.

"I enjoyed meeting your friend," Neal said. "She's . . . well, she sounds like an interesting person."

"That's a nice way of saying it, I suppose,"

"Is she the only lawyer in Farmington?"

"The only one that we know for sure is breathing. Ole Harvin Barnes is still practicing, but we think only his taxidermist knows for sure."

Neal laughed. Good sense of humor, he thought. I like that.

Neal wanted to ask her something. Something meaningful. Or significant. Or just something. "You like the beach?" he asked, quickly adding, "No, I didn't mean that. I guess you wouldn't be here for seven weeks if you didn't. I meant: What do you like about the beach?"

"Gee, I don't know," she said. "Everything, I guess. Maybe not the hurricanes. But I never went to the beach for a hurricane."

"Me, either. But I did drink a few Hurricanes in Underground Atlanta one night. A Peach Bowl, I think. Or maybe a Tech or Braves game."

"We went to the Peach Bowl once," she said. "Almost froze. And then Carolina lost. It was when Jay was in med school. He was so ticked we lost. He takes it much too seriously."

"Kentucky, 21-0," Neal said. "I was there. It was very cold."

"I like the summer better."

"Yeah, me, too."

More silence. To their back the early morning sun cast a bright beam across the sea. Their shadows looked more than fifty feet long. "So what do you like about the beach?" Laura finally asked.

Women like you in bathing suits, Neal thought. "The six *s's*," he finally said. "It all comes down to that. And they're all here."

"Six *s's*? Let me guess . . . or maybe I shouldn't."

"Sun, sand, surf, salt, suds," he said. "and . . . well, you know."

"You know? No, I don't know," Laura said, counting.

"Sure you do. It starts with *s*."

"I think I get it."

"Just a little joke," he said.

"What's that?" Laura asked, pointing ahead and suddenly changing the subject somewhat to Neal's relief.

"What?"

"Out in the water. It looks like rocks."

"That's a jetty," Neal said. "At Little River Inlet. Great inlet. Very calm."

Laura laughed. "I don't even know what an inlet is," she said. "No, I guess I do."

"It's what lets the water from the ocean in."

"That's what I thought," she said, a little embarrassed.

"And lets the boats out," he added. "You guys into boats?"

"Kinda. My husband is. He and Noell's husband keep talking about buying a sailboat. I don't know. It's been going on for two years now."

"No wont no blow bote, mon," Neal said in a Jamaican accent. Man, that sounded stupid, he thought.

"Sounds like you're experienced," she said.

"Oh, hell, nearly drowned on one of those things. But, hey, I shouldn't have said that. I was out with a bunch of drunks and we did a couple of dumb things. I'm sure sailing's great. But when the sky gets dark, I want some power to get me to shore."

"You got a boat?" Laura asked.

"Yeah, well, no . . . sorta," he said. "I have access to one. In the family."

"Must be an interesting family?"

"Why's that?"

"I just meant your cottage is in the family and now a boat."

"Damn," Neal said. "This is embarrassing."

"I didn't mean to embarrass you."

"No, you didn't. I have no problem doing that myself. It's just . . . have you ever heard of a husband-in-law?"

Laura thought a moment. "Can't say that I have."

"That's what I call my ex-wife's husband. My husband-in-law. It's nothing sick. Just a thing. I don't know what else to call it."

Sounds weird, Laura thought.

"We're close," Neal said, "which I guess is good since my daughter lives with him. Anyway, the beach house there actually belongs to Elliot and Susan—that's my ex-wife. And so does the boat. Kind of weird, I guess. A long story."

"I guess it's nice that you have a good relationship with your ex-wife," Laura said. "Could be worse."

"Oh, I don't have a good relationship with Susan," he said. "To be honest, I hate her. Which is OK since she hates me, too. In fact, she hates just about everybody and just about everybody hates her — except maybe Elliot, who seems to like everybody. He has to. He's a stockbroker. But Sarah — that's my daughter — and I get along just fine and we get along great with Elliot. Plus he's rich."

"And generous," Laura said.

"To a point. The truth is he's letting me use the house this summer because I get him photo passes to football and basketball games. He's a camera nut and a sports nut and I'm nutty enough that I've been able to work it out for him to take pictures for us on occasion. He eats it up. I offered to rent the house and Elliot laughed and said, 'Yeah, like you can afford thirteen hundred a week for eight weeks. Just keep getting me the photo passes and this will be my way of saying thanks.' I didn't argue."

"I wouldn't have either," Laura said. "That's a lot of money."

"Yeah, but it's not like he's out the money. You think Susan would ever let him rent that place and someone possibly screw up the drapes or something? She about died when she found out I was going to be here. She'll probably fumigate the place when I leave."

At last they reached the inlet. Neal was nearly breathless. He was hoping she'd want to stop for a rest. She didn't. But they did stop long enough to admire Bird Island. High tide had been at 4:39 A.M. and the inlet was too deep to cross.

"What's over there?" Neal asked.

"You're looking at it, I guess" Laura said. "Except for Kindred Spirit. You really should come back at low tide."

"Kindred Spirit? What's that?"

"If you have to ask, you may not understand," Laura said.

"Well, maybe we'll come back at low tide one day and you can try to explain it," he said.

"Maybe we'll do that," she said. We'll, Laura thought. It made her feel uncomfortable. But overall, Neal was pleasant company. They walked back, chatting about nothing in particular. He had a certain way of saying things—so blunt, so direct—that made her laugh at times and think at others. It was a fun walk.

When at last they reached the Bullish Outlook, an exhausted Neal puffed, "This has been . . . fun . . . even though I'm about . . . outta breath here."

"I can tell," she said. "I guess you don't get much exercise riding around on a golf cart."

"No, I guess not. Thanks for letting me tag along."

"Well, see you around."

"Hope so," he added. As she started to turn up 40th, he said, "I really do hope you'll use the parking space. I'm not here during the day much. So just make yourself at home."

"We'll do that," she said. "Thanks."

CHAPTER SEVEN

Tuesday, June 29

As Laura left for her walk around six-thirty in the morning, she wondered if Neal would be sitting on the walkway again. She didn't see him again Monday after the walk. His car was gone when she and the children parked at the cottage around ten. They went in for lunch around one and came back to the beach from three to five. But his car had not returned when they left.

In a way, she hoped he wouldn't be at the walkway. What if he asked to walk with her again? What if he didn't? Why did it matter? She wasn't sure. It didn't, really. Did it? No.

But she had been thinking about him quite a bit Monday. Wondering where he was. Wondering if he'd come out on the beach. Around four in the afternoon, she had found herself glancing toward the walkway, thinking he might show up with a cooler. It was hot and a beer would have been good.

As Laura approached the beach access, she looked down the path. She didn't see him. His car was under the cottage. But he was not in sight. When she reached the beach, she decided to go east, toward the fishing pier, rather than west toward Bird Island. From 40th Street, it was almost two miles to that end of the island. She would walk at least a mile in that direction. Maybe all the way.

The fishing pier was about four hundred yards away. A few optimists were on the pier, though the fishing in the summer was just fair. As Laura walked along the shoreline, she caught a glimpse of a man standing on the pier, his back to her. He was looking off the east side toward Ocean Isle. But he wasn't fishing. He was on the part of the pier that was over the sand. She walked under the pier. Once she emerged, she heard Neal's voice.

"Good morning, Starshine," Neal said.

She turned and looked up. He was on the pier, about fifteen feet above her. "Good morning, Governor," she said without thinking, then wishing she had left the governor part off. But it didn't matter, she thought.

He started to say something. Then she started to say something. Finally he spoke. "Have a nice walk," he said.

"Thanks," she replied. "Have a nice day."

With that she walked on. She wondered if he was watching her. She felt as if he was. It made her feel uneasy. But in other ways OK. She wanted to stop, turn and see if he was there. But that would seem too obvious. Why did it matter? She saw an interesting-looking shell. She stopped and picked it up, looking casually over her shoulder — to the pier.

He wasn't there.

An elated Neal drove his convertible out of the front gate of Brick Landing and turned left toward Sunset. As he picked up speed, he stuck his right fist in the air and yelled over the

engine and radio, "Yes! Sixty-nine. Mighty fine. Turn it up-
side down if you want to, boys, it's a six and a nine and it's
mine."

A twelve-foot birdie putt on eighteen had netted him his
first sub-seventy round of the summer—his first since that
lucky day at Devil's Ridge in late April when everything had
gone right for a sixty-eight.

He replayed the one-iron on number twelve, a par five.
Two thirty-seven to the middle of the green and he nailed it.
That's got to be tight, he thought. It was. About nine feet,
uphill. The eagle made amends for that stupid bogey on eight.

Neal made a plan. Pack the cooler, head for the beach. It
was only four-thirty. Surely she'd be there.

He patiently observed the twenty-mile-per-hour speed
limit on North Shore Drive before turning onto 40th. She'd
be there, he thought. The semi would be under the Bullish
Outlook. It wasn't.

He hopped out of the Olds. Upstairs first, or to the beach,
he thought. To the beach. Just check. Maybe they walked. He
went quickly down the beach access path, mounted the steps
and looked urgently. East, west. And then again. And again.

She wasn't there.

CHAPTER EIGHT

Wednesday, June 30

Good morning, Starshine," Neal said as Laura approached the wooden steps. "You know, I was thinking about you. Just yesterday afternoon. Thinking about how fast you walk. I'm thinking, Neal, if you would walk with her you could really build up your stamina and then on about number fifteen or sixteen when usually you're starting to get tired, hell, you'd be getting your second wind. Whatta ya' think?"

"I think you should join a health club or something," Laura said with a laugh.

"That would just be so . . . so . . . oh, I don't know," Neal said. "May I walk with you?"

"Sure," she said with a shrug. "If you can keep up."

"If I get tired, I'll just sit down and catch you on your return."

"Which way?" she asked.

"Your pleasure."

She turned west.

Somehow she felt comfortable this morning walking beside him. Laura felt good. Felt relaxed. Felt in place.

"So what's it like to be a famous sportswriter?" she asked.

Neal laughed. "I'm flattered. I never thought of myself as being famous. And a lot of people have told me I'm a poor excuse for a writer."

Laura laughed.

"I will tell you one thing about my job," he said, "if you don't mind patronizing me for a moment."

"Not at all."

"The cheerleaders," he said. And then paused.

"The cheerleaders?" she finally asked.

"Yeah, the cheerleaders," he said. "They keep getting younger. I swear. They're getting younger. Those girls out there today are younger than the ones when I was in college. And younger than the ones ten . . . heck, five years ago. I tell ya', they're getting younger."

"And you're staying the same age," Laura said.

"No, I don't mean that," Neal said. "It's just that . . ."

"Just that what?"

Just that what? Neal thought, wondering how he was going to get out of this.

"Just that I don't know," he finally said.

"Very poignant," Laura said. "Because to tell you the truth, I don't know either. I guess it's like my children. I want them to stay the same age forever. But each day, it's the same. Another day older."

They walked without speaking for about two minutes. She started to say it once. Finally she did.

"So, Neal, tell me about yourself," she said.

He thought for a moment. "OK," he finally said with a shrug. "Where do you want me to start?"

"Start at conception if you like."

"OK, this is it, the deal," Neal said. "For me, it all started with a father who was a bit too fond of the grape. And paid the price."

"What does that mean?"

"My dad drank himself to death. OK?"

"OK," she said slowly. "I guess that wasn't a lot of fun."

"To be honest, no, it wasn't."

"Would you rather talk about something else?"

"No. I don't mind telling you about it," Neal said. "I wouldn't mind telling you anything."

Chapter Nine

Thursday, July 1

I can't believe June is gone," Neal said to Laura at 6:18 A.M. as once again they walked toward Bird Island.

"Me either," she said.

"I've been down here almost a month and haven't even been out shagging yet. Haven't been to the Galleon, Fat Harold's, the Pad—none of them. I keep saying I'll do that. But then I don't. It's disgusting."

Just hearing the names of the beach music clubs in Ocean Drive brought back many memories for Laura: boys, fake IDs and the like.

"Why haven't you been this summer?" she asked.

"I don't know. Hate to go by myself, I guess. And then when some of my friends are down, they prefer other places."

"What other places?"

"Oh, you know. The kind of places some men like to go to."

"You mean topless clubs?" she asked.

"I guess you could call 'em that," he said.

Laura laughed.

"What's so funny?" Neal asked.

"Just thinking about a bunch of drunk guys going to a top-less club and paying women to take off their clothes. It's just funny to me."

"What's so funny about it?" Neal retorted.

"Never mind. I didn't mean to put you on the defensive."

"I'm not on the defensive."

Laura laughed again. Neal felt embarrassed.

"I really don't like going to those places all that much," he said.

"Sure."

"I mean, once you've been a few times, well . . . it's kind of boring."

Laura laughed again.

"Will you quit laughing at me?" he said.

"Sure," she said, trying to get the smile off her face. "But I was just thinking: Wouldn't you guys have a lot better chance of picking up women at a dance club than at a topless club?"

"Who said anything about picking up women?" Neal asked.

"I did," she said. "You're single, right? I figure single people our age are usually out to meet other single people. Sorry. I guess I'm getting too personal."

"No, it's all right. I know what you mean. It's just that I'm still a little too much on the rebound right now. For me, it's a time for caution."

"Oh, I'm sorry," she said.

"But I'll be back in the groove, soon."

"Good for you."

"So you want me to tell you about it?" he asked.

"Sure. After that story about your father, I think you can tell me anything."

IT WAS NEARLY EIGHT when the phone rang at the Laughing Gull. Laura answered.

"Hey, girlfriend. Bored yet?" It was Noell.

"To tears. No, not really. I've had a great time with the kids. Jacob's getting pretty good on the boogie board. And believe it or not, there's this eleven-year-old boy whose been hanging around Meagan a lot on the beach and she kind of acts like she likes it. You wouldn't believe the castle they built Wednesday. We took pictures. It's been fun."

"I bet you've got a great tan."

"It's getting there."

"I just wanted to give you a yell before we left for Richmond," Noell said.

"Can't you come down here instead?" Laura asked.

"I wish. But just can't do it."

"So what's going on in Farmington?"

"Nothing as usual. How about down there? Have you seen him again?"

"Seen who?" Laura asked.

"You know who—Neal."

"Yeah, but so what?"

"Did you talk to him?"

"Yeah. Why are you asking about this?"

"No reason. Just curious."

"Noell, you sound like Meagan talking to one of her friends. I'm not in junior high."

"I know. But I just think it's exciting. Jay up here and you down there with this good-looking guy."

"I'm not down here with him," Laura said, a little exasperated. "You have a dirty mind."

"Yeah, I do," Noell said. "Don't you just love it?"

After hanging up, Laura joined Bonnie and the children on the back porch. As she sat down, she felt the note card in her pocket. Why she hadn't thrown it away, she wasn't sure. Neal had left it on the windshield of the Suburban, sometime that morning while she and the children were on the beach. It was a small envelope with her name written on the front. The note inside read: "The governor of Sunset Beach requests the pleasure of your company to view the setting of the sun over Mad Inlet this evening around 8:30. Beer provided. RSVP. 555-7172."

Laura, Bonnie and the children had driven to Myrtle that afternoon for some shopping. They got home around six, at which time Laura went to the phone in the bedroom and called Neal with her regrets.

"I appreciate it, but I just can't," she said.

"Maybe another night," he replied. "The sun will probably set tomorrow, too."

"I don't know, Neal. I'm not sure," she paused.

"Not sure what?"

"That it would be the right thing to do," she finally said.

"Oh." Neal paused. Then he laughed. "I understand."

"Why are you laughing?"

"Did you think I was asking you for a date or something? That wasn't my intention. I just enjoy talking to you. I'm sorry I gave you the wrong impression. I'm not out to steal anyone's wife. I tried that once. All I ended up with was a thorough ass-kicking."

Laura felt embarrassed. Foolish. She didn't know what to say. "I didn't mean it like that. I don't know what I meant. I'm sorry. I've got to go."

"No, it was all my fault," he said. "But that's not what I meant. Look, if you change your mind, I'll be here. And bring your children, too, if you like. It's a great view from here and I thought you might like to see the house. I have to admit Susan did a great job decorating it. That was all."

How dumb can I be? Laura thought as she rocked beside Bonnie, absorbed in a book as usual. It still wasn't too late to go. She enjoyed talking to Neal. But she certainly was not interested in an affair or even giving the slightest impression she was. No. Definitely not. But of course, he wasn't either. So what was wrong with her going to his house and drinking a beer? They were adults. Friends. If it had been a woman who had asked Laura to her house, she probably would have gone. Why did the fact he was a man make it so different? But it did, even though it shouldn't. She would like to be able to say to Bonnie, "Hey, I met this man on the beach and he's invited me to his house for a drink. I won't be long." And to tell Jay, "I had a drink with Neal Nickelsen at his cottage the other night. It was fun. He's a nice guy." And everyone would say, "That's great." And not think another thing about it. Hell, she was lonely down here. And it would be over a week before Jay came. He hadn't even called but once. This is silly, Laura thought.

"Granny B," she said, standing up. "You mind watching the kids while I go for a little walk?"

"Of course, not," Bonnie said.

"Can I go?" Meagan asked.

"Me, too?" Jacob said.

"Guys, I think we've spent plenty of time together down here. I just want to go for a quick walk by myself. OK?"

"OK," they said reluctantly.

As she walked down 40th, she thought about not even going to Neal's. Go to the Island Market, instead. Maybe they'd have a decent book. She'd buy a six-pack of beer and a book and go back to the cottage and read. But Laura never liked drinking alone. Bonnie, never much of a drinker, had become a near teetotaler after Doc's death. The beer Neal had given her Tuesday afternoon was the only thing she'd had to drink since Sunday. She deserved a beer every now and then. Almost two weeks at the beach and she had actually lost a pound or two.

As she walked up the steps to Neal's deck, the sun was setting. It was a great view. Neal looked surprised to see her.

She shrugged. "Never been one to pass up a free beer," she said. "But just one. Bonnie's with the children."

"I've got a chilled bottle of Asti Spumante if you'd rather have it," Neal said.

She definitely would. It was her favorite. But she seldom drank it. Liquid headache, as she called it. Had she mentioned Asti to Neal? She didn't recall. Maybe so. She wasn't sure. They had talked about so much, it seemed, in just a few days.

"I'd love some," she said. "The sunset really is beautiful."

Neal returned with the Asti and two glasses. He fired off the top. "A toast," he said, handing her a glass.

"To what?" Laura asked.

Neal shrugged. "You name it."

Laura thought a moment. "To friendship," she said, lifting her glass.

Neal nodded approvingly. "To friendship."

WEEK THREE

CHAPTER TEN

Saturday, July 3

So it must not have been too wild last night," Laura said to Neal as they stepped onto the sand at the bottom of the access steps around six-fifteen. "I didn't expect to see you here this morning."

"Actually I was just about asleep when they got here," Neal said. "I welcomed everyone and went to bed. Evidently they kept it down fairly well."

Neal had extended the invitation to the other three couples before he and Julie McAllister had ended their five-year relationship. Ended it for good this time. The others considered canceling, but Neal talked them into coming.

"I'll probably be shacking up with some nineteen-year-old beach bunny by that time," Neal had told them. One of the women, Martha Ann Hyde, was a close friend of Julie. Both worked in the news department—Martha Ann a copy editor and Julie an accomplished reporter. She had come to Raleigh from Boston when she and her husband divorced.

Martha Ann's husband, Bud, was a decent golfer. He and Neal had become friends. Garry and Cathy Davison and Hal and Linda Ward rounded out the group. Garry was a former Carolina football player and now an assistant football coach for the Tar Heels. He and Neal had been friends since college. Hal had been on the sports staff of the newspaper nearly eight years.

Over the past few years, the four couples had gotten together periodically. When Neal and Julie split, it was like a divorce to the other three. Making it worse, sides seemed to have been taken along gender lines. The women didn't want to go to Neal's for the weekend. The husbands had looked forward to the golf. Julie finally came to the rescue and insisted to Martha Ann they go. Martha Ann held out hope Neal and Julie would reconcile. At one point, in early May, Neal would have at Martha Ann's urging. But Julie shut it off. "I wasted five damn years of my life on that man," she told Martha Ann. "It's over. I'm through."

Julie already had started dating again—a physics professor at N.C. State University. They were going white-water rafting in the North Carolina mountains for the holiday weekend, taking along her only child, an eleven-year-old son. Martha Ann, through her husband, kept Neal well apprised of all facets of Julie's new romance, including the rumored ability of the professor to defy the laws of his discipline in the bedroom. Neal didn't blame Julie for being bitter. He should have ended it long before and probably would have had it not been for Jeff, her son. He idolized Neal. And in many ways, the feeling was mutual. Even after the breakup, Neal rarely missed one of Jeff's baseball games. "Hell, someone ought to be there for him," Neal told himself. "Julie's sure not going to lower herself to go to a stupid game."

It was games—sports—that was a deciding factor in the split. Julie hated sports. Thought they were silly. She thought the newspaper's sports department had too big a budget, got too much space. At first, Neal sympathized with Julie's complaints. He agreed philosophically with her. The newspaper probably did make too big a deal of sports. But sports was a big deal to its readers. Readership surveys consistently proved it. But what started out as casual complaining almost had become a crusade for Julie. He felt she had become resentful of his success, his notoriety. Julie was an excellent reporter but received little public recognition.

Neal never told Julie why he was ending their relationship. But he felt she probably knew. It certainly hadn't been because of the sex. Neal missed it. He even embarrassed himself by dropping by her house unexpectedly after the split, hoping for one more night together—for old times' sake. The professor was there. Neal said he came by to see Jeff, who as it turned out was spending the night at a friend's house.

Julie introduced Neal to the professor. He was tall and thin—had a goatee, of all things. He and Julie were watching a show on PBS. Neal considered farting and inquiring of the prof in which direction the odor traveled, at what speed and why. If I'd had a few drinks in me, I probably would have, he later thought.

The visit disgusted Neal—he disgusted himself. He had been the one to dump Julie. And now he was jealous she had someone else.

Since that night, he considered he and Julie finished. He eventually became content with the situation, glad she was with someone else. But he had still not dated anyone, hadn't even really considered it. Someone else would come along in time, he was sure.

In a sense, she already had, Neal thought, looking at Laura stride down the beach. No, Neal didn't hold any false hopes that he and this beautiful doctor's wife would somehow end up together. Not that he wouldn't love to.

Thursday night, for the brief time they were together, Neal found himself more aroused than he had been in months, maybe years. As she talked that evening, Neal had a difficult time concentrating on her words. Instead he imagined Laura putting down her glass, looking at him shyly and saying, "Let's go inside." He would lead her to the bedroom. Unbutton the denim shirt, the same one she wore to the beach shop that day. He wondered if she was wearing a bra. He didn't think so. Once, when she leaned against the railing of the deck, the shirt opened just enough that he thought he could tell. I love it when women do that, he thought.

Their lovemaking would be intense, Neal felt certain. After he removed her shirt, he would sit on the edge of the bed. She would stand in front of him, wearing only the white shorts. He would kiss her stomach, then unbutton the shorts and slowly unzip them. He imagined Laura on top of him. He worried that he would come too quickly. It had happened to him before—had happened the first time he was with Julie. Too much anticipation, too much excitement.

As they walked on the beach that Saturday morning just after sunrise, he played out the fantasy again, frustrated somewhat by his unwillingness to get it out of his mind. It wouldn't happen, he felt sure. Oh, it possibly could. But it wouldn't. And in a sense, it didn't matter. Just being with her was enough. Just walking beside her. Hearing her talk. Though he had been disappointed somewhat when she toasted to friendship, it was appropriate. In just over a week, they had become friends. Had become comfortable with each other. Comfortable with the arrangement. A walk on the beach in the mornings. A beer on the beach some afternoons. And that was it, other than the Thursday night deal. He didn't hound her. He knew she wouldn't like that.

"You're certainly quiet this morning," Laura finally said. Neal almost blushed.

"Getting my mind right . . . for the golf," he replied.

He had wanted to ask her Friday afternoon when he joined Laura and her children on the beach late in the day. He knew Jay wasn't coming back to Sunset until the next weekend. He knew it would just be Bonnie and the kids with Laura for one of the biggest weekends of the year. Neal sensed her disappointment. He understood — the woman wanted to do something, something other than what she had been doing.

"Laura, I was thinking," Neal said slowly. "We're all going out tonight to OD. The Tams are going to be at the Spanish Galleon and . . . do you like the Tams?"

"Neal, that just wouldn't be appropriate."

"I'm not asking you for a date, now," he said defensively. "It's not like we'd be together."

"Not like we'd be together? You, me and three married couples. I don't think so."

She was right. He felt dumb for asking. But she had said she wanted to go dancing.

"I just said that because you said you wanted to go dancing," he said. "That's all."

Laura felt as if she had hurt his feelings. She had been abrupt. She hadn't meant to be. But there was no way she was going out with them. She couldn't imagine it. But then again, she could at least imagine it. She'd wear that short blue slip dress with the gold trim—the one she was going to wear the weekend before had she and Jay gone dancing. But she wasn't wearing that dress just to a restaurant. She and Jay would go out in OD for her birthday, she felt sure. She'd force him, threaten him if she had to. She'd have a good time, even if he didn't.

"Look, I really appreciate your asking," she said. "It's sweet of you. Why don't you get a date next weekend and go out with me and Jay? He'd love talking to you, if you wouldn't mind talking about football and basketball."

"I'm just not in the frame of mind to get involved with anyone yet," Neal said.

"Since when is one date getting involved?" she asked. "I'm sure there will be plenty of available women at the Galleon tonight. Next Saturday night. You and her, Jay and me. That's your mission."

"I wouldn't know what to say to a woman in a bar," Neal said.

"I think it goes something like this: You ask her if she wants to dance and if she says no, you say, 'Then I guess that pretty much rules out oral sex, too.' "

Neal was stunned. Laura even more so. She couldn't believe she had said it. Neal had heard that old joke, in a cruder form of course, hundreds of times. But coming from Laura, it was funny, real funny. Neal laughed—laughed as if it was the funniest thing he'd ever heard.

He looked her way. She laughed, too, but wouldn't look at him. Her face felt so warm she fanned herself.

"I don't know why I said that," she said, thinking it was something maybe even Noell wouldn't have said. "I know you've probably heard it a hundred times."

"Yeah, but never quite like that," Neal said.

"Quite like what?" she asked, still not looking at him.

"I don't know," Neal said. "Just coming from you . . . I don't know. But I promise you this: Next weekend I'm going to get a date and go out with you and Jay. And when I ask you to dance, you know what I'm going to say if you say no. And I'll tell your husband I heard it from you."

"Don't worry, Guv. I'll dance with you," she said. "But only once — and not a slow one."

CHAPTER ELEVEN

Sunday, July 4

Every few minutes, it seemed to Laura as she sat on the beach and watched her children play, Jay was walking up behind her. She felt sure he would come. She held out hope until about three o'clock when she went back to the cottage, calling first the house and then the private line at the office. Jay answered on the third ring.

"Just catching up," he said. "It's been a good week. I've gotten a lot done."

He planned to work at the office until about eight. Then he'd go to the high school and catch the annual fireworks display. He missed her. And the kids, too. Couldn't wait to see them next weekend. What could he bring them? He'd call during the week to check. Miss Pauline was much better. She was released from the hospital Thursday. But Chester Ballance had another stroke. It didn't look good. The farmers were worried about the drought. The tobacco was OK, but the corn would be gone if it didn't rain soon. He loved her. And when he hung up, he was a bit ticked off that she sounded so cool. What was he supposed to do? Surely she didn't expect him to drive all the way to Sunset just for one day. She can't be that unreasonable. And if she is, well, that's her problem. She had unrealistic expectations of him. But of course everyone always had, he thought.

It was after she hung up that Laura decided she was going to Neal's party — unless Bonnie acted funny about it. But Laura felt sure she wouldn't. She had Frances with her and they seemed to be having a grand old time. Maybe she should have mentioned it earlier. Neal was insistent that she attend. But who was he to insist. Nevertheless, it sounded like fun. And sure, Bonnie would understand.

But now, the important stuff. What would she wear? Neal said very casual. But everything she thought about was either extremely casual or very nice casual. What did casual really mean? At one point she was tempted not to go. Neal would be the only person there she knew. But he promised there would be people at his cottage he didn't even know.

"By the time things get going, all you got to do is act like you belong there," he had said. "Because you do. It's my party and my friends. And I count you as one of my friends. So you come. Hell, bring someone with you. But I'd advise leaving the kids at home. Some of these folks may be a little outrageous."

For Laura to go to a party at which she knew only one person — and him for only about a week really — was not a simple undertaking from the standpoint of her psyche. But by golly she was going to do it. But not without something new to wear, she thought, as she loaded up the children around four-thirty to drive to Calabash. She'd go to Victoria's Ragpatch and buy that outfit she'd almost gotten last week but had decided it was too casual. She'd also rent a movie for the children. And Jacob could get some new baseball cards. And he and Meagan could get a pizza to take back to the cottage for dinner. And she'd let Meagan buy something. Maybe she'd pick up something for Bonnie and Frances, too.

She knew it was silly. But Laura, whenever she did something for herself — like go out for the evening — felt as if she had to do something for the children first. For all practical purposes, all she had done since coming to Sunset Beach was do for the children. But she didn't mind. She enjoyed it. And she knew while she was at the party — and she doubted she would stay more than an hour — she would think about them. About what they were doing? Would they be bored? They sometimes complained of being bored when they stayed with Granny B. Why was it she always had to do for everyone else before she could do something for herself? But it wasn't a bad trait, was it? No, not at all.

She didn't buy the outfit. It looked good, maybe too good. It made a statement. She didn't want to make a statement at the party. She just wanted to go. Instead she decided to try the ole reliable: just forget about it until the last minute and then put something on and go.

Bonnie seemed confused about the whole thing at first. I'm not doing a good job explaining this, Laura thought.

"It's just some people I met on the beach and they're having a little get-together for the Fourth and they asked me to go," Laura said. "I'd feel bad if I didn't. They're nice folks."

"You should go," Bonnie finally said. "Would be impolite if you didn't. I'm sure they're fine people if they're staying down here. Stay as long as you like. We'll be just fine."

"As long as you like," Frances said, echoing her sister's words as she had a habit of doing. "We'll be just fine."

"Fine. I've got the telephone number," Laura said. "I'll write it down right beside the phone. Call me if you need me."

"We'll try to stay out of trouble," Bonnie assured her.

"Out of trouble," Frances added.

Yeah, Laura thought, me, too.

NEAL WAS DISAPPOINTED WHEN Laura didn't show for the sunset. Most everybody was there, including Scott Faircloth's secretary. Her name was Joy. Thirty-six years old, twice divorced, three kids. "But you'd never know she had kids," Scott had said. "Dynamite bod. Great tits. Hey, if I thought I could get away with it, but Leigh would kill me if she found out. And she'd find out. Believe me. She'd find out."

Neal was glad he'd invited Scott, his wife, Leigh, and, at last count, eighteen of their closest friends to the party. But he really would have preferred his old college friend stay out of the match-making deal.

Scott was a star soccer player at UNC. He and two others shared an apartment with Neal their last two years in college. They had many wild times to recount, which they often did when Leigh was not within earshot.

It had been Scott who attracted Neal to southeastern North Carolina in the first place. He owned a car dealership in Shallotte and a fashionable home in Brick Landing. Scott was one of those guys who not only could detect opportunity but also capitalize. He had learned the car business from Leigh's

father in Wilmington. He helped set up Scott with the dis-
tressed dealership in Shallotte. With much hard work and
savvy, Scott had turned it into a huge success. It had killed
Scott's golf game—he had only played once with Neal this
summer. Didn't break ninety. Probably not a hundred if
they'd really been keeping score. But Scott was one of those
few awful golfers Neal enjoyed playing with. He was just fun
to be around when he was not on the job.

And he definitely was not on the job this night.

"Look at that butt," he whispered to Neal, pointing to Joy.
"Go for it big guy. She likes you. I can tell."

Before the night was over, Neal thought, I just very well
may. He had become more than irritated that his friend—
some friend—was standing him up. Laura had promised—
that morning as they walked—she would drop by. But it was
nearly ten and Neal was becoming convinced she wouldn't
show. Her husband must have shown up for the day. Which
was OK, he thought, because a guy could do worse than Joy,
especially a guy who hadn't even held a woman's hand in
several months. Oh, she was a little on the trashy side, Neal
thought—he wondered just how long she had spent fixing
that bleached blonde hair and applying the war paint—but
it's not like I'm the classiest guy in the world. And Scott was
right about the body. If only she didn't have that stupid
laugh. And two ex-husbands. She must be hell to live with.
But for one night, it probably wouldn't be bad.

Neal grabbed another beer from the cooler and gulped
down about a third of it in one pull. He was sweating. The
AC was running full throttle, but it was warm in the cottage.
It was full of people now—the breeze had died—trying to

escape the mosquitoes and no-see-ums on the back deck. Just as he started to walk over to Joy—ask her if she needed a refill and strike up an obligatory conversation—he glanced to his left and saw Laura standing just inside the door. She was talking with one of Scott's salesmen, who looked as if he was trying to sell her a lemon. I'm rescued, Neal thought as he wandered over to Laura.

"What kind of beer you want, honey?" Neal heard the salesman, a rotund greaser named Dwayne, ask Laura. "If they don't have one to you liking, I'll jes get in my car and go to the store and gitcha one. That's my Caddy out there. You see it?"

"No, but thanks, yes," she said. "I would like a beer, just some kind of light. Thanks again."

"Hell's bells, honey, when you walked through that door there, I thought I was looking at one of them girls in the Victoria Secrets catalogue," he said.

That's Victoria's Secret, Laura started to say, but instead replied, "Thank you. I'm very flattered."

"Me, too," he said.

"No, I think you're just drunk," she said. "But that's OK. What are parties for."

It was at that point she saw Neal, who seemed to glide through the crowd toward her.

"Starshine!" he said, extending an arm and giving her a cordial pat on the back. "I was beginning to think you couldn't find the damn place."

If he only knew, she thought. Laura had changed clothes no less than six times before leaving the Laughing Gull. She still wasn't totally satisfied with what she had on. But two beers had helped her disposition. She had finished the second one outside the Bullish Outlook.

"I'm nervous as a hooker in church—or maybe a saint in a den of iniquity," she said to herself as she walked up the steps of the cottage. But upon reaching the door and entering the crowded living room—where loud talk and even louder strains of Jimmy Buffett on the stereo enabled her entrance to be made with little fanfare—she felt she could hang.

Dwayne got Laura a beer before Neal whisked her away. "Just got to introduce you to a few friends," he said. "Then I'll let you alone."

Laura sensed Neal also was drunk. Or at least feeling pretty darn good. He was more animated than usual. But of course he was in his element, she supposed.

After a few introductions—an old college friend, he called her—Laura told Neal, "Look, I know this is your party. So don't feel like you have to be my chaperone. Mingle if you must."

"I'm proud just standing here beside you," Neal said.

"I think those women over there are talking about me," Laura said quietly.

It was Martha Ann and Linda.

"I'm sure they are," Neal said.

"What have I done to them?"

"If you want me to, I'll tell them to stop," Neal said.

"No, I didn't mean that," she said. "It just makes me feel uncomfortable."

"Actually you should be flattered," he said. "They only talk about women who threaten them."

"Me? Threaten anyone? I don't think so."

"Laura, you're just one of those women who, upon walking in a room, threatens even the most secure woman," he said. "In the case of M.A. there, not only is she a bitch, she's also very insecure. And she probably also knows that her husband — Bud over there — hasn't taken his eyes off your legs since you got here. Of course, I haven't either. Not for long at least."

"You're crazy," Laura said with a laugh. "And drunk, too."

"Crazy, maybe. Drunk, no," Neal replied. "But the night is young."

Neal tried to lean against the bar in the kitchen, but stumbled, as if the thing had moved. Laura chuckled.

"To tell you the truth," he said, "I think you're right. I am about smashed. Let's grab a couple of beers and go for a walk on the beach. It'll sober me up."

"I wouldn't trust you on the beach tonight if I had a guard dog," Laura said.

"I'm not that bad, am I?" he asked.

"Not yet."

"Actually I've only had a few."

"Yeah. A few six-packs."

"Oh, hell, lighten up. It's a holiday."

"Hey, I've no problem with you getting drunk," she said. "Maybe it'll do you good."

"Do me good? What's that mean?"

"Maybe you'll find yourself a date for next weekend. There's bound to be a few single women in this crowd."

"Indeed, indeed," Neal said. "In fact, see the blonde over there. She's Scott's secretary. He's kind of setting us up."

Laura glanced at Joy and grimaced.

"You can't be serious," she said to Neal, quickly taking a swig of beer and looking away from him.

"Whatta you mean?"

"No, not her. Not even you should—"

"What's wrong with her?" Neal asked.

"You'll have to admit she's rather . . . well . . . trashy looking. Right?"

So I'm not the only one who noticed, Neal thought. "I guess. I think that's what I liked about her. After all, it has been quite awhile, Laura."

"Awhile since when?"

"You know," Neal said, "awhile since I've . . . well, you know . . . been with someone, as they say."

Laura blushed but only slightly. What would Noell say?

"If it means that much to you, go for it," she finally said. "But if I were you, I'd go with the industrial-strength latex."

Neal laughed, trying to stay composed. Should he say it? Maybe not. What the hell. If it doesn't work he'll talk his way out of it. Somehow.

"If I didn't know better, Ms. Babson, I'd say you're jealous," he finally said, looking her in the eye only briefly.

"What?" she asked. "Jealous of what? Surely you don't mean her."

"No, not her," Neal said and then paused. "Of me. I think you're jealous of me."

"Suddenly I don't understand this conversation," Laura said.

"Well, let me rephrase that. You're not jealous of me specifically, but you are a bit envious of my marital situation. Free to date and all that. And I guess I'm equally so of yours."

"Oh, sure. I'm really envious of the fact you haven't had sex in — let's see, how did you say it? — awhile."

"Touché," Neal said. He started to say something else but refrained when Joy walked up.

"So you guys like Jimmy Buffett?" she asked Neal and Laura in a distinctive redneck drawl.

"Sure," Neal said. "Who doesn't?"

"Man, I'll tell ya'," Joy said, "I went to the Buffett concert in Raleigh last summer. At that outdoor place. Man, it was wild. We'd been drinking and toking all day. Man, I got so wasted they had to tote me out of there like a sack of taters."

Since Neal didn't seem to know what to say, Laura decided to help by calmly commenting, "Well for goodness sakes."

"Yeah, shit man, I love Buffett," she said before turning to Neal and asking, "Where's the beer? You got any talls?"

Neal directed her to the coolers on the deck.

"You're a very perceptive woman," Neal said to Laura after Joy had left.

"I think she likes you," Laura said, laughing at the fact Neal had slurred his words a tad. "It's probably that stain on the front of your shirt there that impressed her most."

"Damn! Cocktail sauce," Neal said, looking down. "Did you get any of the shrimp? Obviously I did. I guess I should change shirts. Wanna help?"

Laura laughed. "Now maybe if it was your shorts you were changing . . . just kidding. No, you run along and I'll mingle in your place," she said.

Neal excused himself and went to his room. So much for the bimbo, he thought.

When he rejoined the party, he found Laura engrossed in conversation with Martha Ann. "Shhiitt!!" Neal said, thinking it was under his breath when in fact it was audible to most. There's no damn telling what she'll tell Laura about me, he thought. He turned away from those who looked, searched the kitchen counter and found it. A bottle of the brown stuff — and his favorite at that — Wild Turkey.

At which point, Neal — as he was prone to say — took drunk.

Chapter Twelve

Monday, July 5

Laura was not surprised when she didn't see Neal at the 40th Street walkway. She had gotten a bit tipsy herself at the celebration of the nation's birthday. But nothing like most of the crowd. And certainly nothing like Neal.

She laughed at the thought of him standing shirtless on the coffee table, dancing with a reluctant Martha Ann, who looked as if she was either nauseous or swooning.

As she walked down the beach, she wondered — as she had half the night — if Neal had ended up in bed with Joy. Probably not. He was much too drunk, she thought. Or maybe just drunk enough. He's probably an excellent lover, she thought. He seemed like the type who would take his time. Jay took his time about some things but not about that — at least in recent years. What was it about the beach that made her so horny? Maybe because it was the first place she'd ever made love — or at least came close. She and Robbie Sellars, beach weekend her senior year in high school. They didn't actually do it, but they did just about everything except. At least everything they knew to do. They broke up soon after-

ward. She couldn't even remember why. But she vividly remembered being naked in bed with him on Saturday night.
How good it felt. How confused and nervous she felt. How
guilty she felt the next day. Yes, guilty. She could almost
swear, that Sunday night when she returned home, her parents knew. She swore she would never do anything to make
herself feel that guilty again. And she hadn't. She remained
a virgin until her wedding night. It never really seemed to
bother Jay. It was one of the things she most loved about him.

But where was he now when she needed him?

But Neal was right. She was jealous of his situation. Just
for one month, one week, even one day, she wouldn't mind
being single. She could hang with that. Not that she didn't
love Jay. She really did. She would never leave him. Not that
he was perfect. Who was? Not me, she thought. She could
never hurt Jay. Never. But at times she thought about being
with someone else. Someone caring, a little bit romantic or
something. Who hadn't? She wondered what it would have
been like if she hadn't stopped Bill Sanford that night. But
she did stop him. Thank goodness for that. If for no other
reason, she couldn't have done that to Bill's wife.

She imagined Neal and Joy in bed. It made her stomach
hurt. She really hoped they hadn't. But why did it matter?
Disgusted at herself, she broke into a jog and then a sprint.
She ran so hard her feet were hitting her rear.

Exactly what I need, she thought, a good kick in the ass.

"ARE WE STILL FRIENDS?" Neal's voice startled Laura, who was
sitting in a chair facing the ocean and reading a book. The

children were playing nearby. It was almost three o'clock in the afternoon.

"I'm not speaking to you," Laura said.

"Oh, shit," Neal said slowly, plopping down in the sand beside her.

At first she considered carrying on in that fashion for a time, but after taking a good look at him, she just couldn't do it.

"Don't worry, I'm still your friend," she said. "But I don't feel real good about being seen with you in public."

"Don't say it," he said. "Death warmed over in a defective microwave wouldn't look this bad. I know. I've seen myself in the mirror."

"You do look a little rough," Laura conceded.

"But I don't look as bad as I feel," he said. "What time did you leave?"

"Right about the time the police got there," she said.

"Oh, shit. I didn't know about that."

"But they were really nice. They reminded us politely that Sunset is a family beach — which it is supposed to be in case you hadn't noticed. One of them offered to take me home. Young guy. Sorta cute. I explained to him you were the governor and he explained recall election procedures."

"Thanks. Anybody arrested?"

"No, I don't think so. They probably would have locked you up, but you were locked in the head puking at the time."

"It wasn't the only time I puked," Neal said. "To tell you the truth, I just tossed 'em again about thirty minutes ago. But it did make me feel a little better."

"So I guess your friends have gone."

"Ex-friends. When I got up this morning they were packing. Hurriedly. We exchanged a few unpleasantries and I went back to bed."

"One of the wives was pretty ticked," Laura said. "Cathy, the football coach's."

"She seemed bent. What was her problem?" Neal asked.

"You mean you missed the skinny-dipping? It was quite a show."

"Oh, shit."

"Yeah, the football coach and a few other guys, jumping off the dock into the inlet. And then of course Miss 'Sack of Taters' herself had to join in. I think one of the neighbors saw them and called the cops."

"Oh, shit. You mean Garry Davison went skinny dipping with Joy? With Cathy there? He must have been smoking something."

Laura took a deep breath, said what the hell and asked, "So how did you make out with her, if you don't mind me asking? Did you have to take a number?"

"I do know I can plead innocent to that one. I called Scott to verify. She told him I was stuck up. Didn't speak to her more than once all night. What a relief."

"Too bad. I really hope you can get a date for Saturday. I didn't realize until last night you were such a good dancer," Laura added teasingly.

"Dancer? I don't remember dancing. Did we dance?"

"Oh, no, you didn't ask me to dance," she said.

"So who'd I dance with?"

"Don't play innocent. You know you danced with her."

"Danced with whom?"

"And I distinctly remember hearing you say to her: 'M.A., you're one hot lady.'"

"Oh, shit," Neal said, falling backward into the sand. "Oh, shit."

RIGHT AROUND SIX NEAL heard a knock at the door. He was surprised to see Laura.

"I always wanted to be in the Red Cross," she said.

She held up a large paper bag. "Hangover Helper," she said. "You still don't look well."

"I'll feel like shit for three days," he said. "Bourbon does it to me. Once I start I just can't stop drinking the stuff."

"So why did you start?"

"I don't know. I was drunk. I was under a lot of pressure. It was the heat of the battle. I don't know. I don't want to think about it."

"I thought you were going to say you did it for your country," Laura said, taking first a bottle of vodka out of the bag.

Neal cringed at the sight of it. "I'm not drinking anything for a week," he said.

"Look, I'm a doctor's wife. I know about these things. Wash down three aspirin and a Donnatal with one shot of vodka—but only one—and some Gatorade. Then eat this cheeseburger and these French fries. Put some extra salt on the fries. You're still dehydrated. And drink all the Gatorade you can. If you feel like you're getting sick, take one of these Compazines. Then go to bed. No later than seven-thirty. And then I'll meet you in the morning around six at the corner. It was boring walking alone today."

"What are you trying to do? Kill me?"

"Believe me, this works. At least for Noell. Me, I've never had much of a hangover before."

"You should try it. Loads of fun. And while you're on this mission of mercy, will you promise me one thing?" Neal asked sincerely.

"What's that?"

"The next time you see me near a bourbon bottle, just hit me on back of the head with a blunt instrument. Or maybe the bottle."

"You sound like you mean it," she said with a laugh.

"I do," he said without one.

CHAPTER THIRTEEN

Thursday, July 6

W HAT'S YOUR BOOK ABOUT?" Laura asked as she and Neal —
who actually looked and almost felt like himself again —
headed west down the beach around 6:20 A.M.

"I thought you'd never ask," he said. "I was beginning to
think you weren't interested."

"As long as it's not some coach's autobiography I might
be," she said. "I don't think I'd want to read the Mack Brown
story as told to Neal Nickelsen. But maybe a decent novel. I
haven't found one yet this summer."

"I've considered writing a novel," he said. "About a love-
starved sportswriter who goes to the beach for the summer
and meets this beautiful doctor's wife and —"

"Oh, a trashy romance," she said. "Sorry — not into that."

"You mean trashy romances or books about trashy romances."

"Neither one, wise guy."

"Well, my book's not a trashy romance," Neal said. "It's
just a collection of my columns. Just a collection of trash, some
might say."

"A collection of your columns? You mean stuff that's already been in the newspaper?"

"Yeah," he said. "You know, the best of Neal — something like that."

"You mean some people would buy that?"

"Give me a break here," he said. "I know you don't read the sports, but I'm a very popular writer in some circles."

"I know," she said. "Don't be so defensive. Actually I have been reading the sports the last few days. Read your column in Sunday's paper as a matter of fact."

"Oh, yeah. Did you like it?"

"Sure, it was fine," she said.

"Fine?"

"Yeah, fine. Good. Great. I enjoyed it."

"What was it about?" he asked.

"Sports, I suppose."

"I knew you didn't read it."

"Sorry. I was in a hurry. I like watching sports but have never been one to read about it. But I did read the headline and looked at your picture. It's getting a little dated, don't you think?"

"Some friend you are."

"Friends tell friends the truth," she replied. "I think I read that in one of the children's books."

"Just about my speed."

"Seriously, I'm looking forward to seeing your book. Do I get an autographed copy?"

"You bet. And I'm working on a couple of other books. "

"A novel?" she asked.

"Yeah, one of them."

"Good," Laura said. "It's got to be better than the ones Bonnie's passed on to me this summer. If I read one more time about someone moaning in ecstasy—"

"What's wrong with that?" he asked. "Sounds like fun to me."

"It just doesn't make any sense. People simply do not moan in ecstasy."

After a few moments of silence, Neal finally spoke up: "My ex-wife did."

"I doubt that," Laura said. "Think about it: Moaning is an expression of suffering, right? And ecstasy is like rapture. Complete exhilaration. So how do you moan in ecstasy? Who suffers in exhilaration?"

"I didn't know you were such a wordsmith," he said. "You've got a point there. But I guess it's just a literary device. What is it you call that, an oxymoron? Anyway, I guess if you're writing something like that it's better to say, 'She moaned in ecstasy' rather than 'She emitted an inarticulate sound expressive of suffering, thus indicating she had achieved orgasm.' But I wouldn't know for sure."

"Well, I hadn't thought of it that way."

"What way?"

"That it means someone had an orgasm," Laura said.

"I would guess that's what it means."

"I suppose so."

"That reminds me of the first time with Susan. I had just moved to Raleigh and went to this club and met her and we hit it off pretty well. We ended up back at my new apartment. I didn't have much furniture, but it was a new place and it had this nice thick green shag carpet. Anyway, we ended up on the carpet and, wow, we went to it for about an hour—at least. I was giving it my best, you know, trying to impress her. Anyway, she moaned in ecstasy so many times I thought my eardrums were going to burst. And finally when we got through she moaned one last time and said, 'Neal, I have never in my life. Let's get married.' It was special."

An hour—at least, Laura repeated in her head. "So how long before you got married?" she asked.

"Just about three months. And six months later Sarah was born, if you get the picture," he said.

"Oh, yes. In addition to my English skills, I'm also quite adept at math," Laura said.

"So now you know," he said. "That's the one thing about our happy little family I hadn't told you before."

"Why'd you split up?" she prodded, remembering how Neal had avoided it earlier.

"It wasn't the sex, that's for sure."

"I would guess not," she said.

"It was money."

"That would be bad to have money problems, especially when you're first married," Laura said.

"We didn't have any money problems, really. It's just that Elliot had so much more money than I did. And Susan, well, if there's only one thing she likes better than screwing, it's spending money. It's like the beach house there. She picked it out, decorated it and now never wants to use it. Elliot says she wants to sell it and get something on Bald Head Island. You know something weird? She even told me once Elliot was a lousy lover—especially compared to me, of course—but it didn't matter to her. She wanted to be rich. And now she is. She used to try to get me to go to bed with her after she married him. Can you believe that? But I wouldn't."

"I'm so glad to know you're a man of such upstanding principles," Laura said.

"I was tempted a few times, but I said, 'Hey, Susan, you can't have your cake and eat it, too.' "

"If this island were any smaller, Neal, I don't think there would be room enough for you and your ego."

"Probably not."

They laughed. The talking really made the walking go by fast.

"So what's the novel really about?" Laura asked, finally getting back to the original subject.

"Actually it's about a sportswriter, who like a lot of sportswriters is more a cheerleader for his favorite school than a journalist," Neal said. "Anyway, he discovers a scandal at the school, something that would wreck the athletic program. So there's his dilemma. Is he really a journalist or is he just a fan?"

"Sounds interesting," Laura said. "I'm betting he'll come clean in the end."

"Of course," Neal added.

"And the other book?"

"Now don't laugh," he said. "It's a cookbook."

She laughed anyway.

"My idea is to have a collection of favorite recipes from former athletes and coaches at Duke, Carolina, State and Wake Forest," Neal explained. "And little snippets about what they're doing now. I think it would be on everybody's Christmas list. Besides, I'm really into cooking."

"I didn't know that," Laura said.

"Oh, yeah. I've been wanting to ask you over for dinner, but I was afraid you'd think it was a date."

"I possibly would have dinner with you," Laura said as they reached Mad Inlet. They waded in the edge of the inlet. The tide was too high to cross to Bird.

"Really?"

"Possibly," Laura replied, thinking all the while: Did he really say at least an hour?

CHAPTER FOURTEEN

Thursday, July 8

LAURA WAS JUST GETTING out of the shower when the phone rang. She could hear Meagan talking to Jay.

"Yes, sir," she said. "Yes . . . yes . . . no . . . yes . . . I miss you, too, Daddy . . . I love you, too, Daddy . . . hold on . . . MMMOOOMMM!! For you!"

Laura had been hoping Jay would call. She had wanted to call him, but it always seemed she was bothering him when she did. So she waited. But if he hadn't called by eight, she was calling him. Laura and the children had enjoyed a great day on the beach. Neal even showed up around five and they chatted briefly. He was going to the Galleon that night—by himself—and wasn't coming back empty-handed, he promised. And even if he did, he knew this female golf pro over at Sea Trail who would go out with him, Laura and Jay Saturday night.

"She's really not much to look at," Neal said. "But she's a great gal. Has a great swing, too."

Laura picked up the phone in the bedroom. It was just past seven. She sat on the bed, wearing only a towel.

"Got a big surprise, babe," Jay said to her. He's coming down a day early for my birthday, she thought.

"I think we're getting a boat," he said. "And a real deal at that. If everything checks out, that is. You've seen this boat before. At the marina in Oriental where Darrell's boat is. Anyway, it's a Beneteau 305. Great condition. Sleeps six. It's just what I've been looking for and the price is right. These two brothers around Fremont, or somewhere, own it and they're buying a new 385, but they've got to sell this one first and they're motivated. Anyway, they've got some other people looking at it, but Darrell knows 'em and thinks if we act fast we can get it. Anyway, they're having a little race at Oriental Sunday and Darrell and Jim and I are going down and Jim and I are going to go on the race with the brothers. We're going Saturday night and stay on Darrell's boat and then after the race Sunday we'll come down to Sunset."

Laura just sat and listened in disbelief.

"Are you there, babe?"

"Yes, I'm here," she said coolly.

"Anyway, Darrell and Jim are going to take Monday and Tuesday off and so is Noell. And she and Anna and Anna's kids are going to drive down to Sunset tomorrow night and spend the weekend with you and then we'll all be together Monday. We'll all go out Monday night and celebrate your birthday."

"My birthday is tomorrow, Jay," she said.

"I know that," he said defensively.

"We were going to celebrate Saturday night."

"I know, but this will be even better," he said.

"Oh, yeah, like OD will be hopping on a Monday night."

"Dammit, I can't believe you," Jay said. "Everyone's excited about this. I went to a lot of trouble setting this up. I thought you'd be thrilled to have Noell and Anna with you. And you know our kids will enjoy seeing Anna's."

"They may even enjoy seeing you one day," Laura said. "I'll introduce you to them if you ever get around to seeing us."

"Come on, Laura, don't pull this crap on me."

"I just wish you'd at least consulted me first."

"It's a surprise," he said.

"Damn right it is!"

"Jesus, Laura, this is just like you to throw cold water on everything just because it all didn't work out exactly the way you had planned it."

"Have you even talked to Bonnie about this?" she asked.

"Yes. She's going to spend a few days with Frances in Whiteville to make room for everyone. She's been wanting to anyway. I talked to her this afternoon. She said she wouldn't tell you. She thought you'd really be excited."

Silence.

"Aren't you going to say anything?" Jay asked.

More silence. Then finally she spoke.

"Yeah, I'll say something: Happy fuckin' birthday to me!"

With that she slammed down the phone.

Laura considered breaking something but didn't. She was glad the children were engrossed in a TV show in the other room—and behaving. She had never hit either one of them, but for a few minutes there she probably would have slugged a nun if she had looked at Laura the wrong way. She considered drinking another beer but passed. Her head hurt.

"A damn sailboat race—how stupid is that?" she muttered. "And now Anna's little monsters are going to be running around here all weekend. No wonder Bonnie said she'd go to Whiteville. I wish I could go with her. And if she's gone, who the hell's gonna baby-sit the kids for us to go out? Probably me."

It was a slow, slow burn. And to make it worse, Jay hadn't called back.

"I know I hung up on him, but he should have called back by now," she told herself. "He knows how damn ridiculous this is."

She went into the bathroom and started drying her hair with the blow dryer. She stared at herself in the mirror for several minutes as the dryer whirred in her ear. When her hair at last was about dry, she turned off the dryer and calmly returned to the bedroom. She picked up the phone and called Jay at the office. He answered on the second ring.

"I am such an ass," she said calmly. "I am so sorry. You just caught me off guard. I wasn't thinking at all."

"I understand," he said. "It happens to all of us."

"I really appreciate your lining this up. It'll be a lot of fun. And Monday night will be better for my birthday. Won't be so crowded."

"What do you think about the boat?" he asked.

"Sounds great. I hope it works out."

"Hey, that would be something if we won the race," he said. "Darrell says it's a pretty fast boat."

"That would be great. Good luck."

"I love you, Laura."

"I love you, Jay. I better go. The kids are starving."

"Call me if you need anything. I'll probably be here till midnight. Trying to get all the finances figured out. I'm thinking about selling some of that bank stock Dad left us. It's never going to do anything."

"Whatever you think is best. I trust your judgment."

"I love you, Laura. I really do."

"I know," she said. "Have a good night."

With that she quietly hung up the phone. She took a deep breath, reached for the phone again, then hesitated. Finally she picked it up and dialed. She was surprised her hands weren't shaking. When she heard his voice, she hesitated.

"Hello," Neal said again.

"Hey."

"Laura?"

"Yeah. You still going to OD tonight?" She talked quickly.

"Yeah."

"What time you leaving?"

"Oh, around nine, nine-thirty. Things don't really get going until after ten. Why?"

She paused but only briefly.

"Mind if I tag along?"

"What?"

"Mind if I tag along?"

"Of course not."

"OK," she said. "I'll be at your house by nine-fifteen."

"Great," he said. "I'm looking forward to it."

"I am, too."

CHAPTER FIFTEEN

Friday, July 9

LAURA AND NOELL CLIMBED the steps to the sun deck on top of the Laughing Gull around eleven that night.

"That's the wildest bunch of rug rats I've ever been around," Noell said. "You can't believe what it was like in the car coming down here. I thought if I heard Anna say one more time, 'Stop squealing and squirming, sweeties,' I was going to start squealing and squirming."

"She's a patient mother," Laura said.

"They don't listen to a damn word she says," Noell said. "I can't believe she's going to have another one. Darrell's gonna shit when he finds out."

Anna had sprung the news of her fourth pregnancy during dinner that night.

"Wanna beer?" Noell had asked her.

"No thanks."

"Wine?"

"Nah."

"Shot of whiskey? Some smack? What gives?"

"No, thanks. I guess I shouldn't be drinking."

"Don't tell me you're pregnant again," Laura said, pointing to her.

"You got it," Anna said calmly, pointing back.

"That's great! I guess. What's Darrell say about it?"

"He doesn't know yet. I thought I might take him for a long walk on the beach Sunday night. Then if he wants to kill me he can just throw me out to sea."

Noell, Anna and the children—Jennifer, nine, Matthew, six, and Ryan, three—arrived at Sunset around eight-thirty Friday night. Laura ordered pizza. Noell and Anna surprised her with a birthday cake. It was hectic for a time. But the squealing and squirming at last had subsided. Anna, who guessed she was about six weeks, settled in on the couch to watch a video with the children. Two of the five were already snoozing and the rest seemed not far behind when Laura and Noell went on top to catch a breath. It was one of the few times Laura had been on the sundeck—or in this case, a moon deck.

The island looked peaceful. Just a few cars moving about. They could faintly hear muted voices from a nearby house and occasionally sounds of laughter. And the distinct aroma of a charcoal grill.

Laura, at Noell's insistence, was sipping a White Russian, which tasted more like a clear one.

"So, seen him much?" Noell asked.

"Who?" Laura responded, wishing Noell hadn't asked.

"You know, the Neal-ster."

"A few times."

"And?"

"And what?" Laura countered defensively.

"Just trying to give you a hard time," Noell said. "I mean, you're so perfect. Got to find something to give you grief about, even if I have to make it up."

Laura had told herself she wasn't going to tell Noell about going out with Neal. Not that it was such a big deal. Nothing had happened. Nothing. It was just two friends enjoying each other's company. That's all.

But it was fun. And now, sitting here with Noell and nothing else but the ocean breeze, Laura decided she would talk about it. She needed to. Not that it was that big a deal. But it wasn't every night she had gone out with a man to a club and danced with him and even another guy, too. Twice. His name was Phil. From Winston-Salem. A nice guy. Married. In the area on business. It was just a bunch of adults enjoying themselves but not doing anything wrong. Not that she could see.

"I went out with him last night," Laura said bluntly. "To the Spanish Galleon in OD. North Tower — you remember them — was playing. They were really good. It was fun."

At first Noell didn't say anything. Laura looked away from her and took a drink. Like it was no big deal. Just something she did. Because that's what it was.

Noell quickly broke the silence with the squeal of her own. "Get out! Get the hell out, girl!" she exclaimed.

"It was no big deal," Laura said, as if in protest.

"Get out," Noell said, shaking her head. "I can't stand it. Now, let's start at the beginning. I want to know everything."

"OK. But, Noell, you've never seen me when I was really mad, have you?" Laura asked.

"Not that I recall."

"I'm going to tell you about this, but I swear to you, if you say a word about it to anyone, you will see me mad and you will not forget it."

"Hey, I'm your attorney. Anything you say to me is just like — oh, I don't know — like telling it to your attorney."

"Or my priest?" Laura asked.

"I wouldn't go that far, but for all practical purposes, yes, I suppose so."

With some reluctance, Laura told.

The night out was a pleasant one. Laura firmly decided twice to back out but finally left the Laughing Gull in the Suburban. She told Bonnie she just needed some time alone. She was going to catch a late movie in North Myrtle. Bonnie expressed concern for her safety. Laura assured she'd be just fine. She drove to Neal's and parked way underneath the cottage. He was waiting on the steps for her. They drove to OD in his convertible with the top down. The wind made a mess of her hair, but she didn't care. Thursday night was a busy one at the Galleon. They waited in line to get in, but only for about ten minutes.

Laura was nervous — and quite uncomfortable — until they were inside. She wondered if she would see anybody she knew. She didn't. Not the whole night. That was a relief. And once inside, Laura felt as if she was someone else. Not Laura Babson at all. The place was crowded. Men were looking at her when she walked by. Really looking. Laura figured some women wouldn't like that. Usually she wouldn't. But it made her feel good.

They hadn't been there fifteen minutes before Neal excused himself for the men's room. She wandered around. The club was huge. Two clubs actually. One with a DJ that seemed to appeal to the younger crowd. The music was more rock than beach. But on the other side the shaggers gathered for the beach music band North Tower. Laura remembered them. They got their start at UNC-Chapel Hill.

She felt alive. Laura always disdained cigarette smoke. But on this night she didn't mind it. The mixture of perfumes, colognes, perspiration, beer, fruity drinks and loud bass was hypnotic to her. She felt as if she belonged—as if they were one big family. And so many were so glad to see her. During Neal's brief absence she'd been asked to dance at least three times and been offered a drink a couple of times, too. I really have lived a sheltered life, she thought.

She was standing beside a small table, one foot on a stool, when Neal found her. He admired her from a distance for a minute. Some guy walked up and said something to her. She smiled but seemed to say, "Thanks, but no thanks." She was, at that very moment, to him the most beautiful creature he'd ever seen, just as she'd been twenty years earlier on the varsity tennis courts in Chapel Hill. She wore a blue sleeveless dress, cut above her knees. It had gold trim. She had on gold sandals. She brushed her hair away once in such a manner that Neal felt a shiver come over him.

"Did you kiss him?" Noell asked.

"No!" Laura retorted. "Of course, not."

"Did he try to kiss you?"

"Will you grow up?"

"No."

"We're friends. Neal and I have become good friends. You may not understand that. Being just friends with a male."

"Hey, Laura, back off," Noell said. "This isn't about me."

Silence.

"It's just that I've never done anything like that before," Laura finally said. "But I'm glad I did it. I'm not ashamed."

"Nor should you be, my sweetness," Noell said.

"That's a real comfort, coming from you and all," she said.

"You going out with him again?" she asked.

"Oh . . . well, no, I don't think so. No, I'm sure I won't," Laura said. "This was just an out-of-the-blue thing. It just happened. I'm sure it won't again. It wasn't a date or anything at all like that. Don't even think that. It was nothing like that."

They sat in silence for a few moments. Laura felt as if Noell was going to keep talking about it. She wanted to change the subject. The boat. She'd nearly forgotten. It hadn't been mentioned.

"So it sounds like we may be getting a sailboat after all," Laura said.

"About damn time," Noell added.

"I wonder how much it's going to cost?" Laura asked.

"I think they're asking forty-two."

"Thousand? Damn, that's a lot of money."

"Yeah, but Jim said a new one would be about eighty grand."

"Well, I guess we can afford it," Laura said. "Jay handles all the finances. He said he might sell some of the bank stock his father left us."

Noell laughed. "What's so funny?" Laura asked.

"You," she said. "Wondering if you can afford half of a boat. We're the ones who ought to be worried."

"Yeah, but just because Jay is a doctor doesn't mean he makes all that much money," Laura said. "If he was some kind of specialist, he probably would. But a small-town doctor just doesn't do all that great."

"Laura, you don't have to patronize me. I'm an attorney. I know things, including all about the tidy little Babson fortune. I never said anything about it, and I sure wouldn't want Jay to know it, but I helped Harvin settle Doc Babson's estate. He hires me to do a lot of things for him, but he doesn't want anyone to know. But don't worry, I've never said anything to anyone about your money. I know how people in a small town are about things like that."

Laura looked confused. "I don't know what you're talking about," she said. "What fortune? I have no idea how much money Doc had. I don't know how much we have. All I know is Jay puts some money in my checking account the first of each month and that's what I get to spend. If I ever run out before the month is over, he raises hell."

"You gotta be kidding me," Noell said, shaking her head in disbelief.

"What are you saying, Noell? That we have a lot of money?"

"Just forget it," she said. "I shouldn't have said anything."

"No," Laura protested. "If it concerns me I have a right to know."

So against her better judgment—or was it really?—Noell told. About Doc inheriting a large sum from an aunt in Winston-Salem some years ago. About his wise investments through the years. About the $4.2 million estate he left five years ago. Considering the Babsons' modest lifestyle and the strength of the financial markets in recent years, Noell guessed it probably had doubled since then. She told about the trusts for Bonnie, Meagan and Jacob. Jay was co-trustee with the bank in Greenville and the sole beneficiary of Bonnie's trusts. Bonnie got a set amount per month to live on, indexed to inflation. She could only get more with Jay's approval. Doc even left Bonnie instructions to start an annual gifting program to Jay and his children, to reduce the eventual estate taxes at her death.

Doc did leave Jay and his two daughters some bank stock outright. But not much. For the daughters—both of whom split Farmington at the first opportunity—that was it. Bonnie didn't talk about her girls much. Just that they stayed in touch and seemed to be doing well. And that she missed them but understood.

But others in Farmington talked about them on occasion. What a disappointment—disgrace, even—they were. Blair, the oldest, attended a woman's college in Raleigh after graduating high school. She was three years older than Jay, who was the middle child. Blair was an outstanding student and athlete. She led the Fighting Rebels to back-to-back district championships in girls' basketball. She double majored in drama and French in college, graduating with honors. Then she shocked her many admirers in Farmington by moving to Paris with one of her professors, who just happened to be female. She confided in a letter to one of her old high school friends, Gloria Harper, that she and the woman were lovers. Gloria received the letter on a Thursday. Three days later, the adult men's Sunday school class at the Baptist church— which was taught by Gloria's father—held prayer for Blair.

"What kind of places, Lord, must our institutions of higher learning be to cause a young woman to lose her way like that?" Mr. Harper asked his maker.

The youngest daughter, Beth, was two grades behind Jay. Hers was a different story. She was one of Farmington's first true flower children, excelling in high school only at worrying the hell out of her old man. After her sophomore year at a different woman's college in Virginia, she went to the west coast with a friend, this one a male. Even at an early age, Beth hated both Doc and Jay. She despised Doc's endless put-downs, the comparisons to Blair and Jay. In Doc's eyes, Beth always ran with the wrong crowd. Wore her dresses too short. Wouldn't wear a bra. Smoked marijuana. And probably was a card-carrying commie in the opinion of the ultra-conservative Doc.

Beth used to think getting away to college would make things better. It didn't. But then she fell for a musician/philosopher who was into transcendental meditation and professed to be a Zen Buddhist. His name was Norman, but everyone called him Ice. She followed him to San Francisco, then to LA. Finally they settled in New Mexico on a ranch with a band of like-minded individuals. No one was sure if they ever got married. But they did have a child, a daughter named Water.

Most in Farmington assumed she was living in a hippie commune. There were rumors of satanic worship. And worse. But the truth, Laura knew, was that Ice and a partner formed a creative leadership retreat where executives from major corporations around the country attended workshops on topics such as team building and stress reduction. The business was a huge success and Ice, now known as Norm, was in big demand as a motivational speaker.

Meanwhile Blair and her friend weren't doing so badly, having founded an avant-garde theater in Paris that featured the works of gay French playwrights.

So when Doc, for all practical purposes, disinherited his daughters, it was more a blessing to them. In the case of Beth, she sold the bank stock the day she got it and gave the proceeds—in Doc's name—to a militant left-wing political organization.

The purpose of the bank stock, Noell always guessed, was to make Blair and Beth think they were being treated the same as Jay. And the purpose of the trusts, in addition to basic estate planning, was to make sure Bonnie didn't share the wealth with the daughters. "I think the girls knew the score but just didn't care," Noell said.

Noell talked endlessly about Doc's will and the trusts. About things like the federal estate tax, generation skipping, credit-shelter trusts, marital trusts and so on. Laura barely listened. She thought about the time two years ago when she asked Jay about getting a condo at the beach and he had said maybe one day they could afford it, but not now. About the extra ten thousand Ted Parker had wanted to join the practice.

She felt as if there was something pressing against the right side of her head. It was intense. But it wasn't the money, she thought. Her father had been a successful partner in a large accounting firm. They had never wanted for anything. There had been times when Laura felt guilty about having so much when so many in the world had so little. No, it wasn't the

money. It was the basic dishonesty of it all. The absolute ab-
surdity of it.

"Why would he do this?" Laura asked, as if to no one in
particular. "And why didn't I know? How dumb can I be?"

"If you want my opinion, he's just like his father," Noell
said. "You know what a miser the old man was—tight as
Dick's hatband. Jay's probably afraid if you knew about the
money you'd want to spend some of it."

Laura was sitting on the deck's built-in bench. She pulled
her feet up on the bench and placed her head on her knees.

"For someone who just found out she's a multi-million-
aire, you don't look too happy," Noell said jokingly, hoping
to break the sudden tension. She looked at Laura and saw a
small stream of tears making their way down her cheek.

"Oh . . . Laura," Noell said in a soothing tone that was un-
characteristic.

Laura barely heard her, but she did feel the sympathy. It
was appreciated, though she couldn't respond. She was thinking about a time she was in the sixth—or was it seventh?—
grade when she was the brunt of a practical joke played by
that bitch Mary Alice Kiser. She remembered the mixed feelings of pain, anger and embarrassment. As then, she felt be-
trayed and alone—an empty, almost hopeless, feeling she
couldn't explain. She put her face in her hands for a second,
shook her head, then looked up at Noell and said softly, "I
feel like such a fool."

WEEK FOUR

CHAPTER SIXTEEN

Saturday, July 10

LAURA SURPRISED NEAL BY not showing for the morning walk. It made him uneasy. Confused. Disappointed. Downright pissed.

"What'd I do?" he asked aloud with a shrug.

But then he consoled himself in the thought Laura had stayed up late talking to Noell. Maybe they talked about him? He wondered what they would say. He imagined her saying, "He's such a good dancer. So much fun to be around. God, that man could make a woman lose her religion. I mean, he's just something."

But instead she could have said, "He thinks he's such a good dancer. I couldn't tell him he's not. He acts like he thinks he's God's gift to women. Believe me, he's not."

He thought about the kiss. In a sense, he felt remorse about it. He did kind of sneak up on her. But she did kiss back.

And man, could she kiss. She wasn't a sloppy kisser. Neal hated sloppy kissers. And she wasn't one of those tight-lipped kissers. The woman could kiss. And probably wasn't even trying.

Would she tell Noell about the kiss? No, he thought not. She probably wouldn't tell Noell anything about the evening.

He wondered about his own kissing skills. He was glad he had quit smoking. Seven years now. He remembered the time he and Jill Adams were having an argument. Ah, Jill, that blast from the past. Where did it go wrong? He couldn't even remember. Didn't care now. But he did recall the time she said, "Neal, you're a great kisser, but your tongue really does taste like an ashtray."

"Like you've tasted an ashtray?" Neal responded. "What possessed you to do that?"

He knew it sounded defensive—it was—and from that point, it seemed, the relationship began to crumble. But I learned from it, Neal always told himself. Either date smokers or quit. As the former became less available, he quit. In the long run, it made his life simpler. And maybe it would make it longer. Though at times he considered that aspect of quitting a negative.

"You've added ten years to your life," his doctor told him.

"Does that mean I get to go through my twenties again?" Neal asked.

I've never asked anybody for much, Neal thought as he gave up waiting for Laura and headed back to the cottage. But just one time. One time with Laura. Or maybe two, while we're at it. My life would be so complete I'd probably start smoking again, he thought.

"HE MADE ME QUIT playing tennis," Laura said almost nonchalantly to Noell as they sat side by side watching the children play in the surf. It was just past noon. They had all slept late—what with Bonnie away.

"Who are you talking about? What are you talking about?" Noell asked.

"Jay. He made me quit playing tennis. In college."

"Made you quit?"

"No, he didn't make me. Not really. But I let him talk me into it."

"That was dumb," Noell said bluntly.

"I'm well aware of that, thank you," Laura responded coolly.

"I'm sorry. I just don't understand. Why did he want you to quit playing tennis?"

"I don't know. When we were dating, back in college, he was so possessive. We were together all the time. After our freshman year, he got an apartment and I stayed in the dorm. After class in the afternoons, we'd go to his apartment and study. And then I'd cook dinner for him and usually his roommate, too. And after we ate we'd study some more and then he'd drive me back to the dorm."

"You mean you didn't spend the night with him?"

"No! My mother would have died."

"How would she know?"

"She'd know. She called almost every morning. And sometimes late at night. I still remember my dad bitching about the phone bills."

"So college was just one party after another for you, huh?"

"Really," Laura said. "Almost every weekend, except when there were football games, we went to Farmington or Charlotte. God, I look back on it now and just can't believe it. Jay was so serious about studying. It's all he thought about. If he hadn't gotten in med school, he would have killed himself. I'm not kidding."

"So what did that have to do with tennis?"

"I don't know. I guess I was like his support system. I always took care of the details. The cooking, the laundry. I couldn't have done that if I'd been playing tennis. For me to quit, it made life simpler. And I was tired of it, too, I guess. It was just a lot easier to quit. It wasn't my knee. It was OK. It was just easier for everybody concerned."

"I don't think you were tired of it," Noell said.

"Of what?"

"Tennis. I think you just wimped out."

"You don't understand," Laura said. "You see, Jay is somewhat of an insecure person. He can be very sensitive about certain things. I have to handle him cautiously at times."

"How so?"

"Oh, I don't know. Like back in college one time. He asked me what I made on the SAT. I started to tell him, but instead I asked him what he made. So he tells me and I realized I made higher than he did. So I made up a score—about a hundred points lower than his. It just worked out better to tell him I made less."

"Like I said, you're a wimp."

"I am not."

"Laura, let me ask you this: Why did you marry him?"

"What kind of question is that," Laura said.

"You can't remember, can you?"

"Sure I can. I was in love with him. I still am."

"What do you love about him?"

"Can we change the subject?"

"No. Why did you marry him?"

"It seemed like the right thing to do. OK? And it was. He was a doctor's son and he was going to be a doctor and he said he was going to become Catholic, too, and that was all it took for my parents."

"I didn't know your parents married him."

"This isn't as simple as you make it sound, Noell."

"It never is," Noell said. "But I will tell you this, Laura: My life, for better or worse, is what I've made it. I don't have anyone to blame but me. Oh, sure, my parents screwed with my head and so did my brothers and my boyfriends and my law school professors and on and on ad infinitum. Mind-fuckers, every one of them, if you let 'em. So I made up my mind a long time ago that I could do just as good a job fucking up my mind as anyone else. So you know what I tell people who try to fuck with my mind today?"

"I can't imagine."

"I tell them, 'If you want to fuck with my mind, have at it, bucko. But just remember my mind's like a steel trap. So be careful what you try to stick in it. You might not get it back.'"

Laura laughed. "Well said, counselor."

"And just for the record, your honor," Noell added, "it's no piece of cake being named after a damn holiday either."

As NEAL'S CAR APPROACHED the Bullish Outlook, he clinched his fist and let out a big, "Yes!"

It was nearly five, but the Suburban was underneath the cottage. He quickly climbed the cottage's steps, put some beers in a cooler and headed for the beach. Laura, Noell and Anna sat together, the children playing all about. It was an intimidating sight and Neal thought about backing out. But it had been twenty-four hours since he had talked with Laura and dammit, he wasn't waiting any longer. He walked up behind them without being noticed.

"Afternoon, ladies," Neal boomed. And then added, "You, too, Laura."

"Thanks, jerk," Laura said. "I hope you've got something cold in that cooler."

Laura introduced Neal to Anna and re-introduced Noell, as if he had forgotten.

"Could I interest anyone in a beer?" Neal asked.

"No," Noell responded quickly. "But a bottle of Dom Perignon would sure hit the spot."

"You lawyers," Neal said. "Much too expensive for my budget."

Noell finally settled for a Bud Light, as did Laura. Anna, of course, refrained.

"So what's a charming single guy like you do for fun on a Saturday night on the Grand Strand?" Noell asked. "Strip joint or beach-music club?"

"Actually the Original Drifters are gracing Fat Harold's tonight. Thought I'd check 'em out and see if they're still breathing."

"Great," Noell said. "What time you picking me up?"

Neal laughed. "The last time I went out with a lawyer, I got a bill in the mail the next week for three hundred dollars. Fifty bucks an hour."

"So she worked cheap, huh?"

"I'll say. I sent her a check for twelve-fifty and wrote on it I was only paying for the fun part," Neal said.

Damn, Laura thought, now it's only fifteen minutes.

IT WAS AROUND EIGHT when the dinner dishes were cleared and Noell made her announcement.

"Girlfriend," she said to Laura, "it's about time we gave you your birthday present."

"I think the cake was enough."

"It wasn't," Noell said.

"How much time have you spent away from those kids since you've been here?" Anna asked.

"Not much," Laura said, wondering what was next and why that statement was relevant.

"It's time for you and me to go out on the town," Noell said. "So go get your pretty self ready."

"What are you talking about?"

"Go get ready. You and I are going out. OD-ville. I can't decide what to wear. But I've got it narrowed down."

"I'm giving you a birthday present Laura," Anna said. "I'm keeping the children while you and Noell go out and live it up."

"Where?" Laura asked.

"Oh, I don't know. Fat Harold's maybe?" Noell said.

"No, not there."

"OK. Wherever. You name it." Noell said.

"But I promised the kids—"

"What? That you'd play fifty-two pickup with 'em? Laura, get a life. And get your butt in gear while you're at it."

"Don't worry," Anna said. "If the husbands call, I'll tell 'em you've gone shopping for matching sailing outfits. You know how they love that kind of shit."

"WHY DO I LET you get me into situations like this?" Laura asked Noell as they waited for the bridge light to change so they could exit the island. Noell was driving her BMW. Laura figured she would end up driving it back.

"Because you always do what people tell you to do," Noell said.

"What is it about me that makes people want to tell me what to do?"

"Most people want to tell everybody what to do. And then once they find someone who will go along with it, the demands just keep coming. So I'm telling you to go out and have a good time tonight. I plan to."

"I don't feel good about this," Laura said. "I feel guilty about Thursday night already. I'm not dancing with anybody."

"Oh, c'mon. Lighten up a little. As your attorney I advise you to drink a beer. There should be some in that cooler in the back seat."

Maybe that would help, Laura thought. She just had a bad feeling about this. Which in a sense made her feel better. If the evening was indeed a bust, she wouldn't be disappointed. Maybe it would be fun. Just watching Noell in action in a bar without Jim would be worth seeing, Laura supposed. In a way she wished they would see Neal. But in other ways it would be better not to.

"Can you imagine living in that house?" Noell said, motioning to a new huge colonial-style structure that had been built on the Intracoastal across from Oyster Bay. "I wonder what the market's like for lawyers and insurance agents down here."

"I'm sure they're welcomed with open arms," Laura replied. "Aren't they always?"

"Hey, don't knock it," Noell said defensively. "When folks get in trouble, who do they turn to first? Either their attorney or insurance agent. As long as people keep screwing up, we'll keep coming to their rescue."

"It must be comforting to make your living off other people's misery."

"Beats having a real job."

They drove on mostly in silence for a few miles, through Calabash and then onto U.S. 17 South to Ocean Drive.

Noell finally asked, "You going to say anything to Jay about the money deal?"

"Nope."

"Why? You ought to spring it on him and then milk it for all it's worth."

"I don't care."

"Bullshit, Laura."

"No, I do care. I'm just not going to get mad about it and let it ruin this vacation."

"You are such a wimp," Noell said. "It's the nineties, woman."

"All I said was I wasn't going to get mad," Laura replied. "But I didn't say I wasn't going to get even."

"I heard that!" Noell said.

"But it's not what you're thinking."

"What am I thinking?"

"I know what you're thinking. But I'm not. That's not what this is about."

"So what is it about?" Noell asked.

"I think you said it best when you said, 'Get a life.' Hey, you're right. I've got nobody to blame for this but me."

AFTER ABOUT FORTY-FIVE MINUTES of sitting on the sidelines alone and watching Noell dance with some stud who couldn't have been more than twenty-five—my god, was she going to screw the guy right there on the dance floor?—Laura was ready to leave. She'd been asked to dance a few times but each time gave the same reply: "I'm waiting for my husband."

Noell at last took a break and introduced Laura to Ben.

"Zup?" he asked.

"You, I guess," Laura said.

"Yeah, I guess so," he said. "Can I get y'all something to drink?"

"Sure," Noell said. "Here's a ten. A couple of light beers for us. Keep the change."

Ben looked confused but headed for the bar as he was told. "I gotta get rid of him," Noell whispered to Laura.

"I don't want to put a damper on this, but why don't we just leave? I'm just not into it," Laura said.

Noell's eyes suddenly lit up as she looked beyond Laura. "I think you might change your mind," she said smiling.

Laura glanced over her shoulder and saw Neal approaching.

"Oh, shit," Laura mumbled. She was not amused. She could sense this was Noell's doing. It was so juvenile. This just wasn't a good weekend.

Ben returned with the beers just as Neal walked up. Noell introduced everyone and then not so politely brushed Ben off.

"Look, it's been fun," she told him. "But I get out like this about once a year and you're just not my type. But good luck at college next year."

Ben, looking even more confused, just shrugged and sauntered off. Noell excused herself to "powder my nose."

Laura was disgusted. She wouldn't look at Neal.

"So how are you?" he finally asked cautiously, sensing something was awry.

"I've been better," she said.

"What's wrong?"

"This," she said. "This . . . situation is what's wrong. Did Noell tell you we were coming here?"

"Well, she may have said something," Neal admitted. "What's the problem?"

"This whole thing. It's just not right."

"What are you talking about?" Neal was beginning to get a bit defensive.

"I wish people would stop trying to manipulate me. This is so sophomoric."

"Nobody's trying to manipulate you, Laura. At least I'm certainly not."

Laura looked down, put her left hand on her forehead and shook her head slowly.

Neal broke a long silence. "What? What? Talk to me."

"Look, Neal, Jay's coming down for the week tomorrow — as you know — and I think we just ought to cool it. I've enjoyed the walks on the beach and all, but I think it should end here. It's getting too complicated."

"Do you always get this upset when you're about to see your husband?"

"That wasn't fair," she said. "Jay and I are having some problems and to be honest you're not making things any easier."

"I didn't know that was my job."

Laura was getting more and more irritated by Neal's cavalier attitude. Couldn't he be a little more understanding? She wished Noell would get back so they could leave.

And Neal — he didn't feel much better about the situation either. What was it Laura had called it? Sophomoric. Yeah, it was.

"It's not that I would mind being here with you tonight," Laura at last said, "but it's like you and Noell set it up. I don't like being set up. I just wish people would be honest with me. I shouldn't have come here with you the other night."

"OK, Laura," Neal said, taking a deep breath. "I'll be real honest with you, if that's what you want."

"That's up to you," she said.

"OK. I think that indeed you do have a few problems with your husband," Neal began in an unbecoming tone of voice that to Laura seemed nearly belligerent. "Three to be exact. Number one, you're under-loved. And for someone as loving as you, that's a shame. Number two, you're underappreciated, which also is a shame given all you do in running your household and raising your children. And then number three — which is the biggest damn shame of all given the fact you've got to be one of the best-looking women I've ever had the pleasure of knowing — you are most definitely under-fucked."

"What did you say?" Laura shot back.

"You heard me. I don't stutter," he said.

"You asshole!" she said in disgust as she got up from her seat and collected her purse. "When Noell gets back, tell her I'm waiting at the car."

"Wait, Laura," Neal said, reaching for her arm as she walked away. "Just calm down."

When he touched her arm, she spun around quickly and glared at him. Neal quickly realized he had made his second strategic blunder of the evening. If looks could kill, he thought, that one would be an Uzi.

"Leave me alone," she said through clenched teeth. "Just leave me alone."

CHAPTER SEVENTEEN

Sunday, July 11

Neal was almost certain it was a hopeless cause. But he decided to go to his usual rail on the walkway and wait nonetheless. Just in case.

"God, why did I say that?" he asked himself for about the five hundredth time in the last ten hours.

Though he figured she would be a no-show for the morning walk—two days in a row now—the ocean breeze would do him good. Though the sun was just beginning to appear on the horizon, it already was hot. He sat in stillness as he watched the glory of the ever-lightening sky beyond the fishing pier, which would soon be silhouetted by the piercing rays. The beach was all but deserted. The breeze was calm, as was the surf. The breaking waves had a laziness about them. On the railing he placed a yellow rose he had purchased for three dollars in a convenience store in North Myrtle the night before. It had a small card attached on which he had written, "I'm sorry."

As Neal studied the sand below, wondering if maybe a walk alone would do him good, Laura turned right off Bay

Street onto 40th, steady strides moving her along the asphalt toward the beach. She wondered if he would be there. She considered turning left on North Shore Drive, walking over to Sunset Beach Drive and then past the stores and two tiny motels to the beach access at the fishing pier. From there she could go east and he'd never see her. Down to First Street. She had really not explored the eastern end of the island as much as she would like. She felt comfortable on the west end, even though over half of the island's homes were on the east side. Maybe it was time for a change, to explore a bit, she thought. How could this have happened? In just three weeks. She felt as if it had been longer.

As she approached North Shore, even from that far away, she could see that someone was sitting on the railing of the wooden walkway—in his usual spot. She knew it was Neal. Could he see her from here? What the heck. It wasn't that big a deal. She'd think of something to say. Or do. To make things right. But what? What could make this right? She didn't know.

Neal glanced to his left once and saw her approaching down 40th. He quickly looked back to the ocean. He would pretend not to see her. What would she say?

Nothing, as it turned out. Laura simply walked by him without slowing up. When she was no more than ten feet past, he said, "Hold on, Starshine. What's the hurry?"

Laura didn't let up, instead taking the steps down to the ocean without breaking stride, turning west toward Bird Island. Neal was right behind.

"Nice morning, huh?" he asked.

Nothing. She just kept walking, a little faster than usual.

"Hey, look, ah, Laura, about last night, well, I'm sorry. Really sorry. See, I got you a rose. The whole deal was uncalled for. I mean, Noell, I guess she thought it would be kind of like a joke, or something and then when you acted upset, I got upset, but instead of trying to see it from your perspective, I was like, 'Wait a minute. What in the hell did I do?' So I kind of got in that mode and well, I guess I've had better nights and I guess you have to. Well, that goes without saying, of course."

Laura really was walking fast, Neal thought. And getting faster. He kept talking. She kept silent. He noticed he was breathing heavy. The sand felt particularly heavy on his feet. Why didn't she stop and say something?

"But . . . really . . . I'm sorry and . . . Jesus, Laura, I'm about out of breath here. Will you slow down just a little?"

She sped up.

"C'mon, Laura . . . please!"

Finally she stopped.

"Neal," she said politely, "if you're going to keep walking with me this summer, I suggest you get in better shape."

With that she turned, leaving him not in a quick walk but instead a fast jog, almost a sprint. But he wasn't letting her off that easy. The tide was nearly high. She couldn't go but so far. It took him ten minutes to reach Mad Inlet. She was seated with her back to him, her feet in the water.

"So what's going on?" he asked casually, sitting beside her, but not too close. Like Laura, he put his feet in the water.

"I wonder that myself," she replied, "as I sit here in my under-fucked state of existence. Who says something like that to somebody, Neal? Think about it. It's so degrading."

"It was a joke."

"I didn't get it."

He didn't know what to say. Knew what he wanted to say. Didn't know how to say it. He noticed a broken sand dollar nearby, picked it up and placed it on her forearm.

"Half-dollar for your thoughts," he said.

Laura chuckled.

"Neal," she finally said. "I get this feeling that you may be thinking this is leading to something it really shouldn't be—something it really isn't going to lead to. Oh, I don't know what I'm saying."

"OK, I think I get the picture here," Neal said. "I think. What do you want me to do? What do you want me to say?"

"I don't know," she said. "Nothing. You say whatever you're thinking. I don't want you to say or do anything, not on my behalf. It's just that . . . I'm married, Neal. I'll admit I'm attracted to you. You've given me more attention the last few weeks than Jay has in five years. And in some ways there's nothing I would rather do right now than go back to your house and make love. OK? Does that make your male ego feel better? But for a lot of good reasons, I just can't."

"Name one," he challenged.

"OK, smart ass, I'll give you one even you'll understand. I'm having my period."

"That's a good one," Neal conceded.

"But that's beside the point."

"Is it?" he asked.

"Yes. Look, all the hell I did was come down here for a simple vacation with my children and mother-in-law and next thing I know my life's become very complicated."

"Because of me?"

"Partly," she said. "But there are some other things, too."

"The problems with your husband."

"His name is Jay. Why do you always call him my husband?"

"Calling him by his name would seem—I don't know—too personal."

They sat in silence for over a minute.

"I'm not going to be here this week," Neal at last said. "I'm leaving tomorrow and I'll be back next Monday."

"Where are you going?"

"I'm going to cover the seniors' tournament in Ohio."

"When did you decide this?"

"Right now to tell you the truth. I've been wanting to go to one this summer. And I sure don't want to be here this week when your husband's here. Maybe that will make your life simpler."

"Yeah, maybe so," she said, thinking how strange it would be not to see him.

"I hope you'll still park at the house."

"Maybe."

"I'll leave the key."

"Why?"

"I'd appreciate it if you'd check on the house."

"Whatever," she said, standing up. "I better get back. The kids will be up soon."

"Laura, let me ask you something," Neal said as he rose to face her. "Twenty years ago, when I asked you out, if I had been more persistent, more assertive—like kept asking you and done things to let you know how important it was to me, how much you meant to me — do you think you eventually might have gone out with me?"

Laura shrugged. "Maybe."

"Probably?"

"Maybe!" she repeated before turning and jogging away from him on the beach.

THE HUSBANDS ARRIVED AT the Laughing Gull around ten-thirty that night. The children having settled down, the wives were sitting on the screened porch talking. Anna had just remembered some new gossip. She only knew bits and pieces. But it involved one of the male high school teachers — a coach, she thought — and a female student. She felt sure either she or Darrell would get the scoop once they got home.

Earlier in the day Laura and Noell made up. Both agreed they were wrong. Laura gave her a hug, to which Noell responded by saying, "Hey, let's not turn this into a sorority party."

Jim and Darrell ascended the steps first. Both gave their wives kisses. Then Darrell, as was his habit, kissed both Laura and Noell on the cheek. Jay finally showed, patted Laura on the head and said, "I gotta go to the can."

"So do we own a boat?" Noell asked Jim.

"It's a long story," Jim said in what seemed to be disgust. "I better let Jay explain."

"Oh, god," Laura said. "Not again."

The story was indeed a long one. The race was called off for lack of wind. So Jay and Jim tooled around the river with the boat owners. Just as they were about to turn back to the marina, the wind finally picked up and they managed to sail. But then a storm came up—"I knew we should have gone in," Jay said—and they had a difficult time getting the sails down. They motored into South River, seeking shelter in a certain cove. They found the cove just as the rain stopped but then ran aground on a shoal.

"It was a nightmare," Jay said.

"Oh, it wasn't that bad," said Jim, who then whispered to Noell, "Jay was scared shitless."

"I thought we'd never get back," Jay said.

"It was fun."

Noell finally broke it up. "Enough. So did we buy a boat?"

Silence.

"It's up to Laura," Jay finally said.

"Me? What have I got to do with it?" Laura demanded. "If you want it, get it."

"No, I want you to see it first."

"I saw it. You said it was at the same marina as Darrell's boat."

"Yeah, but you don't remember."

"I'm sure it's fine if you and Jim like it."

"What about me?" Noell asked.

"Please, Noell, stay out of this," Jim cautioned.

"You can drop by the marina Sunday on the way to taking the kids to camp," Jay told Laura. "You can follow me. You check the boat out and then take the kids."

"Oriental is not exactly on the way to Salter Path, is it?" she asked.

"Not really," Darrell said. "But it won't be bad. You can take the ferry at Minnesott over to Havelock and then up to

Morehead and then to Salter Path. It won't be bad. It'll probably be fun."

"The kids will like the ferry," Jay said.

So why don't you and Darrell take the kids to camp, Laura
thought. It sounded like an all-day ordeal, which indeed it
would prove to be.

"Please, Laura," Noell said. "Let's get this thing over."

"I for one don't want to make a purchase like that without Laura checking it out first—am I wrong here?" Jay said.

Noell cleared her throat and tried to read Laura's reaction.

"I agree," Jim said. "But I'm sure you'll like it and in a
little over a week we'll own a sailboat."

"Good," Noell said. "That settles it."

"Yep, I guess it just about does," said Laura, who then politely excused herself for bed.

CHAPTER EIGHTEEN

Tuesday, July 13

Y ou've got grounds," Noell said as she and Laura — taking a break from their husbands, Darrell, Anna, and the children — strolled down the beach in the direction of the fishing pier around eleven in the morning. "You've definitely got grounds."

"Grounds for what?"

"You name it: divorce, murder, caning, Chinese water torture. I'm telling you, you've got grounds."

"He was doing the best he could."

"Oh, so now you're going to be on his side. Cute."

"I've come to face it: Jay simply has limited capacity for irrational, though meaningful, sentiment. Of course, it's taken me seventeen years of marriage to figure it out."

"So that's why he took us to that country music place for your birthday. Wow, what a meal. They fried everything but the napkins."

"It wasn't that bad."

"How would you know? You didn't eat a thing."

"I don't eat fried food."

"Right. So that was pretty dumb to take you there for your birthday."

"Yes, but the men and children enjoyed it. I'm sure he considered it a good value: dinner and entertainment at a reasonable price. The show wasn't all that bad."

"You don't even like country music."

"I can take it or leave it. It was all right."

"You're letting him off easy, Laura. He owes you."

"No, he doesn't. He doesn't owe me a thing. He's a good husband, father and provider. He has his shortcomings, but who doesn't? I certainly have mine."

"I don't get it."

"Sorry."

"But he lied to you."

"About what?"

"The money, Laura"

"No he didn't. He never once lied about it. He just didn't tell me. I'm sure he had his reasons. I'm sure it's all for the best."

"All for the best?"

"Yes."

"And your tennis."

"All for the best. Who cares about tennis?"

"I just don't get it."

No, Laura thought, you probably don't. For even though she considered Noell her best friend, there were some thoughts—some feelings—you just don't share with even your best friend. Besides, Laura never considered herself one of those best-friends types. She never saw the need to bounce things off someone first. She considered herself an intelligent, capable and independent person. She could make up her mind on her own. Make her own decisions. Make her own mistakes. And live with the consequences. Good or bad.

"So what are you going to do while the kids are at camp next week?" Noell asked.

"Oh, I don't know. Just hang around here and continue to prematurely age my skin."

"Just you and the old rich mama-in-law, huh? Maybe you'll have a chance to talk her out of some of those bucks."

"No, she won't be here either. Frances has talked her into going to Williamsburg next week with a group of women from Whiteville."

"Oh, so it'll just be you and Neal down here. Now that should be interesting."

"Very funny. Actually, he won't be here either. He's gone for two weeks."

"I thought it was only for this week."

"Some special assignment he got. He called this morning. I told him I'd keep a check on the house. His last week here ends on the twenty-eighth. Then his ex-wife's husband is entertaining some clients at the place. He said he might not even be back at all except to pick up his stuff."

"Don't tell me he's given up on you."

"He never had any designs on me."

"I think he did."

"He's just a flirt. And I'll admit that was fun going out that one night. Please, Noell, don't ever tell anybody about it. I shouldn't have gone. Jay would die if he found out."

"I won't tell. And once again, I'm sorry about the deal Saturday night. I get carried away at times. I guess I have this fear I'm the only woman in Farmington who's ever run out on her husband."

"You probably are."

"Give me a break."

"Well, the whole thing's of no matter now," Laura said.

"And you probably think it's all for the best."

"Most definitely," Laura said.

Even though she felt it was absolutely necessary to do so, Laura really didn't enjoy lying to her friend. But Noell had a big mouth at times, especially when she was drinking. No telling what she might say if she knew. And at this point, Laura thought, who knows what I might do.

THE BEAMANS AND THE Lanes left Sunset around five in the afternoon.

"We really ought to try to get home before dark," Jim had said. And, of course, everyone agreed, though if pressed on it no one could have come up with a valid reason for trying to get home before dark. It was just one of those things people often said and then translated into purposeful action.

"I wonder if they made it home before dark," Jay would say to Laura later that night as they sat on the back porch, saying practically nothing, staring through the screen at practically nothing.

"Huh?" she replied.

"I wonder if Jim and Darrell made it home before dark."

"How would I know?"

"I was just wondering."

"Why?"

"I dunno," he replied defensively. "I was just wondering. That's all."

"What difference would it make? It's not like they don't have headlights. And even the streets in Farmington don't roll up at nightfall. But if you're really concerned about it, we could call 'em."

"Hey, back off, Laura. I was just making a statement here."

"Oh, I'm sorry, Jay. You know how I am when I'm having my period."

"Oh," he said, then adding upon reflection, "So when did it start? Today?"

Jesus, Laura thought, he's been here since Sunday night and hasn't even realized it.

"Just this afternoon," she said, somewhat surprised at her newfound ability to fabricate so comfortably.

"You think it'll be over by Sunday?" he asked with a tinge of helplessness in his voice.

"Probably not," she said in a disappointed tone, knowing full well it would be.

"Too bad," he said.

"Yeah, too bad."

Chapter Nineteen

Thursday, July 15

Around three in the afternoon, Laura and Jacob were walking along the beach in the direction of the pier, collecting a few shells. They had left Jay and Meagan at work on an intricately designed sand fortress. Meagan's new friend Jeremy had joined in. Laura sensed Jacob, who had been relegated to order-taker status, felt left out.

She had whispered in his ear, "Go for a walk with me and we'll get ice cream at the Trading Company. But don't tell the others. It'll be our secret."

Besides, Laura thought, it'll be good for Jay and Meagan to spend a little time together. She thought about Jay's sisters. What must it have been like for them growing up in the Babson household? Even Jay had admitted his father wasn't always fair to them. But he always insisted the old man was just as tough on him, maybe even tougher. The girls just couldn't take it, he'd say. That statement always infuriated Laura, though he never knew it.

It was often hard for Laura to realize—to even consider the notion—that in just ten years her youngest would be in college. How would it turn out for this generation of Babsons? Laura sometimes would look at Bonnie whenever her daughters were mentioned and notice a look on her face that others seemingly could not see. She couldn't imagine going months, years at a time without seeing Meagan. Or without seeing her own mother. Though it was difficult, Laura often made the nearly five-hour drive to Charlotte. She hadn't seen her mother since early May and missed her. She had promised Laura she would visit her at the beach. But things kept coming up and just Wednesday she had admitted they wouldn't be able to make it. Laura promised to take the children to Charlotte for a few days after the vacation, but before school started back.

Laura placed a hand on top of Jacob's head, rubbing his head. "You're getting tall, Jay-Bo," she said, using her pet name. "So tell me, what do you want to be when you grow up?" she asked. It was a question she often posed to her children. She'd kept a mental record of the multitude of answers through the years.

"A professional football player," he said, "for the North Carolina Tar Heels."

"Carolina's a college," she reminded him. "Colleges don't have professional players. At least they aren't supposed to."

"Oh, yeah," Jacob said. "I forgot. The Panthers. I could play for the Carolina Panthers."

"After college," she said. "But you know you can't play football forever. What about after then?"

"A doctor, I guess," he said.

"That's nice," Laura said. "Meagan wants to be a doctor, too. It'll be nice having two to look after me in my old age."

"Meagan can't be a doctor, can she?"

"Sure, she can."

"I thought girls could only be nurses."

"Boys can be nurses and girls can be doctors," Laura said. "You know I've told you that before."

"I forgot. So why aren't you a doctor?"

Good question, she thought. "I guess Daddy and I figured one doctor was enough in our family," she said. "That way I get to spend more time with you and Meagan."

"If Meagan's a doctor who's going to spend time with her children?" Jacob asked.

"Her husband, I guess," Laura said. "I'm sure it'll all work out."

They exited the beach at the walkway near the pier, made their way through the large public parking lot on Main and then up Sunset Boulevard about a block to the Sunset Beach Island Trading Company, one of the few commercial establishments on the island.

Jacob loved to visit the Trading Company. In addition to ice cream, beachwear and water toys, the business featured an amiable owner who during slow times would entertain younger patrons with magic tricks. Laura was looking through some T-shirts—both Meagan and Jacob could use some new ones—when Jacob came up behind her quickly and slapped her on the leg.

"Mom," he said quietly. "Look." He opened his hand to reveal a fifty-dollar bill.

"Where did you get that?" she asked.

"On the floor, over there. Can I keep it?"

"I don't know," Laura said. "Just hold on to it a minute."

Jacob was so excited his hands shook. He shirked back in a corner of the store. Fifty dollars. He wasn't sure he had ever even seen a fifty-dollar bill before. He'd had a fifty-dollar check before. Laura's mother, whom all the grandchildren called Nana, had sent him one his last birthday, having doubled her usual birthday ante in the last year.

Laura looked around the store. It was fairly crowded. At first she considered blurting out, "Anybody lose a fifty-dollar bill?" But she quickly realized how dumb that would be. Maybe she should give it to the owner. But what would he do with it? They could just leave. But that wouldn't be right, would it? Just then she noticed an older woman at the cash register, looking through her purse frantically, then saying something to a younger woman beside her, who was about Laura's age.

"Just calm down, Mother," the younger woman said.

"But I know I just had it," the older woman replied.

"Then let's retrace your steps. Where were you last? Over at the toys?" The women went to the toy section and were looking around on the floor. Laura motioned for Jacob.

"Excuse me," Laura said politely as she approached the women. "Did you lose something?"

"My mother thinks she may have lost a fifty-dollar bill."

"I know I lost it," the older woman said. "I just had it. I took it out—"

"We found it—no, my son here did."

Jacob, without reluctance, handed the woman the money.

"Oh, thank heavens," the older woman said.

"Isn't it nice to know there are a few honest people around?" her daughter added, patting Jacob on the head.

"I'm just glad we found it before you left," Laura said.

"Because you were so honest, young man," the mother said, "I'm going to give you a five . . . no, a ten-dollar bill."

"You don't have to do that," Laura said.

"No, I insist," she said, handing a ten to Jacob. "Good deeds deserve reward."

"That's very nice of you," Laura said. "What do you say, Jacob?"

"Thank you," he said. "I'm glad I found your money."

Laura let Jacob pick out anything he wanted in the store for ten dollars. It took a while, but he finally settled on a snorkeling mask that went for $9.95. Laura sprang for the tax.

As they left the store, she told Jacob she was proud of him.

"You know, some people would have just kept that fifty dollars," she said. "But doesn't it feel better to have ten dollars and know you got it for doing a good thing rather than have fifty dollars just because someone lost it. Losing that money probably would have ruined that woman's vacation."

"Yeah . . . I mean, yes, ma'am. If I had lost fifty dollars, I'd be mad if someone had found it and not given it back."

They walked back to the beach, Jacob licking a cone of chocolate; Laura, fat-free strawberry yogurt.

"Mom," Jacob said after they crossed Main, "I'm glad you're not a doctor."

"Why?"

"Because I like spending time with you."

"Well, thank you, Jacob. That was very sweet. I like spending time with you, too."

When Jay and Meagan were in sight, Jacob darted ahead. He couldn't wait to tell about the money. But he was out of breath when he got there and Jay couldn't make much sense of the story.

"Go try out your new mask," Laura told him. "I'll tell 'em all about it."

At the conclusion of a detailed recounting of the visit to the Trading Company, Laura remarked, "Aren't you proud of him?"

"Yeah, that's neat," Meagan said.

"I think it's lame," Jay said, seemingly in disgust.

"What do you mean lame?" Laura retorted.

"He should have kept the fifty."

"But he made ten dollars."

"Better check your math on that one, Laura. Sounds like to me his Mom stiffed him out of forty."

"You can't be serious."

"Hey, finders keepers, losers—"

"Never mind. I don't care what you say, I think we did the right thing."

"I'm sure you do," he said, "but I'm just talking about the way things are in the real world. You know, Laura, for a woman your age you really are naive."

"Whatever," she said as she headed down to the water to help Jacob with the mask. And this, she thought, from a man who suggested she buy *The Book of Virtues* for the children.

JAY LIT THE CHARCOAL around eight. He had rolled the grill out to the short dock behind the house. It had been high tide around five-thirty that afternoon. As such, the marsh was still under water. A pleasant southwest breeze kept the bugs away. He sipped on a gin and tonic and was just considering dropping a line in the water below when Laura emerged from the house with a magazine and a beer.

"Mind if I join you?" she asked him.

"Of course not. What are the kids doing?"

"I told them they could watch TV until dinner. They're pretty tired."

"I know the feeling."

They sat together in silence. Laura read. Jay occasionally would fiddle with the fire. Suddenly the silence was broken by Meagan, who ran out on the deck and called, "Mom, telephone. I think it's Mr. Neal."

Laura winced.

"Neal Nickelsen?" Jay asked. "Why would he be calling?"

"I guess to check on the house," she said as she headed inside.

Laura picked up the phone and said, "Hello."

"Afternoon, Starshine. How's it going?"

"Fine."

"Did you get the flowers?"

"Yes, they were beautiful. Thank you."

"Is the doctor in?"

"Outside. Cooking on the grill."

Laura looked through the sliding glass door to make sure. There was nothing wrong with Neal calling, but it made her feel uncomfortable.

"I've missed you," he said. He waited a moment for a reply and finally, "You been walking every morning?"

"Yeah. Look, I better go. The house is fine. I went inside. Everything is fine."

"So you got the invitation."

"Yes. It was very nice. And funny, too."

"So," he said.

"So?"

"So, can you have dinner with me Monday night? I really am a decent cook. I make this great seafood and pasta thing. I think you'll like it."

"I guess so."

"Good. I'll get all the stuff. My flight gets into Wilmington around three Monday afternoon. I'll look for you on the beach late in the day."

"Sure."

"Laura, is something wrong?"

"This just isn't a good time to talk."

"I understand."

"Good."

After she hung up, Laura went to the refrigerator for another beer. She realized her hands were shaking slightly. It was good to hear his voice. But she wondered what Jay might say.

When she returned to the dock, Jay immediately asked, "What did he want?"

"Just wanted to know if the house was all right," she said. "He gets real nervous about it. I guess it's because it belongs to his ex-wife and her husband."

"Oh, yeah," Jay said, recalling Laura's explanation when they had parked at the cottage. "So when's he coming back?"

Laura thought for a second. "He's not sure. He knows he won't be here next week. He said something about some special assignment or something. After that, I don't know."

"Well, good," Jay said.

"What do you mean, good?"

"Good that he's not going to be here."

"Why?"

"Nice-looking single guy like that down here. He's probably on the prowl for good-looking women whose poor husbands are at home working their asses off—not that I don't
trust you."

"Well for goodness sakes, Jay, I'm so honored that after
four years of dating and seventeen years of marriage, I've
earned your trust. Maybe this calls for a celebration."

"I was just kidding, Laura."

"Believe me, you don't have anything to worry about. I
don't think I'm his type—if you know what I mean."

Jay looked puzzled. "No, I don't know what you mean."

"Oh, I guess you don't know."

"About what?"

"About Neal Nickelsen."

"What about him?"

"It took me a little while to figure it out, but it's like this:
He's single and doesn't have a girlfriend. He's really into
cooking. Real fancy things. And the only visitors he's had
this summer have been men. There's a different man over
there with him every time you turn around. Sometimes two
or three. And think about it: For a living he hangs around
men's locker rooms."

Jay thought for a moment. "You think he's gay?"

"What do you think, Sherlock?"

"I don't doubt it. There was this column he wrote about
Dean Smith one time. Man, did that piss me off. I don't know

now exactly what he said, but I remember thinking at the time, 'What kind of queer would write something like that?' Damn, I can't wait to tell Jim. He'll love it."

Laura stood up and glanced at the grill. She took another sip of beer and realized her hands weren't shaking anymore.

"You ready to put the steaks on?" she asked.

"Sure."

"Good. I'll get 'em," she said, thinking all the while: Laura, for a woman your age. . . .

CHAPTER TWENTY

Friday, July 16

Neal woke up confused. Though he was miles from the ocean—on a bed in an Embassy Suites in Cleveland, Ohio, of all places—he could taste salt water. It seemed to be on his tongue. In the back of his throat. Bubbling up through his nostrils. He looked for the clock, which faced away from him. He turned it to read 4:47, the deep red standing out in an otherwise darkened room.

He attributed the vivid dream to excessive intake of alcohol. He really had overdone it. Why had he let those other writers talk him into taking a cab to that strip joint? But he hadn't made a fool of himself. Just had a good time. And he remembered full well that Letterman was still on when he got back to his room so it wasn't but so late.

He recently had read somewhere that a symptom of over-indulgence—or alcoholism as they called it—was vivid dreams. Neal didn't consider himself an alcoholic but knew he was a prime candidate, what with the family history.

"At least I'm a nice drunk," he told himself. "Never hurt anyone much but myself—at least not that I can remember."

He thought about Sarah, his daughter. He often did at times like these. But she was OK. He was sure of it. Her European summer—Susan and Elliot's idea of properly prepping her for prep school in the fall—was almost over. Neal looked forward to seeing her. Hearing all about it. What an opportunity. It was important, he felt, to take advantage of opportunities. He wanted her to do that.

He went to the bathroom and brushed his teeth. He had a habit of doing that when he woke up during the night. He was glad he had purchased a two-liter Pepsi the day before and had stored it in the refrigerator in the suite. He was thirsty. Dressed only in his boxers, he grabbed the Pepsi, found the remote, sat down on the couch, the large bottle between his legs, and turned on the TV. He took a big hit. As the screen began to lighten, he thought again about the dream.

It was so stupid. Or was it? So surreal. But also real.

He had been walking about ten steps behind Laura on the beach. She wore a bright orange two-piece. They were going in the direction of Bird Island. The tide was low. When Laura reached Mad Inlet, she waded across effortlessly, the water no more than two feet deep.

But as he followed behind, it was as if he stepped in a hole. Suddenly the slow-moving water was flowing quickly toward the ocean. His head popped up from below the water and he could see her, just ahead. She kept walking, though it looked as if she might be watching him from the corner of her eye, a smug look on her face.

He tried to call her name, but the out-going current overtook him. He felt himself being pulled out to sea. Into a cold void of nothingness. When he woke up, for just a moment there in the dark, he thought he was dead.

ABOUT TWELVE HOURS LATER on Sunset Beach, Laura realized she was out of laundry detergent.

"I'm going to run to the Island Market," she told Jay. "I've got at least two loads to do to get them ready for camp."

It was a little thing — just a trip to the store — but the break from Jay and the children was a welcomed respite.

Once in the store, she took a few moments to browse through the T-shirts and souvenirs that adorned the left wall. She found a print she liked, a reproduction of a painting of the Sunset Beach bridge.

"That would look nice in the rec room at home," she said to herself. "Or maybe our bedroom."

On the back was a brief history of the bridge. The island's original developer, Laura learned, built the first bridge in 1958 and privately maintained it until 1961 when the North Carolina Department of Transportation replaced it. The state replaced it again in 1973 and yet again in 1984 with the current bridge. It measures 508 feet, six inches and is manned around the clock by a crew of bridge tenders. For several years, the state has had plans to replace the one-lane span with a high-rise, fixed bridge. Replacement of the bridge was a source of constant controversy.

"If they ever replace that bridge," Laura had heard a man say on the beach, "the next thing will be a sewer lines, then condos and finally high-rise hotels like at Myrtle. Think of it: the Sunset Beach Hilton. It's enough to make me puke."

Close to the door of the island market was a large note-book in which residents and visitors wrote comments about replacing the bridge. Most seemed to oppose it, by a margin of about five to one. Most of the comments were succinct:

No, never.

Please keep our bridge!

It's a hassle. We need a new bridge.

Laura skimmed through the pages and was just about to write her opinion. There are plenty of beaches around with fixed bridges, she thought—if you don't like the Sunset Beach bridge, don't come to Sunset Beach. Just then she spotted a rather lengthy treatise in familiar handwriting, written just three days earlier. Oh, brother, she thought as she began to read:

July 13

To: Whom It May Concern

Re: Sunset Beach Bridge

I am a medical doctor on vacation here with my family. While this beach seems to be an adequate one, I for one feel uncomfortable staying here because of that antiquated bridge. My profession requires me to be accessible to others. In the event of a malfunction of the bridge (I understand it has happened on many occasions before) I could be stranded here at a time when my services are desperately needed on the mainland. I am equally concerned that in the event of some life-threatening emergency, fire and/or rescue person-nel could be needlessly detained by the bridge when their services are required on the island. In addition, I also own a sailboat and know what an inconvenience it is for boaters en route on the Intracoastal Waterway to be delayed at this beach when such is not the case at other beaches.

I fully understand from reading some of these other well-intended (though somewhat irrational) comments that the bridge holds a certain sentimental and nostalgic value to some. That is all well and good for them. Perhaps a worthy monument could be erected in memory of the bridge or some other appropriate gesture made to appease them. But in this day and time I find it not only ludicrous but totally unacceptable that the proper authorities have not attended to this matter in a sensible fashion. Therefore I urge those in a position to impact this pressing issue to take action post haste. Failure to do so would leave me no choice but to insist that my family vacation in another locale in the future. I am sure many, if not all, of my fellow professionals would support my position.

Sincerely,

J.W. Babson Jr., MD

Farmington, NC

Under it someone had scrawled:

Get a life, dude. This is the beach.

Laura decided against the print for the time being, just bought the detergent instead.

WEEK FIVE

CHAPTER TWENTY-ONE

Sunday, July 18

THE BABSONS LEFT SUNSET around seven-thirty in the morning, right on schedule. Jay had it all planned out. He led the way in the Mazda, Jacob seated beside him. Laura followed in the Suburban with Meagan. Jay had filled both vehicles with gas the day before. He planned but one stop, the McDonald's off U.S. 17 just before they got to Wilmington. *Why do we have to go to McDonald's for breakfast?* Laura thought, but she did not question the plan. From there — Jay had ordered the Big Breakfast, the kids each a Breakfast Burrito and hash browns, and Laura, of course, only a fat-free muffin — they followed 17 through Wilmington, past Topsail Beach and Camp Lejeune Marine Base, through Jacksonville, finally reaching New Bern, where after crossing the bridge over the Neuse River, they picked up N.C. 55, taking it to Oriental and at last Sea Harbour Marina.

"There's the pool over there," Jay said to the children.

"Can we go swimming?" Meagan asked.

"We're not here to have fun," he replied.

Got that right, Laura thought.

One of the boat's owners, a pharmacist from Fremont, was waiting for them. He showed the Babsons around. The children were impressed. And even Laura was, too. The Beneteau was even nicer than Darrell's boat. A cabin in the bow, another in the stern and benches on either side of the galley's table that were just right to double as children's bunks.

"I figure all six of us can sleep on this," Jay said to Laura.

"I'm sure Jim and Noell will be thrilled."

Finally the owner asked, "So, does the ship meet with the first mate's approval?"

First mate? Laura thought. Get real.

"Well?" Jay asked.

"I think it's wonderful," Laura said politely. "Now I better get the kids to camp."

"Stay for a sail," the owner said. "There's some pretty decent wind out there."

As it worked out, Jay did stay, which didn't surprise Laura, whose job it now was to finish the journey alone. She promised to call Jay when she got back to Sunset that night.

"I'll miss you this week," Jay said as they stood by the Suburban around noon, just before she left.

"I'm sure you'll have enough to keep you busy."

"Yeah. Between work and ironing out the details on this boat, it'll be a nightmare."

"Can you make it next weekend?" Laura asked.

"I don't know yet. I'll try. So what are you going to do all week by yourself? When's Mom coming back? Saturday?"

"I think so. And I'm picking the kids up Friday afternoon. I don't really have any plans except to go down to Myrtle and see Katy McLachlan. You remember her. From Winston?

They're going to be at her parents' place for the week. I'll probably spend some time with her."

"Sounds good."

"Would you rather I come home for the week and stay with you?" Laura asked.

"Oh, no. No need to let that place at the beach go to waste."

"OK," she said. "Take care, Jay."

"You, too. And don't forget to use sunscreen."

"Aye, aye, captain."

LAURA LEFT THE CHURCH camp around five in the afternoon. Thank goodness Jenny James, a college student from the church in Farmington who sometimes baby-sat for the Babsons, was a counselor. It wasn't until Jenny got the job that Laura consented to Jacob attending camp.

"Don't worry, Mrs. Babson," she assured as she just about forced Laura to the Suburban. "I've got your number at the beach and your car phone number and Dr. Babson's office number and his private line at the office and the house number and his car phone number and his beeper. Y'all sure got a lot of phones, don't you? And you can call me at any time. But they'll be fine. They'll love it here."

Meagan had been to the camp, held at the Episcopal beach retreat called the Trinity Center, for two years. But this was Jacob's first time. He was the one she worried about.

"It'll be good for him," Jay had said.

"How so?" Laura had asked.

"I dunno. What you can't think of to ask sometimes. It'll just be good for him. And maybe you, too."

Laura crossed the bridge leaving Emerald Isle around five-thirty. Sunset was still nearly three hours away. She didn't feel well. She hadn't eaten much all day. After the ferry ride, Laura and the children had stopped at yet another McDonald's. She ate half of a grilled chicken sandwich and drank a Diet Coke. Even then her stomach felt queasy. And now, even more so. But she kept on, taking a left on 24, past Swansboro. She followed Darrell's advice and took the short-cut, Highway 172 though Camp Lejuene, finally picking up 17 South on the other side of Sneads Ferry.

It was a tedious drive. Laura never really liked traveling alone. It was boring, too much time for self-reflection. She thought about the children, finally satisfied they would be fine. She thought about Farmington—how living there was beginning to grate on her more and more, especially after being away. But it probably was better for the kids than a big place like Charlotte, so long as she took them places. She had to do more of that. The art museum in Raleigh. The symphony. She should take them to Washington or New York. And they also wanted to go to Disney World. But to Jay, the thoughts of spending a vacation, let alone money, at places like that were beyond consideration. She would just have to do it herself. Maybe Noell would go with them. She thought about Jay and the money. About Bonnie, Beth, Blair and Doc.

But mostly she thought about Neal Nickelsen. She tried not to, but she did anyway. About the way he would say things. About the way in which he genuinely seemed to care about her. About what she thought. How she felt. Who was she kidding? She knew what Neal really cared about. Or maybe not. She wondered if she would go to his house for dinner Monday night. How could she get out of it at this point? What would happen? Nothing probably — though the thought of it happening really wasn't all that bad. Or was it?

By the time she reached the edge of Wilmington, not only did her stomach feel worse, her head hurt and she was sweating. She felt feverish. Was she coming down with something? Surely not.

To her right she spotted a familiar pair of golden arches. Three times in one day, she thought. She could use a Diet Coke. And really needed to go to the bathroom, too. She parked the Suburban and went promptly inside to the rest room. She was glad no one else was in there. She looked at herself in the mirror. I look like hell, she thought, just before walking into one of the stalls and throwing up.

She washed her face with a paper towel, left the rest room, went to the front counter and ordered the drink. Once back in the Suburban, she pulled down the visor and looked at herself again in the vanity mirror on the sun visor. I look worse than hell, she thought, just before saying aloud, "So this is what adultery is like." It was as if she was making a simple, matter-of-fact observation.

She then started the vehicle, backed out of the parking space, pulled back onto the highway. A few miles down the road she saw the exit sign to I-40 West. It would be so easy, she thought, just to take the exit and go home to Farmington. Spend the week at home — at home with her husband. She even put on the blinker, as if she was going to take the exit. But at the last possible moment, she switched it off and continued on her way to Sunset Beach.

CHAPTER TWENTY-TWO

Monday, July 19

LAURA DIDN'T MAKE IT to the beach until around three-thirty in the afternoon. She decided not to drive. The walk would do her good, even though she was tired. She had packed a small cooler. One soda and at first one, then two and finally three Bud Lights. She felt she could use one—or two or three. She could have just waited for Neal. He said he'd look for her on the beach. But what if his flight was late. Who knew when he would get there?

She packed light: two magazines, a towel and a sand chair. She felt funny going to the beach alone. She couldn't remember having done it before. But it felt good, too. No one to keep an eye on. She was on her own. And so far the day had been a good one, even though she had developed a nagging blister on her right index finger. She was determined she would turn it into a callus in time.

She picked a spot well west of the walkway, away from the crowd. She read. She considered walking to Mad Inlet but was too tired. She tried to resist the beer but couldn't for more than about twenty minutes.

By the time Neal got to the beach, she had emptied two cans and decided to take a little swim. To cool off. And of course empty her bladder. She always felt funny about going in the ocean. But everyone else did it, didn't they?

She saw Neal first. She felt good. Real good. Two beers on a near-empty stomach had a way of doing that to her. Plus she really had sweat a lot that morning.

Neal look bewildered. Don't tell me she's not out here, he thought. When her car wasn't parked at his cottage, he drove down to hers and knocked on the door. No answer. He figured correctly that with the children gone she had decided to walk. Finally he heard her.

"Come on in," she said. "The water's great."

The swim was fun. They floated over waves and talked mostly about the golf tournament. A few times he started to touch her but decided not to. They finally retired to the chairs. It was after five.

Laura felt the swim had sobered her up a little. So she drank another beer.

"You coming for dinner tonight?" Neal finally asked.

"I guess."

"Great. What time?"

"It's your deal. But I do need to check on the kids. Jenny — she's a girl from our church who's a counselor at the camp — she's expecting me to call around eight."

"OK. Eight-thirty. Just right to catch the sunset."

AT FIRST LAURA WASN'T going to wear a bra, but then she thought she really should. "I don't know," she said aloud as she stood in the her bedroom at the Laughing Gull. "This is crazy. Somebody ought to just shoot me."

She already had decided she wasn't going to dress up. She considered not wearing makeup. But that seemed dumb.

It was eight-fifteen. She ought to be leaving in five minutes. Yes, she should wear a bra. With what she was wearing, he might notice. And that might give the wrong impression. She was glad she'd gotten in touch with Jenny. The children were fine. And Jay, too. She'd talked to him around seven. He was fine, excited about the boat. She just wasn't sure about Laura.

Meanwhile, just down 40th at the Bullish Outlook, Neal was in a quandary.

"If I hadn't quit smoking," he said, "I'd have some damn matches or a lighter or something."

Finally, in one of the drawers in the kitchen, he found a book of matches. For the candles. Candles. Was it too much? But that wasn't that big a deal, was it? And music. They had talked about music some. She liked beach. And Bonnie Raitt, he remembered. Not too crazy about country, even though she said she really did like Mary Chapin Carpenter. And classical? He wasn't sure. He went through his tapes. And then he found it. Just right. James Taylor's *Greatest Hits*. Perfect. And Carole King's *Tapestry*. How could he go wrong with those? But first some beach music. To keep things lively. And then over dinner, the serious stuff.

He checked the bottle of Asti in the freezer. He'd bought it — and three more which were in the fridge — at the IGA on Ocean Isle on the way in, along with the pasta, sauce and garlic bread. And one of those packaged salad deals. And five kinds of salad dressing, three of which were fat free. He knew she was into that fat-free thing, which really did become her. He felt his gut. He'd been dieting all week. And even doing sit-ups. It felt pretty good.

The seafood came from Bill's, just over the bridge. Shrimp, scallops, clams and mussels. Enough to feed the masses.

At eight-twenty he walked outside and glanced down 40th. He didn't see her. At eight-twenty-six he did the same — same result. When she wasn't there at eight-thirty-three, he thought about calling.

"Back off," he said. "Chill out and sit on the deck."

The sunset was looking good. The southwest breeze was just right for keeping the bugs away. He packed the Asti on ice in an ice bucket. A white hand towel lay on top. I feel like a Frenchman, he thought. Two glasses, which he had washed by hand to remove the dishwasher spots, sat nearby. He was considering grabbing another beer from inside but thought maybe he'd had enough what with the Asti on the way. Was she ever going to get here? It was eight-forty-two by his watch. But of course it was always a few minutes fast. And just then he heard her. Walking up the steps. He turned and looked at her.

"It's me," she said, waving her hand.

"Evenin', Starshine."

"Good evening to you."

"Can I interest you in a glass of Asti?"

"Probably so."

"Good. I'll get it."

"Good."

"I hope you're hungry."

"I am."

"Good."

"Yeah. Good."

He opened the Asti, poured two glasses and handed her one.

"You know, you really look great, Laura," he said sincerely. "That color's good on you. Especially with the tan."

"Thanks. You look nice, too."

"A toast?"

"Sure," she said. "To friendship?"

"Nah. I'd rather toast to you, Laura. Cheers."

THE MEAL LIVED UP to its billing—with Laura's help. "I know how to cook, like the recipes and all that, but coordinating it, that's the problem," Neal said.

"That's why an orchestra has a conductor," Laura said.

"You conducted very well. Thanks."

"Thank you. It was a great meal. I really enjoyed it. Can I help you clear the table?"

"Oh, sure. I guess. I hadn't really thought of that."

Laura was trying her best to hold it together. She wanted to drink some more but thought maybe she shouldn't. Knew she shouldn't. Two bottles of Asti were almost gone. And she didn't remember him drinking much of it. She was so nervous. In some ways. In other ways not. But she was tired. Would another drink wake her up? Yeah, maybe it would.

"Oh," Laura said with a with a look of pain as they got up from the table.

"Problem there?"

"My knee. It stiffened up on me. And my shoulder, too."

"Does that happen often?" Neal asked.

It was then she decided to tell him. She started to about half a dozen times but each time something else came up.

"If you must know," she said slowly, "I'm a little sore. You see, well, I took a tennis lesson today."

"What?"

"A tennis lesson. I've decided to start playing again."

"Wow."

"Is that all you're going to say?"

"I don't know what else to say. I'm taken aback, as they say."

"You and me both," she added.

"But I really think it's great. Really."

They cleared the table. Laura led, Neal followed.

"You know," he finally said, "you may not know this, but I really am quite adept at the time-honored art of massage. For medicinal purposes only, of course."

"Massage?" she asked slowly. It sounded to her as if she was slurring her words slightly.

"Yeah. I can't do much about the knee, but when it comes to shoulders . . . now, shoulders, I can do wonders for shoulders—and spines, too."

"I bet."

"No, really. I read a book on it. You know, a sports medicine book. I know about every injury in the book. Tricks of the trade."

"So what are you saying?" she asked as he opened—she distinctly remembered him opening another Asti—a third bottle of Asti!

"I'm just saying I'll give you a massage. If you would like for me to?"

"I think I'll survive."

"You sure?"

"I don't know. I mean, this tennis-lesson thing. I guess it was dumb. But I did it. Got another one tomorrow."

"So tell me about it," he said.

"Well, I told you before, about Jay making me quit tennis. Not making me. People don't make you do things, do they?"

"Maybe not. But I guess they try. I like to think instead we all do what we want to do."

"Yeah, I guess. Anyway, I called the racquet club this morning in Myrtle Beach. Asked if someone would give me a lesson and this guy said he would and I went over there and spent, oh, gosh, I don't know, over six hundred dollars, I think, and anyway I bought two tennis outfits — I really like 'em — and two rackets. You know, you're not a real player if you don't have at least two rackets, right? Anyway, I charged it all on my Master Card. Jay's gonna die. And I took a lesson from this young guy named Keith. Kinda cute. Great legs. And I think he was impressed, too. Not with me, I mean, but with the way I played. Anyway, now I'm sore and I got this blister. But hey, it was fun. I mean I really didn't do all that bad. If only we'd had these big high-tech rackets back when I was playing. When I quit playing, seriously anyway, we were still using wooden rackets. With those damn presses, you know."

"I remember those," Neal said. "So why'd you take the lesson?"

"I don't know. I just wanted to."

"Sounds good. Now. You want a massage or not?"

She thought a few seconds. "Yeah. Sure. I guess so."

"Only one stipulation," he said.

"What?"

"You have to take off your shirt. Or blouse or whatever you call it. And your bra, too."

"Oh, cute."

"And right here in front of me," he demanded, though it sounded to Laura as if he might just be teasing.

"Double cute."

They looked at each other briefly, then looked away.

"You don't think I'll do it, do you?" Laura finally asked.

"I don't know."

"You don't, do you?"

"I guess not."

"Well, Neal, ole buddy, old pal, I'm calling your bluff on this one."

"You are?"

And with that she got up from the bar stool she was seated on at the counter, took another sip of Asti and said, "So you going to get a sheet or blanket or something I can lie on. I assume the floor is the best spot. Unless you've got a massage table."

"Yeah, oh, yeah. Hang on," he said.

He came back from the back of the house with a quilt and a bottle of aloe vera cream Susan evidently had left down there. His hands were shaking. He couldn't believe it. He spread the quilt on the floor, sat down on a bar stool and said, "OK, Ace. Ball's in your court."

"You don't think I'll do it, do you?" she said.

"If it'll make you feel any better, no! I don't think you'll do it."

She looked him in the eye and began to unbutton her blouse, starting at the top. He still couldn't believe it. She was going to do it. Which she did. So casually. As if he wasn't there. The bra. Did it snap in the front? he wondered. No, it didn't. She reached behind her, undid it and then dropped it on the bar. She stood in front of him for just a second. Her untanned breasts seemed to stare at him, though later he realized that he was doing the staring. And then she turned and lay face down on the quilt.

"I'm waiting," she said after a few seconds.

"Oh, yeah, sure. Where's the lotion? Oh, yeah. There. OK. Yeah. Be right there."

He wasn't sure what to do. I guess I gotta give her a massage, he thought. He gave it his best. He started with the shoulders. Had to move her hair out of the way. It felt like, oh, he just didn't know. But it felt good.

"That feels good," she said.

"Good."

He kept on. Working his way down her back. It wasn't easy, but he stopped at the top of her shorts and worked his way back up. Her legs. He wondered about them. Should he? He started to but refrained. But she said her knee hurt. He just kept working her shoulders. And then the middle of her back. He was getting tired. He rested by strumming her back gently, as if it was a guitar. He started to say something when he heard something. Did she sigh? It sounded like it. Maybe that's good. He thought maybe he should say something. Do something other than what he was doing. God, this woman is gorgeous, he thought. He studied her shoulder blades. And her vertebrae. And sometimes looked lower. He tried to concentrate on a few freckles he had spotted. They were cute, he thought. He was seated to her left. He just kept on.

Then suddenly it dawned on him. No, he thought. This can't be. But indeed the answer was yes.

"Laura?" he asked quietly.

No response.

"Laura?" A little bit louder.

"Yeah, good," she murmured, though it was barely audible. He moved his fingertips up and down her spine for a few more seconds.

"Laura?" Again. No response.

Then he resigned himself to the fact — the bitter truth as it were — that she was asleep. Out like a lamppost, he thought, whatever that meant. The woman was a goner.

He stood up and looked at her, looked at her for a long time. He gritted his teeth. He thought about her breasts. No, they weren't big. But very nicely formed, he thought. He looked for something to drink. No, not the Asti. He didn't really even like the stuff. He started to get a fresh beer from the refrigerator — even though he figured he had an unfinished one sitting around somewhere — but instead opted for Pepsi. He stepped over her, walked on, opened the door and went to the deck. He ran his fingers through his hair and exhaled deeply. And then sat down in a rocking chair.

IT WAS ON THE deck Laura found him, the deck overlooking Mad Inlet. In the distance, silhouetted somewhat by the lights of North Myrtle Beach, was Bird Island. It was nearly two in the morning. The southwest breeze made it pleasant. What time had she gone to sleep? Probably before eleven, she thought. Had anything happened? Not much, she figured, considering she was still wearing her shorts. The blouse and the bra were neatly draped on a nearby chair.

"What's up, Guv?" she asked. She tried to sound upbeat but knew it was a weak effort. She could still taste the garlic, lots of garlic—and the Asti, too.

"Not much, Shine. What's shakin' with you?"

"Oh, just trying to figure out how big a fool I made of myself. Sorry. Something about bunches of alcohol and pasta, along with a massage, that puts me out. I don't get that sort of treatment every night."

"Was the meal OK?" he asked.

"Very nice. Thanks for the invite."

She stood beside his rocker.

"Been out here long?" she asked.

"Just about three hours."

"Sorry."

"No. It's OK. Been thinking. It's OK."

"Whatcha thinkin' 'bout?"

"Lots of things."

"Like what?" she asked—and sounded sincere, almost demanding.

"OK. First, I guess—or most recent—the moon and the stars."

"I'm touched."

"I'm serious here. Look to your right. Way up. It's the Big Dipper. I come out here and look at it on clear nights. Such a perfect view. You know, its always up there, but somehow when I'm here, down here at the beach, and I look up and see it, I think . . . I'm not sure what I think. It just does something to me."

"I can understand that."

Laura sat down in a rocking chair beside him, to his left. She rocked a few times. She actually felt pretty good. The nap had done her good. She knew she'd have a hangover in the morning. But right now she felt OK. So she decided to talk. She needed to talk, or at least listen intently.

"So, Neal, what do you believe in?"

"Not sure."

"Who is? But if pressed on it. Pinned to the wall. What?"

"Ping putters and Big Bertha drivers."

"Get serious. What?"

"Not religion."

"Oh, yeah. Why not?"

"I'm un-churched, as they say. What about you?"

"I want to know about you. I babbled on enough about me tonight at dinner. I wonder if there's anything about me you don't know. I tend to do that when I'm drinking too much. Talk a lot. So I'll be quiet now and you can tell me why you don't believe in God."

"I didn't say God. I said religion. It can be dangerous."

"How so?"

"Well, I remember this time back in Henderson, it wasn't all that long after my father left, when Mom took me and Dave—that's my brother—to church. I told you about Dave, didn't I?"

"Yeah. Career military. I remember."

"Right. Anyway, we were sitting there at the First Baptist and during the silent prayer — I even remember we were supposed to be praying for this old woman in the church who was about to die or something — right out of the blue, Dave farts. Real loud."

"Impressive."

"He was about seven and I was about nine, I guess. He looked at me and laughed and knowing better I held it in pretty well even though I was about to die. Anyway, Mom didn't do anything. She just sat there like she didn't hear it. But everyone heard it. I'll bet the preacher even heard it. Then he started praying and then after he finished we all stood up to sing a hymn and Mom took us by the hand and led us out. We didn't say anything and she didn't either. We just got in the car and went home. And once we got there, she beat the ever-loving shit outta Dave. I'm not kidding. I mean, at first it was funny, but then I got worried. I was in the other room laughing at first and after a while I started getting worried. I thought she was going to kill him."

"What'd you do?"

"I stopped her. I was pretty strong, even at that age. I grabbed her arm with both my arms. And stopped her. Later she thanked me. It was weird. But I guess Dave and I learned a lesson."

"Yeah, don't poot in church," Laura said.

"Well, I hadn't thought of it that way. We just figured we better stay away from church. No need going somewhere you could get your ass whipped just for farting."

Laura laughed. "You're too much," she said.

They sat in silence. Neal finally broke it.

"But I know why she whipped him. She wasn't whipping him, she was whipping my father. Only too bad for Dave dear ole Dad wasn't there."

"What do you mean?"

"I mean there she was, living in this small town and everybody knew Dad was a drunk and a philanderer. And then he runs off and leaves her with these two wild-assed boys and I think she just lost it that day. She couldn't take it anymore."

"Maybe she was just thinking Dave could do better than that," Laura said.

"Maybe so. But I know what it's like—to be pissed off at somebody and take it out on a kid. I remember one time Susan pissed me off so damn bad and every time I tried to get at it—you know, the problem—and fix it, she would come up with some other bullshit and finally Sarah, she was just about two at the time, started crying and I'm standing there— I remember this—standing in the middle of the living room in our apartment looking at Sarah, this little two-year-old, and saying, 'Will you shut the hell up or I'll give you something to cry about?' And then it hit me. I was taking it out on this little girl. All my frustrations with Susan. I was taking it out on her. I guess that's why I've always been glad about Elliot. He could handle Susan. And Sarah, too. I couldn't. I don't know. I just couldn't."

"It sounds as if Sarah's turning out all right," Laura said, looking for something good to say.

"God, I hope so," Neal said. "I mean, I hope everyone does."

"But they don't, do they?"

"I don't know. But I hope so. And if you don't hope, what the hell good are you?"

Laura was taken aback a bit. She'd never heard Neal being quite this open.

"You seem to be an excellent parent," he said. "Your kids are very lucky."

"I'm not so sure about that. But I do try. I really try."

"I'm sure you're the perfect mom."

"But hardly the perfect wife, huh?"

"I wouldn't say that," he said.

"You mean, Neal, if you were married to me and knew what I had done tonight you'd be very happy about it."

"What's the big deal about tonight? All we did was have dinner."

"And then I took my blouse off as I recall."

"So what?"

"I don't know."

"Don't know about what?"

"About us. I don't know. I really didn't have a very good week with Jay last week. But in a lot of ways, it wasn't his fault, I don't think. It was like I was looking for things to get mad at him about. Looking for every little thing he did wrong. We just don't seem to see eye-to-eye on anything anymore. Like that bridge over there. We can't even agree on something like that. What do you think of the bridge?"

"I like it. Keeps the riffraff off the island."

Laura laughed. "That's a good one coming from you. But really, Neal, I don't know how I've gotten myself into this."

"Into what? Having a friend?" he asked.

"I'm just very confused."

"Lighten up, Laura. Go with the flow, as they say."

"Yeah. Maybe I should."

"So I guess this wouldn't be a good time for me to ask you what you believe in," he said.

She laughed again. "I guess not."

They sat in silence for nearly a minute. Looking at the stars. Watching the grass in the marsh sway with the steady ocean breeze.

"You know, last week was a pretty shitty week for me, too," he finally said.

"How so?"

"First, I was at the tournament, you know, and sometimes I think I can make it—that I can do it. There really are times I'm a pretty damn good golfer. I've got the length—I know that. I've always been long."

"Is that so," Laura remarked.

"Oh, yeah. I can hang with any of those guys off the tee."

"Good."

"But then I watch 'em play and they're so damn good. I mean really . . . they're good. So consistent. So focused. And if I had the monetary wherewithal to quit work today and hire the best damn teacher in the world and work up to it for the next seven years, well, even then, I'm not sure I could do it."

"Sure you could," Laura said with a sincere tone of encouragement. "Sure you could."

"No. Physically, yes. But it takes more than that. I don't think—I know I can't—do it."

"Don't be so hard on yourself."

"I'm not. I'm just being realistic. I know me."

And at that point Laura felt as if she was beginning to know him as well, even to feel a part of him.

"And now more bad news for Neal," he said.

"What's that?"

"I talked to Lou Friday. They've already hired a columnist to take Fred's place. Some damn Yankee. I swear, those Yankees are moving in on us in droves."

"I was born in Connecticut," Laura said. "Dad got transferred to Charlotte when I was three."

"Oh, I'm sorry."

"It's not like it's a disease, Neal."

"Not one there isn't a cure for, I suppose," he said. "Anyway, I'm out."

"I'm sorry. I know it meant a lot to you," Laura said.

"Well, it did," Neal said. "But only to a certain extent."

"How so?"

"Get with me here. Last week I realized I'm such a long shot to make senior tour that I might as well forget about it — that was on Friday — and then I found out I'm not getting the job I wanted — that was on Saturday. Do you think I then had a lousy weekend?"

"I would guess so," Laura said.

"No. I really didn't. Just knowing — or at least hoping — that you would be sitting here beside me tonight, I really didn't care about that stuff. I really didn't."

"Is that true?" she asked.

"Yeah. It is. And I must say, for me at least, this has been a wonderful evening. Thank you for coming."

"Thank you. It's been fun. But I guess it's past time to call it a night."

"Can I walk you home?" he asked.

"I can manage, well, no, I mean yes. You can walk me home. That would be nice."

It was quiet. They saw only one car on the street. Lights were out in most of the cottages as they headed up 40th to Bay Street. They didn't say much. About halfway there, he asked, "Laura, this may sound dumb, but do you mind if I hold your hand?"

"Sure. I mean no. That would be nice."

They walked on. It was the first time he had touched her hand. He was on the left. The fingers of his right hand intertwined with those of her left. Her skin was soft, but her hand seemed to exude a certain amount of strength. His skin was a bit rough, lots of calluses. But his hand also seemed to have a certain softness.

"I've got an idea," Neal said. "Let's rent bikes tomorrow — at that ice cream place — and ride on the beach."

"That's funny," she said. "I've been thinking about doing that all summer. I've never ridden a bike on the beach. It looks like fun. We could even ride on Bird Island. I've been wanting to go to the end of it, to the South Carolina side. That's where the mailbox is. I haven't been this summer. I walked once last year. But it's a long walk."

"What mailbox?"

"You know. Kindred Spirit's."

"Oh, I forgot about that."

"I told you I'd explain it to you sometime."

"Great. So what time?" he asked.

"What time is low tide?"

"Around four, I think."

"Great. We can make it after my tennis lesson. Unless you're playing golf."

"Just hitting a few range balls in the morning. That's all. So maybe around two?"

"Sure," she said. "I'll come down to your place and we'll walk to the bike place."

"Sounds good."

They reached the Laughing Gull and stopped at the bottom of the steps.

"Should I walk you up?" he asked.

"I think I can manage. Thanks again. I had a nice time."

He let go of her hand and started to turn before saying, "Laura."

"Yes."

"Ah, well, never mind. It's nothing."

"What?"

"I was going to ask if you would mind if I kissed you goodnight. That was all."

She thought for a second and then said, "Sure. Gosh, I mean no. I wouldn't mind. That would be nice."

Chapter Twenty-Three

Tuesday, July 20

Y EAH!" L AURA YELLED AFTER nailing a two-fisted backhand down the line that even the young pro on the other side of the net, had he been trying, would have had a tough time handling. She slapped her thigh. She had a habit of doing that back when she playing competitively. A little pick-me-up after either a particularly good or bad shot.

"Way to go, ma'am," Keith said.

"Will you quit calling me ma'am? It's Laura."

"Yes, ma'am. I mean, yes, Laura. Good shot."

They were about thirty-five minutes into the hour-long lesson. It was hot. Noon in late July was not an ideal time for a lesson to most. But Laura liked the heat—and the sweat.

"I need to sweat some of that poison out of my system," she told herself, all the while swearing off Asti. But despite drinking more than she should have the night before, she actually felt good. Had slept to almost ten. When had she ever done that? And the more she played, the better she felt.

"Bend your knees," Keith reminded after a forehand hit the net four inches below the tape.

Laura was impressed with Keith's teaching style. She listened intently to every instruction. No, it wasn't her intention to start playing tennis competitively again. But she knew a couple of youngsters in Farmington she planned to have on the court soon. She always had felt Meagan would be a natural. She had considered lessons for her several times but always had let it slide. But no more. She planned to buy them rackets next week. She planned to spend some of that Babson money.

So intent was Laura on the lesson, she didn't notice a spectator had sauntered up and was leaning against the small set of bleachers beside her court.

"All right," Neal said loudly after she ran down a sharp cross-court forehand from Keith and sent it back cross court with a good deal of pace.

Laura looked his way. At first, she felt embarrassed. She shrugged, grinned and gave him a wave with her racket.

Neal watched her carefully. She wore a beige tennis skirt and a sleeveless white shirt with matching trim. The coat of sweat seemed to make her tanned arms and legs shine. On the court, she looked just as he remembered her: that determined look on her face when the ball approached, the casual, confident manner she carried herself and the grunt when she hit the ball. She had a good grunt. It wasn't one of those little girl grunts. But not an obnoxious macho grunt. It was a good grunt.

"You must really be desperate for a column," she said to Neal when the lesson had ended.

"Actually I was looking for a lunch partner. Hungry? I know a great place nearby."

"I could stand it. Just don't sit too close. I probably stink."

"Laura, you really looked great on the court. I mean it."

"I know," she said, before gulping some water from a plastic bottle. "I could tell by the way you were looking at me."

"And I thought I was the one with the big ego."

The Suburban followed the Olds out of the club onto 17. He led her to a restaurant at a marina on Little River. They chose to sit outdoors, under a big canopy on the second floor, overlooking the boats.

"I guess we're getting a sailboat," she said. "Did I tell you I saw it Sunday?"

"Yeah, you told me."

"Oh, yeah. My memory's still a little fuzzy."

She had the shrimp salad. He went with the grilled chicken sandwich. She drank about seven glasses of water. He considered ordering a beer, but when she didn't, he didn't.

"I just thought of something," she said. "What if I see somebody I know? I wouldn't know what to do. How would I introduce you?"

"As your male prostitute."

"Get serious. Think about it?"

"Laura, all we're doing is having lunch. I'm repaying you for keeping a check on the house. I'm an old college buddy. After all, that's it, right?"

"Yeah, I guess so."

"Good. And Laura, relax, OK?"

IT WAS PAST THREE before they got the bikes. "Wind's not too bad, but I'd ride into it first," the man at the rental place said.

"No problem. We're headed for Bird Island," Neal said, knowing that the wind was once again out of the southwest. The ride back would be easy.

"Please don't ride the bikes through the inlet," the man said. "Salt water's bad on these things."

"No problem."

They crossed the street and entered the beach at the fishing pier. The sand near the dunes was too thick to ride on, but that lasted just about thirty feet. With the tide out, the beach was nearly as good as asphalt for bikes. Perhaps even better, Neal thought, figuring if he fell off he probably wouldn't kill himself.

Laura led the way. She often rode bikes at home with the children. She could never talk Jay into it. Though he hadn't ridden a bike in years, Neal caught on quickly.

"I guess it's like riding a bicycle," he reasoned.

The movement and the moderate breeze kept them cool. The beach was crowded in places. Laura navigated it with ease. But Neal nearly crashed into a young child when he was looking at Laura, who was riding without using her hands some of the time. He started to try it but quickly realized he would fall. How did she do that? he wondered.

By the time they got to the 40th Street access—about a fifth of the journey completed—Neal was beginning to tire a bit. He finally had to stop for a rest about two-thirds of the way to Mad Inlet. Laura rode around in a large circle, laughing.

"Maybe you should quit golf and take up tennis," she said.

When they reached the inlet, Laura found a spot, built up speed and rode through the water with relative ease. Remembering what the man had said—and fearing he would fall on his face in the inlet—Neal got off the bike, picked it up and walked through.

"Wimp," she said.

"Yeah, yeah."

Neal had never been to the western end of Bird Island, though he had seen the backside by boat a few times. Laura had been only once before. She slowed down and they rode side by side. The beach was nearly deserted.

"I can't believe they would develop this island," she said, referencing plans by the island's owners to build a bridge from Sunset and sell residential lots.

"I know. I think they should build a golf course instead. Call it Birdie Island."

"Get real."

"I am. Hell, if they own it, they ought to be able to do what they want. Right?"

"As long as it doesn't mess up the environment."

"I didn't know you were a dune-hugger."

"I didn't know you were a scum bag."

"Hey, I was just kidding. And no, I don't think they should develop the island either. The last I heard they were trying to get the state to buy it. Maybe they will."

"Maybe so," Laura said. "The state of South Carolina owns the other end. I hope it stays just the way it is now."

"If that's what you think, that's what I think."

"Truth is you don't give a crap, do you?" she asked.

"Laura, you know me so well it's scary."

They continued on, finally to the mailbox. It was located on a dune, offering an excellent view of the beach. A young man and woman were sitting on the bench. She was writing in a notebook, which she soon closed and put into the mailbox. The couple headed off for the backside of the island.

"I wonder what they're going to do," Neal said. "Let's go watch."

"Will you grow up?"

"I tried that once. I was miserable. So what's the deal with the mailbox?"

"People come out here and write to Kindred Spirit on those notebooks," Laura explained. "I guess he's like the mystical guardian of the island or something."

There were about six notebooks in the mailbox. Laura and Neal each grabbed one and started flipping through. Laura eventually read one aloud:

July 15

Dear Kindred Spirit,

The beauty and solitude of this place puts me at peace with myself. Thank you for allowing this respite from the craziness of humanity. Peace and harmony to you.

Bill

Neal just continued to thumb through the pages, shaking his head. "I haven't seen this much horseshit since I covered the Kentucky Derby that time," he finally said.

"You're terrible," Laura said. "Some of 'em are good."

"I haven't found one yet."

Laura had. It was written by a woman in late June whose husband had died earlier that year. It was touching. She started to read it to Neal but decided not to. Some dealt with lost love. Others with new love. Some pleaded for the Spirit to stop the development of the island with divine intervention, while others wrote of their devotion to God. Sometimes Kindred Spirit would respond, little notes at the bottom of the letter such as: "Peace be with you."

"Hey, this must be the one that girl just wrote," Neal said. "What's it say?"

Neal read aloud:

July 20

Dear Kindred Spirit,

This is a beautiful place. My boyfriend and I like it so much we're going to go screw in the dunes.

Thanks for everything.

Betty Lou

"You are awful!" Laura said, though she couldn't help laughing. "Well, make fun of it if you must, but I think it's neat. I'm going to write something."

"OK, OK. I will, too."

They got pens from the mailbox. In a few minutes they were finished and exchanged pads. Laura read his to herself:

July 20

Dear Kindred Spirit,

This is a beautiful place made even more beautiful by the presence of my lovely biking companion. I am at peace with myself today even though I'm not playing golf or drinking.

Neal

Meanwhile he was reading hers:

July 20

Dear Kindred Spirit,

I believe in you, but my friend here doesn't. Please send him a sign. Thanks.

LB

"I can think of a sign that would make me believe," Neal said slyly.

"I bet you could," Laura said, bopping him on the head with one of the notebooks. "But don't count on it."

Having seen enough, they left. With the wind at their backs, the ride was easy. Laura pedaled slowly to allow Neal to keep up.

"So what's on for tonight?" he asked about halfway back.

"What do you mean?" Laura responded.

"I mean, what are we going to do tonight?"

"Neal, are we going steady or something?"

"Very funny. I just meant . . . oh, never mind."

"Don't get defensive," Laura said. "And don't be offended, but I was thinking I might just go back to my place and take it easy."

"We could go out to eat. Those restaurants just over the bridge are very good."

"Maybe tomorrow night. I don't know."

"And Thursday night, the Galleon. It's slow during the week until Thursday. We should definitely go to the Galleon Thursday. Or maybe 2001. Ever been to that piano bar there? It's a blast."

"Neal, I think you missed your calling. You should have been the social director for a cruise ship."

Laura felt good. The break from the children, not that she didn't miss them — would Friday ever get here? — had, as Jay predicted, done her good. And Jay. He was just hours away but also so far away. It was frightening. The man she had lived with for all these years. Shared so many moments with, the most significant of which, the birth of the children. But where was he today? And where was she? Don't do anything stupid, Laura, she thought. You're not stupid. No, I'm not. Am I? With the wind behind her, she rode. Effortlessly. For a time she forgot about everything else but riding the bike. As fast as possible. Then she heard Neal. Puffing behind her.

"I got my second wind," he said enthusiastically. "I'm hell on wheels when I get my second wind."

Laura sped up, but he was already past her. His legs ached. His chest hurt. If I die, he thought, so be it. And just barely, though it was close, he beat her to the still shallow inlet and rode through it, only to fall off the bike and into the sand as he was about to clear it. Laura made it through unscathed.

"Neal," she said, "you were so close. Very close. But as usual, so far away."

"If this damn motor doesn't work," Neal said, "I'm gonna, gonna . . . not go very far."

Well, miracle of miracles, he thought as the tiny outboard started.

"The sign," Neal said aloud though no one could hear. "Maybe this is the sign."

The fifteen-horsepower motor cranked on just the third pull. It was attached to an eleven-foot Zodiac inflatable boat

Elliot had purchased on a whim and kept hidden away below the cottage in a large storage room. About a four thousand dollar toy that he had used not more than twice, Neal
thought. Elliot had another one just like it that served as the
dingy for a forty-two-foot cruiser he kept at Myrtle Beach
Yacht Club.

Once comfortably situated aboard the Zodiac, at the dock
of the Bullish Outlook, Neal took off. He had been on the little
vessel before with Elliot. They were careless and almost
turned it over. On the Zodiac, he could traverse the inlet and
the intricate tidal creeks around Sunset. He took a while to
get the feel of the throttle then headed up the creek toward
the back side of the island, toward Bay Street. It was nearly
dark, nearly nine in the evening.

Laura, having declined all invitations, and Neal—having
declined to be done in and somewhat encouraged that she
said, "If you must," when he asked, "Do you mind if I stop
by on the boat?"—weren't going to see each other this night.
Neither knew why.

But he gave it a chance.

And by chance, she was there, sitting on the back porch
of the Laughing Gull reading a book by the dim light, thinking she might turn in any time now. But she wasn't really
tired, having slept late. She had tried to call Jay earlier. No
answer. Office. Car. Home. Then she remembered it was Rotary night. Maybe he went. He often did. To Little's Cafe—
"the little place for big appetites." Laura often thought about
the take-out window on the side of the restaurant where Jay
said once was "for the colored people" and where even today most of the blacks went to place their order. It was so

silly. But yet it still happened today. And then finally, out of the blue, Jay called. Yes, he had gone to Rotary. He evidently felt good, having knocked down greasy country-style steak, green beans with fatback, mashed potatoes and gravy and, yes, a bunch of those famous Little's little biscuits. He had "jewed down" the boat owners to thirty-six-five. It was done. They would own the boat by Thursday. Could she work it out for this weekend? Spend Friday night on the boat with the children. She didn't know. She'd work on it. And that was it.

When she finally retired to the porch, it was beginning to get dark. But it was still light enough to read. Her latest book was a mystery. But she'd had a hard time concentrating on it. Indeed, all seemed to be a mystery to her these days. But at least the kids were OK. She'd talked not only to Jenny, but also Meagan, who had met some "neat kids." And how was Jacob? He was taking to camp quite well, both assured, which pleased his relieved mother to no end.

And it was just then, out in the marsh, in the narrow creek that ran beside the Laughing Gull's dock, she saw a bright light and thought she heard her name. She wasn't wrong.

Neal tied the Zodiac up and casually strolled along the little pier as if he had done it many times before. He mounted the stairs and found her sitting there, alone in the twilight, looking at him in what seemed like amusement.

"You were serious about that boat, huh?" she said.

"Works like a charm," he said.

"That Elliot thinks of everything. I'd like to meet him sometime."

Neal laughed. "He's something all right."

Neal took a seat in a rocker. It was his first time in the Laughing Gull, though he wasn't really inside. Just on the porch. It was enough.

"So you want a ride?" he asked.

"Maybe sometime."

"No, I mean tonight. Over to Bird Island. The tide's just right. We can make it in ten minutes."

"You're not serious."

"Sure I am. That's a great little boat. I packed a cooler. No Asti, I promise. Just a few beers. Take the boat over to Bird, sit out on the sand and ponder nature," he said.

"I better not."

"Oh, come on, Laura," he said.

"I don't think so."

"Don't do this to yourself," he said.

"Do what?"

"Put yourself—some one, five or ten years down the road, when that island is the playground of the rich and famous—in a situation, where you say to someone, 'You know, once, a year or five or ten ago this guy offered me a ride to Bird Island at night, back when it was uninhabited, and the chance to sit on the sand, hear the ocean, smell the salt, drink a few beers, have interesting conversation and look at the moon and the Big Dipper. And it was a beautiful night. Just right for it. Couldn't have been better But I declined. I read a book instead.' Please, Laura, don't do that to yourself."

"You are so full of yourself."

"Yeah. You gonna go or not?"

"Neal—"

"Yes or no."

She thought a minute. "Yeah," she said finally. "I'll go."

And so they went. To Laura it was a perilous journey: If he turns this boat over, she thought, I'm going to kill him. To Neal a tedious one: If we don't get there soon, he thought, I'm going to die.

By the time they were situated on the boat and had passed the houses on Bay Street, it was dark. Laura held a large portable spotlight. Its wide beam lit the way well as Neal navigated the creeks. He knew once he got past the Bullish Outlook, the ride would be easy, the channel clearly marked with long poles. He feared that beaching the boat on Bird Island would be a problem, but it wasn't. It took longer than ten minutes, but no one was timing it.

They stepped off the boat, Laura first. Neal managed to drag it ashore easily, well out of the water's reach. He grabbed the cooler and a beach bag. Together they walked, chilled slightly by a brisk south wind that came in directly off the water.

"Over here, on the other side of that dune," he said. "That looks like a good spot. We'll be out of the wind."

"I thought it was illegal to be on the dunes," Laura said.

"I don't think the dune police are out tonight."

It was a nice spot, Laura thought, not realizing Neal had earlier scouted the location, just in case the proper occasion should ever arise. He spread a quilt—Susan's quilt, the same one from the night before—on the sand.

For nearly an hour they sat there, talking, looking and listening. They talked about nothing in particular. They looked at sea oats quivering in the wind, stars getting brighter and a three-quarter moon ascending over the ocean, covered at first by a film of thin lacy clouds but eventually emerging, its beams lending a surreal glow to the white sand around the quilt.

They shared a few beers, a few laughs and a few observations on nothing and everything. And just as both were thinking of asking about the time—was now the time to turn back?—they looked at each other.

"This has been fun," Laura said. "Thanks."

"Yeah. Fun. Thank you."

Laura wondered what if. What if he moved toward her? Would she move away? She really should, she thought.

Neal moved toward her cautiously. She didn't move back. She was surprised she wasn't nervous. She thought she should be. But she wasn't, just wasn't. And then . . . there— then and there on Bird Island, under the careful scrutiny of that Carolina moon, the Big Dipper and perhaps even Kindred Spirit, too—Neal and Laura made love.

CHAPTER TWENTY-FOUR

Wednesday, July 21

I WAS DRUNK," LAURA said.

"Bullshit!" Neal said. "You didn't have but two beers—and didn't even finish the second one."

"I have a very low tolerance for the stuff," she said.

"Look, Laura, I've seen you when you were drunk—you don't make love, you make lumber. Remember?"

It was around six-thirty in the morning. True to their word, they met at the beach access for the morning walk.

"We shouldn't act as if this changes anything," Laura had said when Neal dropped her off at her dock at nearly midnight. "Though I guess it does. It shouldn't, but it does."

To her surprise, she had slept well, so well that she was glad she had set the alarm.

They had walked east and were just about to the fishing pier when Laura finally spoke her first words of the day. She figured she would make light of it. Go ahead and get it out in the open and make light of it. It happened. So what.

"You know, Neal, it's a good thing for you we weren't on the South Carolina side of Bird Island," she said. "I hear the penalties for getting a man's wife drunk and taking advantage of her are pretty archaic and severe down there."

"What are you talking about?" Neal asked. "You weren't drunk."

"Mandatory public castration, I think is what Noell told me once. Right on the courthouse steps."

"Very funny. And in North Carolina?"

"About the same thing, I guess. Only it's done in private."

"I think I have a defense," Neal said.

"What's that?"

"How can you say I took advantage of you when I know for sure, at least once, if not twice, you moaned in ecstasy?"

"I did not."

"Did, too."

"You so love to flatter yourself."

They walked on, footprints soon to be washed away by the incoming tide.

Eventually, Laura stopped, faced him and put her hands on his shoulders.

"Neal," she said.

"Laura," he replied.

"Let's get something straight, OK?"

"OK."

"What happened last night was . . . I don't know. I should not have done that. But I did. I feel OK about it and guilty about it. I just don't know."

"Relax."

"Relax?"

"Yeah, relax," he said. "It was just one of those spontaneous things that can happen in one's life from time to time.

They say it's totally accepted in most European cultures. As usual we're a little behind the times in the states.

"Spontaneous? That was hardly spontaneous, Neal."

"Sure it was."

"Well tell me then," she said, "which was more spontaneous: the fact you took a quilt, of all things, to Bird Island, or the fact that in addition to the quilt you also took condoms?"

"Spontaneity is a many splendored thing," he said with a smile, holding his arms open.

They laughed.

"Why is it you always make me laugh?" she asked.

"You're easily amused."

"OK. Call it, blame it, credit it, whatever, on what you will. I'm OK with it. I did it. But let's get one thing straight."

"What's that?"

"It was a one-time thing. OK? One time. No more. Are you OK with that?"

"Do I have a say in this?"

"No."

"Then I guess I'm OK with that," Neal said. "That'll be just fine. Of course, it would be even finer, I think, if I could have my say about it, but if that's what you want to do—or not want to do—that will be fine. Not as fine as it could be, but fine nonetheless. Are you sure you're sure about this?"

"That's the way it has to be," she insisted.

LATER THAT DAY, LATE in the afternoon, Laura asked Neal, "What time is it?"

"Around six, I think."

She lay to his right, her head on his chest, his right arm draped over her neck and shoulders. They were clad, though partially, only in a king-sized sheet on the bed in the master suite of the Bullish Outlook.

She had taken her tennis lesson earlier in the day. He had played golf. She was on the beach when he returned. He packed a cooler and paid her a visit. When it came time to leave the beach, he invited her inside. One thing led to another.

"God's gonna get me for this," she said.

"Will you let up on that? I would think He's got more pressing matters to deal with."

"I just know it. God's gonna get me."

"Look, you're Catholic, right?"

"Used to be."

"You should switch back. I understand when y'all commit a sin or something, all you gotta do is go to the priest and confess, right? And then that's it. Over. Done with. Isn't that how it works?"

"Well, sorta. If you really mean it and all, I guess."

"So what's the big deal. When I do something like this, I'm wishing I could go tell someone about it—though maybe not a priest."

"Neal," she said, "I don't think you ever have to worry about being a theologian."

"I guess not."

They lay in silence for a time. He eventually broke it by saying, "Three times, maybe. At least twice I know for sure. But I think maybe three."

"What are you talking about?"

"You moaned in ecstasy at least twice. But I'm thinking three was more like it."

"Will you get off that," she said. "Why must you always keep score?"

"I'm a sports journalist, a professional sports journalist. It's my job to keep score. Numbers. That's what games consist of. Numbers."

"So this is a game to you," Laura said.

"No, I didn't mean it that way. I just keep up with things. With numbers. I can't help it."

"Well, in that case, you really should get your facts straight."

"What do you mean?" he asked.

"It wasn't twice and it wasn't three times," she said. "It was four."

Neal looked up at the ceiling, smiled and said, "I am so proud of myself."

AROUND TEN-THIRTY THAT NIGHT Neal got up from the rocking chair he had been seated in beside Laura on the deck of the Bullish Outlook. He climbed up on the railing of the deck and looked intently toward Bird Island, hands on hips.

"What in the hell are you doing?" Laura asked.

"I'm getting ready to make an announcement, a proclamation," he said as he turned to face her.

"If you fall off that railing somebody's going to be proclaiming you dead," she said.

"I've thought about this a lot, Laura. The time has come for me to fulfill my true and sovereign destiny."

"Good. But can't you do it sitting down?"

"Attention citizens of Sunset Beach," he said loudly.

"Will you hold it down a little?" Laura asked.

"No," he replied. "This is the sometimes honorable but always sincere Gov. Neal Nickelsen, Esquire. Let it be known to all present that as of this day I hereby do resign my position as governor of this fair state and do give up all rights and privileges of said office. And let it further be known that tonight I will no longer deny my throne, my place in history. For tonight I do lay claim to that which is rightfully mine. For tonight, I shall become the King of Bird Island. King Neal the first, also known as Neal the Notorious. And let it further be said that my first official act of royalty is the naming of my queen. Queen Laura. Laura the Lovely. The Queen of Bird Island. And now if her highness will join me here on the podium, we will commence with the coronations."

He held out his hand to Laura.

"You are a nut! But what the heck," she said, joining him on the railing.

"Look at it," he said, pointing to Bird Island. "It's just like *South Pacific*. It's our island."

"Are you going to sing to me?" she asked.

"No. I can't sing."

"Too bad."

"But if you like," he said, "I could hum a few bars of *There is Nothing Like a Dame*."

Chapter Twenty-Five

Friday, July 23

For Laura, it seemed at times as if Friday would never come, though she now realized how the week really had flown by.

"You know what they say," Neal had said late Thursday afternoon as they sat on the beach watching the waves. "Time flies when you ain't doing shit."

The camp's closing ceremonies began at eleven and promised to be over by noon, thus saving a meal and giving the staff time to prepare for a weekend retreat planned for the facility.

Though she well remembered the way, Laura felt disoriented as she made the same drive she'd made the weekend before. When she crossed the bridge at Sunset around eight-thirty, she was thinking about so many things that she felt as if she could think about nothing.

"I can't believe I've done this," she had said to herself time and time again. But she had.

But now came the hardest part, she figured. Dealing with the guilt. She had to feel guilty, didn't she? She felt she should feel more guilt. She probably would, she thought, but then it would go away in time. And of course there was the matter of dealing with Neal. Would he go away? He had to. Soon. If not soon, then possibly not at all.

In many ways, she wished his time at Sunset was over. Or hers. But he still had a week left. And there were two to go for the Babsons. And now she had to spend the night on a sailboat with her husband and two children. Mighty close quarters for someone who already felt as if the world was closing in on her. She wished she could just pick up the children and head back to Sunset. Do the laundry. Cook them a meal. Take them to a movie or the video store. Just do the kinds of things mothers are supposed to do on vacation.

She tried to put the last few days into perspective, maybe view it as a learning experience, a growing experience. After all, no one would ever know. She certainly wouldn't tell. And for sure he wouldn't either. She figured she was just another statistic to Neal. And when he had said it—or tried to—she had stopped him. It was such an easy thing for him to say. Even Neal probably couldn't remember how many times he had used that one—the ultimate line, the ole clincher.

It was just the night before, on their way back from Myrtle. They had been out to eat and then to 2001. She had consented to go but was worried at times she might see someone she knew. What would she say? What would they say?

"Tell 'em you're Laura's evil twin sister," Neal said.

As it worked out, she hadn't seen anyone she knew, though a few people had recognized Neal at the club. He just spoke briefly and didn't stop long enough to introduce Laura.

"This has got to end, Neal," she had said as they waited at the bridge.

"But you don't understand."

"Don't understand what?"

"Don't understand that I'm in love with—"

"Don't say that to me. Don't even think it. That's not what this has been about and you know it."

Neal had just shrugged. Once they got to the Laughing Gull, the goodnight kiss was a quick one.

"Are we going to see each other next week?" Neal had asked.

"I don't think we should," she had replied.

"C'mon. Just to walk on the beach at least. I'll be waiting for you Monday morning just after six. I'll probably be back by ten or so Sunday night."

"I'll think about it," had been her only commitment.

Neal was bound for Atlanta the next day, to cover the pre-season gathering of the Atlantic Coast Conference football coaches over the weekend. Laura was relieved. His absence would make the transition to her old world much easier.

She couldn't wait to see the children though she knew she would feel funny. She felt as if she had let them down. And then sleeping tonight on the boat beside Jay. Would he want to make love? Was she ready for that? She figured not, what with the children on board—even though the boat's sleeping berths probably provided adequate privacy. But he probably wouldn't.

As she drove on she tried to rationalize as best possible. She remembered reading an article in one of those women's magazines earlier in the summer about infidelity, a survey claiming that nearly sixty percent of women had committed adultery at one time or the other. So at least she wasn't in the minority, even though the article had pointed out that other surveys had disputed the number—one claiming even higher, many others much lower. One less than twenty percent. Laura didn't feel good about being in the minority.

The survey had listed the reasons. Some did it for the thrill of it. Some to get back at an abusive husband. Some because their husband had seemed to lose interest in them. In many ways, she and Jay had lost interest in each other. Maybe that was why she had done it, she thought.

But she actually thought otherwise. It didn't have anything to do with Jay. To some extent, yes. But not really. And it wasn't just for the sex, though Neal had not failed to live up to most of her expectations. She knew the reason she had done it. It could only be attributed to one thing. And what she was going to do about it now, she just didn't know. For as much as she wished it to be otherwise—and for as much as she wasn't really sure why—Laura knew she was in love with Neal Nickelsen.

WEEK SIX

Chapter Twenty-Six

Saturday, July 24

I$_T$ WAS NEARLY FIVE in the morning when Laura finally gave up on trying to get some sleep. She had dozed fitfully a few times, but for the most part the first night on the sailboat had been rough. The day had been fine. She'd never forget the smiles on her children's faces when they saw her at the camp. She hugged them at the same time, the trio nearly falling over.

"I bet we look like a bunch of fools," Meagan said. "But I don't care."

They arrived at the marina in Oriental around four after a quick visit to Beaufort and stayed at the pool until Jay arrived around seven. Laura had to make the children take turns telling all the wonderful—and a few not-so-wonderful—things they had done at camp.

"What did you do all week, Mom?" Meagan once asked.

"Oh, not much. Just the usual."

It was when Jay arrived the trouble started. He snapped at the children constantly.

"Don't touch that."

"What is it, Dad?"

"I don't know what it is. It has something to do with the boat. But don't touch it. And will you please just sit down and be quiet a minute and let me figure this out?"

The plan had been burgers on the boat's gas grill. But either Jay was not lighting it correctly or it was out of gas. He finally went to the store for charcoal and then had a difficult time getting the coals going.

"Calm down, Jay," Laura tried to say in a comforting tone.

"Don't tell me to calm down," he shot back. "You calm down. Damn. At this rate it'll be midnight before we eat."

"It's OK. The kids and I had a late lunch."

After the meal, Jay finally did settle down a bit. At first his irritable mood made Laura suspicious that maybe he was suspicious. But that was foolish to feel that way, wasn't it? Laura satisfied herself that he was merely nervous about the boat, which he later confessed was the case as they sat in the cockpit around eleven, the children below playing cards, much too excited about sleeping on a boat to actually sleep on a boat.

"It's like camping, only better," Meagan observed.

"Much better," Jacob agreed.

The children finally crashed around midnight. Jay and Laura retired just minutes after to the larger of the two berths, the one in the stern.

Jay slept but was restless. Finally Laura got up, grabbed a light blanket and went up top to sit in the cool early morning air. A light breeze stirred, the masts of the many boats in the harbor emitting a familiar clang as they rocked methodically. Among other things, it had been their conversation just before going to bed that kept Laura awake. Jay had laid out the plan in detail. Darrell and Jim were coming down around ten Saturday morning. Darrell had promised a thorough sailing lesson. Jay and Jim had a lot to learn.

"What about Noell?" Laura had asked.

"I don't know. She was supposed to come, but at the last minute Jim said she had something to do. I don't know. You know how unreliable she is."

Unreliable? Laura had thought. She had never thought of Noell in that way. But she didn't question Jay.

"I'm looking forward to it," Laura had said. "I want to learn to sail. I think the kids will love it."

"I thought you and the kids were going back to the beach in the morning. Mom will be there by herself."

"I thought we were going sailing first then all four of us were going to Sunset."

"I can't fit in the beach this weekend, Laura. I need to get by the hospital Saturday night and then catch up at the office Sunday. But maybe I'll get down there next weekend."

Laura had broken a long silence by asking, "Jay, have you even missed us this summer?"

"What kind of question is that? I was there for a whole damn week. I've got work to do, Laura. I'm not the one spending the summer away from home."

How could it have gotten to this point? Laura thought as the first vestiges of daylight began to creep into the harbor. Something had to be done, she knew. But what?

LAURA AND THE CHILDREN were treated to an enjoyable, though somewhat abbreviated sail. She listened intently to Darrell's instructions, watched even his most subtle movements. She knew the basics, having sailed a Sunfish in her younger days at camps and up on Lake Norman with a friend whose parents had a weekend retreat there. But a thirty-footer was another deal. Nevertheless, by the end of the cruise she figured with practice she could get the hang of it.

She wished Noell had been there and really didn't understand Jim's explanation of her absence, only that something had come up at work requiring her to travel out of town for the weekend. Given Noell's daring, Laura guessed the two of them probably would be better sailors than their husbands if they put their minds to it.

They left Jay with the men around two to head back to Sunset. She was relieved he was in a better mood. The first voyage had been flawless, the children well behaved.

"Daddy, thank you for getting us this boat," Jacob had told Jay as they were leaving.

"Yeah, thanks, Dad," Meagan had added. "Maybe we'll see you again sometime."

On the way back, Laura popped the question. "How would you guys like to learn to play tennis?"

They looked at each other.

"Sure," Meagan said enthusiastically.

"OK," Jacob added.

"Good," Laura said, "because I'm going to teach you."

"Really?" Meagan said.

"Yeah. Really."

SEEING THE CHILDREN AGAIN seemed to thrill Bonnie as much as it did Laura.

"You spent too much on them," Laura said as they sat on the back porch admiring the loot. "It looks like Christmas around here."

"It's my money and they're my grandchildren," Bonnie said with a laugh. "It's my job to spoil them."

The first order of business had been opening the numerous gifts from Bonnie's shopping spree. She also got Jay and Laura a few things.

"I was hoping he'd be here," Bonnie said to Laura. "Y'all haven't had an argument or something, have you? I'm sorry. I guess I shouldn't have said that. It's not my job to be nosy."

"An argument?" Laura said. "No! Why?"

"Oh, some florist delivered a beautiful arrangement for you this afternoon. I figured Jay must have sent it and the only reason . . . well, it's none of my business."

"Is there a card?"

"Yes—and no, I didn't open it. You know I wouldn't do that. I left them in there on the kitchen table."

Laura went inside and found the flowers. She could tell the handwriting on the small envelope it was Neal's. This is too much, she thought.

She opened the envelope quickly and read the words: "I hope these flowers are fit for a queen, for I'm already having a fit to see the queen again."

She quickly stuffed the card in the right pocket of her shorts.

ABOUT THAT SAME TIME, around seven-thirty in the late afternoon, the men were still sailing the new boat.

"The name ought to have something to do with medicine and insurance," Jim said as they continued on their quest for an appropriate new name for the vessel. The pharmacists had named it Legal Drug.

"How 'bout Malpractice?" Darrell offered.

"Ouch," Jay said. "A dentist should know better."

"Major Medical," Jim said. "Or maybe Life Prescription."

"Why don't you just let Laura and Noell name it. That's what I did with our boat. I let Anna name it. Somebody told me that was a good way to make the woman take some ownership in the deal. You know, make them feel a part of it— even though the main purpose of a sailboat is to get away from them of course."

"It is nice out here without 'em," Jay said. "No wife, no kids, no patients, no drug salesmen. Boys, this is the life."

"Amen to that," Darrell said. "But unfortunately it's getting on. We better turn it in for the day. It'll be past eight before we get back to the marina. Why don't we go over to the Trawl Door for dinner? There's usually some fine young ladies posting up around there."

"I really need to get back," Jay said.

"You mean you're not spending the night?" Jim asked. "We're gonna raise a little hell tonight. Those guys from Fremont are down here with their new boat—and they've got a couple of their friends with them. We'll get up with them. Those guys are always wide open."

"No, I've got a bunch to do at the office tomorrow."

"Oh, bullshit, Doc. Look, you got yourself a boat here," Darrell said. "Put it to good use. Might even find us some senoritas who'd like to take a moonlight cruise."

"Speaking of that," Jim said, "did you get a look at the lungs on that bitch two boats down from us?"

"How could you miss them?" Jay said.

"Whatta you say, Doc? You spending the night or not?"

"I don't know. Laura would really be pissed if she found out. She wanted me to go back to the beach with her this weekend. But that beach stuff is boring as hell to me. All we'd do is sit around the house with Mom or on the beach with the kids getting fried. There's just nothing fun to do down there."

"I can promise you tonight will not be boring," Darrell assured.

"Yeah, but I don't know what I'd tell Laura."

"Don't tell her shit. How's she going to know?" Darrell asked.

"Noell's not going to know. That's for sure," Jim said.

"And you know I won't tell Anna," Darrell added.

"Well, all right," Jay said. "I'll stay. Just need to make a few phone calls. And hell, if I ain't driving home tonight, throw me another beer out of that cooler."

"Doc, ole buddy," Darrell said, "welcome to the wonderful world of sailing. Gonna have some fun tonight."

CHAPTER TWENTY-SEVEN

Sunday, July 25

M<small>OM, HOW OLD WERE</small> you when you had your first boy-friend?" Meagan asked.

Thirty-nine, Laura thought but instead replied calmly, "Why do you ask?"

"Just wondering?"

"Meet somebody at camp?"

"Yeah, sort of."

"Want to talk about it?"

"Yes, ma'am. I guess so."

They were on the beach, Sunset Beach, on a beautiful Sunday afternoon under a brilliant blue sky with bright white clouds drifting by. Laura felt in place again. Jacob was playing in the water with some children who had moved in Saturday for two weeks. They were staying right down the street on the right. The parents seemed nice. And now Meagan had a boyfriend of sorts, Laura thought. She couldn't wait to hear about it.

"What's his name?" Laura asked.

"Eric."

"That's a nice name."

After a long silence, Laura finally asked, "Anything else?"

"No, ma'am. May I go swimming now?"

"Sure. I'm certainly glad we had this little talk."

"Me, too. Thanks, Mom."

As Meagan ran off, Laura called out, "Where's he from?"

"Greenville. I've got his address. Is it OK if I send him a postcard from Sunset?"

"That will be fine. We'll pick one out tomorrow."

If only relationships always stayed that simple, Laura thought.

BEFORE DINNER, BONNIE AND Laura sat on the back porch read-ing. Meagan and Jacob were down the street visiting. Laura was considering checking on them when Bonnie said, "I think I'll have a glass of wine before dinner. Would you like one Laura?"

"Sure," Laura said. "I didn't know you liked wine."

"When I go to see Frances, we always have a glass of wine, sometimes two, before dinner. I think it helps me sleep bet-ter. Or maybe it helps with digestion, I don't know. So I was thinking, at my age, it probably won't kill me to drink a little wine before dinner. They say the French are very healthy for it. Or is it the Italians? One or the other, or at least that's what I've read."

They went inside and Laura helped open the bottle. Then they retired to the porch. For reasons Laura never could ex-plain, she asked her mother-in-law a question she had never asked before—had never dared to broach the subject.

"What was Doc like?"

"What do you mean?"

"I mean, I never really knew him until after he had the stroke. I just wondered what he was like. Y'all never talk about him much . . . well, never mind. I shouldn't have asked that."

"For heaven's sakes, Laura," Bonnie said. "You can ask me anything."

"I was just wondering what he was like. That was all."

Bonnie took a deep breath. "You know, I don't think I've ever said this to anybody before, but it's the truth: He was not a very nice man. I mean, it's the truth. I might as well say it. Is there anything wrong with saying it if it's the truth? Now he was a good provider and left me very well taken care of, as I'm sure you know. And by and large a good doctor, I suppose. But when it came to his family, well . . . I'll just say he wasn't always a very nice man and leave it at that."

"I'm sorry."

"But despite it all, and despite what others say, my children turned out all right, I think. Oh, I know what people in Farmington think of the girls. I know they all think they were the bad Babsons and Jay was the good one. But all in all, I think they have it better than Jay. And that's not meant to be a reflection on you, Laura. You're one of the best things to ever happen to our family. It's just that Jay, it seemed, always thought it was his place to try to please his father. And I tried to tell him, no one could ever completely please him— that's just the type of person he was. And sometimes even today, I feel like he's still trying. The girls, on the other hand, they figured him out a long time ago. A long time ago."

"Do you miss them?"

"What do you think?"

"Let's invite them for Christmas this year," Laura said.

"I don't know, Laura. You know, this may sound silly, but when I rented this place for this summer, I held out hope they would come. They said they would try. I think they would like it here. I know they don't like coming to Farmington. But the beach, well . . . that's a different thing, isn't it? I told Blair to bring her friend. I've accepted it, even if Jay hasn't. I think they would have come, but they're busy with a new play or something. And Beth wanted to come, I think, but they already had planned a big trip to Alaska. She even wanted me to come and I thought, imagine that, Bonnie Babson in Alaska."

"It would probably be fun," Laura said. "It's funny, I was thinking the same thing, that maybe my parents would come down and my brother and his family. But it's almost impossible to get my parents out of that house on Lake Norman now that Dad's retired. Now I guess I'll have to drive out there before school starts back so they can see the kids."

"That'll be nice," Bonnie said.

"But I still think we ought to try to get everyone together for Christmas this year. In Farmington or somewhere. You think there's a chance?"

"God only knows," Bonnie replied. "But I never give up hope."

CHAPTER TWENTY-EIGHT

Monday, July 26

GOOD MORNING, MY HIGHNESS," Neal said.

"Morning."

He took a deep breath. "Smell that salt air. Look at that sand and water. And look at you. Gosh, I missed you. I really did."

"I missed you, too," she said.

"Great! Let's go make love."

"Will you get real?" she said, slugging him in the arm.

They walked on the beach.

"I'm starting the kids' tennis lessons today," she said.

"Taking them to that pro?"

"No. I'm teaching them. Mother knows best and all that."

"That girl of yours will probably be good," Neal said. "But the boy's a bit stocky for it, I think. He'd make a better nose guard."

"His father played guard," Laura remembered.

"Yeah, I would think so."

"What's that mean?"

"Never mind."

"You're terrible."

"I know."

After the walk Laura faced an unexpected decision.

"You think your kids and mom-in-law are awake?" he asked as they reached the Bullish Outlook, where they washed the sand from their feet under a spigot beneath the cottage.

"Probably. Why?"

"I was just thinking, that's all."

"Pretty dangerous. So what were you thinking?"

"I was thinking what difference would it make if you got back in five minutes or fifteen minutes or thirty minutes or even an hour for that matter. You know, a lot could happen in five, fifteen, thirty or sixty minutes."

"Are you serious?" Laura said. "You really think I would go in there and make love with you this morning. Is that what you think?"

"Well, if I had to bet on it, I probably would say no. But I'm one of those optimistic types when it comes to some things. And if I had to hope on it, well, yeah, I'm hoping."

Laura shook her head.

"You should have bet on it," she said as she calmly walked over and ascended the steps leading up to the main level of the house.

"THAT WAS UNBELIEVABLE," NEAL said about thirty minutes later. He was lying on his side beside her, gently scratching her back. Laura lay on her stomach, her face away from him. "Awesome. Incredible. What can I say?"

"I don't know but keep on," Laura said.

"I just don't know what to say."

"You are such a flatterer. Is that a word?"

"Who cares? But is it flattery if it's the truth? I mean really, Laura—"

"OK, enough," she said. "My ego's been adequately stroked."

They lay there in silence. She knew she needed to get back to the house. But what for? They were still asleep, she felt certain. A few more minutes.

"Neal, let me ask you something?"

"Shoot."

"How many women have you made love to?"

"Made love to or had sex with?"

"Now don't hand me that line: 'My darling, I've had sex with many but only made love to you.' I've heard it before."

"From whom?"

"In some movie or something."

"Damn. Somebody stole my line."

"Really. How many?"

"You know you shouldn't ask that."

"Why?"

"Because you shouldn't. It's not permitted."

"Well, excuse me," she said. "Sorry, but I've never had an affair before. I didn't know there was some protocol to it."

"No, it's not that. It's just that you've put me in an awkward spot here."

"As if I'm not."

"Whatever. But it's just something you shouldn't ask. I would never ask you that."

"I wouldn't mind if you asked me," she said.

"OK. So how many men. Sex or love, whatever you want to call it."

"Counting you?"

"Yes. I hope I count."

"Two."

"Counting me?"

"Yes."

"Bullshit."

"Whatta you mean?"

"I mean I don't believe it."

"It's true."

"Well, you'd never know it."

"What's that supposed to mean?"

"It's a compliment. Really. I just meant, well . . . I think I better shut up."

"Good. OK, then. I told you. Now you tell me."

"Men don't feel comfortable with a question like that. Or more specifically, that question."

"Why?"

"I dunno. We just don't."

"So suddenly you've joined this big brotherhood-of-man thing. We men this and we men that. I'm talking about you."

"It's like this, Laura: First, if I don't answer the question, you're thinking I've got something to hide. Second, if I do answer the question, there's no way the number's going to be right. I mean, if I said seven—is that high or low? Or three or twelve or four-hundred and seventy-eight?"

"That would be high."

"What?"

"Four-hundred and seventy-eight. I would classify that as high," she said.

"Yeah. Me, too. But it's not that many. Not even close. Why are you asking this anyway?"

"Just wondering, that's all. I think I've been quite honest with you. Looks like you could do the same. So how many?"

"How many what?"

"You know. How many women? Tell me."

"Why —"

"Forget the why. Tell me."

"I don't know."

"You're lying, Neal Nickelsen. I bet you know exactly how many. Maybe how many times with each."

"Well, yeah," he said with a boyish reluctance.

"So how many?"

"Counting you?"

"Yes!" she said impatiently.

"Twenty-two."

"TWENTY-TWO!"

"It's not like I'm Wilt Chamberlain."

"Twenty-two. Jesus. What a special girl am I?"

"You see, I told you. There's no right answer."

"I guess not."

"But if it'll make you feel better —"

"I don't think it will," she said.

"Yeah, probably not."

LATER THAT AFTERNOON, AFTER golf, Neal stopped by the beach to check on Laura. The children were playing just down the way.

"Neal," Laura said reflectively, "do you think things happen for a reason?"

"No."

"Oh."

"Why do you ask?"

"No reason, I guess."

"It's like us," Neal said. "There's no reason we fell in love. We just did."

"Neal, we're not in love. In heat, maybe. But not love."

"I disagree."

"Let's change the subject," she said.

"Why?"

"Because I said so."

"But Laura—"

"Shut up!"

"OK."

CHAPTER TWENTY-NINE

Tuesday, July 27

W<small>HAT TIME IS IT?</small>" Laura asked.

"About two hours past high," Neal said.

"What are you talking about?"

"I was just looking at the tide clock over there. Looks like it's about four hours till low. Or about two hours after high. I'm running on tide time these days."

It was actually around 7:45 A.M. As had been the case the day before, Laura had come inside after the walk. They lay together on the bed in the master suite of the Bullish Outlook.

"Tide time?"

"It makes you younger."

"Sure."

"I'm serious."

"OK, I can't wait. Explain it to me."

"Well, as you know, the tides are caused not by the gravitational pull of the sun but instead the moon—for the most part at least. Anyway, the earth goes around the sun every twenty-four hours, but it takes the moon about twenty-four hours and fifty-one minutes to go around the earth, see. So that's why the tide cycle is about fifty-one minutes later each day. Anyway, to make a long story short, I decided, at least when I'm at the beach, to live on tide time."

"Why don't you call it moon time?" Laura asked.

"Don't confuse me. Anyway, it's really neat because on tide time you're younger than you are on sun time."

"Because the days are longer."

"Right. You're pretty smart."

"I know. So how much younger?"

"I figured that out one time, but I can't remember. Hold on a minute and I'll get my calculator. It's over here on the desk somewhere."

"That's OK."

"No, really, it will only take a second. Or maybe a minute."

"In regular time or tide time."

"I'm ignoring that. Let's see, let's assume it's next July and you've just turned forty and you're down here — with me of course, sitting on the beach and soaking up rays — but you really won't be forty. Let's see, forty times 365, that's 14,600 days, plus ten for the leap years, so you will have lived by that time . . . 14,610 days, times twenty-four, that's 350,640 hours, times sixty that's 21,038,400 minutes. Let's see, here, how many minutes are there in a regular day, sixty times twenty-four, that's 1,440 plus fifty-one, that's 1491. So we divide 21,038,400 by 1491, so in tide time you will have lived only 14,110.3 days, divided by 365.25: that's 38.7 years. See, if you turn forty at the beach, you'll really only be thirty-eight. Almost thirty-nine. But not forty. There's a very big spiritual difference there."

Neal did some more quick figuring. "So the factor here is .9675. You just take your age and multiply it by .9675 and that's how old you are in tide time. The trick is you can only live on tide time if you're at the beach, I think. So for instance, let's see, you're thirty-nine times .9675, that's 37.7 years old. But as soon as your vacation is over and you cross that bridge for the last time, bam, just like that you age more than a year and you're right back to thirty-nine again. Kind of makes you want to stay here, doesn't it? So what I'm looking to do is figure out a way to live on tide time all the time. Then when I turn fifty in regular time, I'll only be, let's see . . . 48.4 years old in tide time and I'll be so much younger than all those other geezers on the Senior Tour I'll be kicking butt."

"So I guess you think this makes you the King of Tides or something," Laura said.

"Hey, I hadn't thought of that," Neal said. "Think that means I might make it with Barbra Streisand?"

"Are you through?"

"Through? What do you mean?"

"Through. With all this tide stuff. The only reason I asked you what time it was because if it wasn't too late I thought we'd have time for a quickie before I had to get back."

"It's just seven-forty-eight."

"Darn. If it had only been seven-forty-six. Well, maybe another time."

"Wait. Can't we work this out?"

"I gotta go. Maybe you should give Babs a call."

LAURA DIDN'T LET IT show — at least she thought not — but she was nervous. She had waited for it to cool off. No need for the heat to discourage them. She had thought about early in the morning would be a better time, but they had grown accustomed to sleeping late and even though she hated to admit she had quickly become accustomed to other activities in the mornings.

So finally, around six-thirty in the afternoon, they crossed the bridge and went to the courts at Sea Trail. Late Monday they had ridden to Myrtle and bought rackets at a discount golf and tennis store. Laura let the kids ride bumper boats and eat at Fuddruckers at Barefoot Landing.

"Say 'Fuddruckers' five times real fast," Meagan had said to Jacob.

"Don't you dare," Laura warned.

Despite her anxieties, the lesson went well. Meagan listened better, but Jacob made better contact with the ball, twice hitting "home runs," as he called it when the ball went over the fence. Laura quickly broke him by making him run down the homers and sit out a few minutes.

"That was fun," Meagan said when they concluded. It was nearly eight when they got back in the Suburban.

"Yeah, but Mom's a lot better than us," Jacob said. "How'd you get so good?"

"Practice. And I had a good teacher."

"Do you think you would have been a pro if you hadn't hurt your knee?" Meagan asked.

"I doubt it," Laura said.

"I betcha would've been," Meagan said.

"That would be neat," Jacob said. "I could get your autograph. Do they have tennis cards? Like baseball cards?"

"I don't know."

"That would be cool. Mom on a card."

"Mom, tell us about that time you beat that girl — where was she from? Maryland? — tell us about that," Meagan said.

"Oh, your father makes too much of that. He wasn't even there. He just heard about it."

"Tell us, Mom," Jacob demanded.

"You've heard it a hundred times."

"Please!"

"All right, I'll tell you. We were playing Maryland in Chapel Hill and it was our first conference match and I was playing number six. Anyway, being a freshman I was real nervous and this girl I was playing was a real . . . oh, let me see: How can I put this? It starts with a 'b' and it rhymes with a lead character in *The Wizard of Oz*. That's what she was."

"A bitch!" Meagan screamed.

"I've told you about using language like that," Laura said.

"Was she really a bitch, Mom?" Jacob asked.

"Yes, she was. And watch your mouth, too. Anyway, I was playing terrible, but she didn't help matters much because every time I hit a ball close to the line she called it out."

"Cheat-er, cheat-er," Meagan chanted.

"Cheaters never win," Jacob said.

"Do I get to tell this story or not?" They agreed to let Laura proceed without interruption.

"So I lost the first set 6-2 and was down 4-1 in the second and I just knew I was going to lose, but then I hit this really good forehand cross-court. I mean a real screamer and she called it out. Well, it was ridiculous. The ball was in by a good foot at least. So I walked up to the net and just stood there and looked at her for a few seconds and finally put my hand behind my ear and said, 'What did you call that?' And she said, 'Out.' And I said, 'I'm sorry, but I must have misunderstood you. It sounded like you said out.' And then she said in this whinny, Chesapeake Bay, I suppose, accent, 'Yeah, bitch. I said it was out.'

"She was serving and I walked back to receive and she hit the next serve in and I just let it go and said in my best whine, 'It was out.' She stared at me and then hit the second serve and it was definitely in and I just let it go and whined, 'It was out.' Then she went into a tirade and I just kept saying, 'Yeah, bitch. I said it was out. Yeah, bitch, I said it was out.'"

The kids always loved that part.

"What happened then?" Jacob asked.

"Finally we had to get one of the coaches to call lines, which is exactly what I wanted. We usually played on the honor system, but I could see this person was not so honorable. Anyway, the whole thing seemed to shake her up. And because there was some controversy a lot of people started watching the match and since we were at home everybody was pulling for me. So at that point I just got real charged up and I just creamed her. Won the second set 7-5 and the third 6-1. By the time it was over I almost felt sorry for her, but then she wouldn't even shake my hand. Like I said, she was kind of a . . . well, you know. It was fun."

After a pause, Meagan put the back of her hand to her forehead and said romantically, "And the next day Daddy sent you flowers."

"Yes," Laura said quietly, "he certainly did. I remember it well."

Chapter Thirty

Wednesday, July 28

AROUND FIVE-FIFTEEN IN THE afternoon, Laura snapped. Almost. "I'm gonna snap," she said emphatically.

"What's wrong, Mom?" Meagan asked.

"I'm gonna snap."

"What's that mean?" Jacob asked. "Why are we just sitting here?"

She thought she had timed it just about right. But something wasn't right. The bridge was still open for boat traffic and Laura and her kids were waiting in the Suburban in a long line of traffic headed for the mainland. At least twenty cars were ahead of her. But they'd been waiting there for nearly ten minutes and nothing was happening.

"What am I supposed to do?" Laura asked no one in particular. "Sit here and wait? I don't know. I gotta do something."

"Maybe the bridge is messed up," Meagan said, sensing her mother's discomfort. "Maybe we should turn back."

Yeah, maybe so, Laura thought. But at this point there was no turning back. Or was there? What is wrong with me?

Laura wondered. An anxiety attack? Me? The tension had been building. I'm coming undone, she thought. Over this bridge? The two-lane causeway leading to the bridge was narrow, flanked by salt marshes. Some cars ahead of her were turning back.

"I hate turning this tank around," Laura said.

"What should we do?" Meagan asked.

"I don't know! Just sit there and keep your mouth shut."

"There's a policeman," Jacob said, pointing ahead.

"You, too."

She couldn't believe she was talking to her children like that. Yes, I'm just having an anxiety attack, she thought. Just calm down, calm down. But it didn't help. Her hands were shaking and she could feel sweat on her forehead even though the air conditioner was wide open.

"Pull up, Mom."

Those cars that hadn't turned back were moving forward. Laura hadn't noticed. She was biting down on the knuckle of her left index finger.

"OK. I said be quiet."

They sat in silence. The children were restless. They hadn't seen their mother like this often. What was the big deal?

More and more cars were turning back. A policeman on foot was stopping at each one. Most turned back. Some just moved up in line.

He finally approached the Suburban. Laura rolled down the window.

"What's wrong?"

"Bridge is out, ma'am," he said. "Sorry. Could be ten minutes, could be an hour. They're working on it. It's up to you if you want to wait in line. Unless you really need to get some-where, I'd turn back."

Turn back, Laura thought. But how? How could she turn back?

"I'm not too good at turning this, this . . . thing around," she said. "I don't know if there's room." He sensed she was worried.

"No problem, ma'am. I'll direct you."

"Are you sure?"

"Sure. You can turn around here. No problem. Right this way," he said motioning.

Calm down, she thought, just calm down.

It took several shifts from forward to reverse, but finally the Suburban was headed in the opposite direction. Laura drove straight to the Laughing Gull without a word. When she pulled underneath the cottage, she said to her children, "Maybe later we can play tennis. I don't know. I'm sorry I acted like a jerk."

"Can we go play with Cora and Max down the street?" Meagan asked.

"Sure. I'm going to sit out on the dock. Be careful."

Laura proceeded to the dock, sitting down on the wooden railing, the sun shining on her skin.

"What am I going to do?" she asked herself.

Chapter Thirty-One

Thursday, July 29

Y<small>OU KNOW</small>, L<small>AURA</small> . . . I'<small>M</small> leaving tomorrow," Neal said as they walked toward Bird Island again, this time around six-thirty.

"Like I'm dumb. I know."

"Don't you think we ought to talk about it? About what's going to happen?" he asked.

"I figured you would leave by car."

"Very funny. I was talking about what's going to happen to us?"

"Don't worry, Neal. You're off the hook."

"What are you saying?"

"Number twenty-two says you're off the hook. We'll say good-bye and that will be it. And I'll just be another statistic in the Neal record book. Maybe I'll even make your hall of fame one day."

"You really think that's all this has been to me? You're wrong there, Laura. Dead wrong. What I said earlier is true. I'm in love with you."

"Give me a break."

"I'm serious, dammit. And I know you won't admit it, but I think you're in love with me, too."

"Oh, you do, do you?"

"Why are you being so glib about this?" he asked.

"I'm not being glib. I'm being realistic."

"I am, too. And I was thinking, well . . . we could continue this."

"So that's what you were thinking."

"Yes. That's what I was thinking."

"So tell me, Neal, just how were you thinking we could continue this? Were you thinking maybe I'd leave Jay and then me and the kids would move to Raleigh and we'd all live together in your condo? You did say you have a condo, didn't you? And then we could start house hunting. What fun! The one we live in now has five bedrooms and a big rec room for the kids with a Ping-Pong table and a big-screen TV. And we also have a huge yard. I bet we could pick up something like that in Raleigh for a song. And of course, there's the schools to contend with. I'm not real thrilled with the prospects of sending my children to public schools in a city I know nothing about; so we'd have to do the private-school thing, of course. How much money do you make anyway? We haven't talked about that. Of course, that hardly matters. I mean, Jay would be so thrilled with the whole arrangement I'm sure he'd be more than willing to heap all kinds of lavish child support and alimony on us — don't you think? Is that what you were thinking?"

She didn't give him a chance to answer.

"But then again, I'm really not being fair to Bonnie and the children. Bonnie hardly ever sees her other grandchild and my kids sure don't see my parents much. And the children have all their friends there in Farmington. It has its faults, but it really is a pretty decent place to raise kids. Hey, I've got it: I'll kick Jay out and you can move on down to Farmington and we'll get hitched at the local church and a fine time can be had by all. We'll cook a pig — that's mandatory for weddings in Farmington. Of course, you'd have to quit your job. We're nearly two hours from Raleigh — too far to commute. But don't worry, we've got a newspaper in Farmington. It comes out once a week — most of the time. They could use a good sportswriter. You could cover Jacob's Little-League games. Is that what you had in mind, Neal?"

"Come on, Laura," he said.

"Or let me see . . . maybe you were thinking ole Starshine here would just drive up to Raleigh every week or so and we'd get together and fuck?"

Neal wasn't sure what to say but decided to take the easy way out, putting his arm around her and declaring enthusiastically, "Queenie, now you're talking!"

They both laughed. They stopped walking. Laura pulled away from him and looked out to sea, then turned, placed her hand on his arm and said, "I think you know the score here, Mr. Sportswriter."

"Laura, don't say this," he said. "We can work this out."

"No. Tomorrow's the bottom of the ninth. Then that's it. What is it you sports guys like to say: 'The fat lady's going to sing?' "

He put his arm around her again. As much as he would like it to be otherwise, he was afraid there wasn't much to say to make her change her mind. Not now at least.

"But tell me something," he finally said, "because I've got to know."

"Know what?"

"Do you love me?"

Laura slowly looked away from him and then quietly said, "No."

"Look at me and say it."

She looked at him and said loudly, "No!"

"I don't believe you."

"That's your problem."

"You mean to tell me that all this has been to you is just sex. Nothing more than a purely physical relationship. Is that what you're saying?"

"Yes," she said.

"Never, ever, have I felt so degraded, so used, so, so—"

"And you loved every minute it of, didn't you?" she said.

"Damn right."

They both laughed again. They just seemed to make each other laugh.

"Bottom of the ninth," Neal finally said. "But I guess it's for the best."

"I think so," she agreed.

"Because I'll tell you, Laura, I'm not as young as I used to be. If I had to go to extra innings with you, I'd probably have to call on a relief pitcher."

LAURA WAS RELIEVED TO get that conversation behind her. It was the only way, wasn't it? Yes, for her it was. Back at the Bull-ish Outlook, she declined his invitation to come inside.

"Maybe tomorrow," she said. "Or maybe I'll see you tonight if I can work it out. I just don't know, Neal. This isn't exactly easy."

"Tonight would be better," he said. "I don't want to see you walk away from me in daylight."

"I'll see you on the beach later," she said. "We'll talk."

When she got back to the Laughing Gull, Bonnie and the children were still asleep as usual. She quietly poured another cup of coffee, sat down on the porch, glanced through a magazine for a few moments, placed it on her lap and stared out at the marsh. It was beautiful at any time of the day, but she liked it best in the early morning. So quiet. So still. So calm. And so unlike the things going on inside of Laura.

She laughed. Shouldn't have let him off so easily, Laura thought. Should have told him I was leaving Jay and expected him to marry me. That would have shook him up. Or would it? Yes. He's just not the marrying kind. Or is he?

But she could at least imagine it. After all, people get divorces all the time, right? Certainly. All the time. Yes. But she didn't. Not Laura. It wasn't like Jay was an abusive husband. Neglectful, maybe. But not abusive. How could she tell Jay she had fallen in love with someone else and was leaving him? How could she tell Bonnie? And her parents? And what would people in Farmington think. The place would probably turn into a big sinkhole and be swallowed by the earth in the matter of hours.

But she probably could tell Jay. She knew she could. She could imagine herself saying, "Jay, I'm sorry. I'm really sorry. But I've fallen in love with someone. I'm sorry. It's not your fault. It's mine. I am truly sorry."

And she could tell Bonnie, too. Given all that woman had been through, she'd probably understand it. Maybe condone it. And even her parents, too. No, they wouldn't like it a bit. But they're adults. They'd get over it. And to hell with what people in Farmington thought — as if many of them are even capable of thinking.

But it was all moot. For she knew there were two people — two children, her children — she could never tell. And she never would, because there would never be anything to tell. And that's all there was to it. She'd made a commitment. Of her own free will, she did it. Not to Jay. Not to Meagan. Not to Jacob. But to Jay, Meagan, Jacob and Laura. Their family. The four of them. They came first.

Laura went back to the magazine for a few moments before glancing up at the dock — the dock from which she had carefully stepped, with Neal's help, onto an inflatable boat for a simple yet complex ride to Bird Island. She thought about the first time he had held her hand and the way he would look at her at times. And the kisses. Killer kisses.

Then she closed her eyes, rested her head on her left hand and cried.

"This is crazy," Laura said.

"I don't think so," Neal protested. "I think it's perfectly sane in my opinion. But I guess I'm being redundant."

It was nearly eleven o'clock at night. Laura had convinced a half-asleep Bonnie, now accustomed to Sunset's safe environment, that taking a late-night walk alone would be harmless. Neal had greeted her on the deck at the Bullish Outlook and told her he had the boat ready—ready for one last run to Bird Island.

"Neal, there's something I need to tell you," she said.

"If you're not going to tell me you're dumping your husband and eloping with me to Jamaica, then don't say it."

She slapped his shoulder.

"Listen to me," she said. "This has to be it. After tonight do not contact me. Don't call. Don't write. Don't think about me."

"But I have written," he said.

"What do you mean?"

"A letter. To Kindred Spirit. You'll find it in the mailbox over there. Just read it and write a response in the notebook. I'll come down Labor Day and find it. Then that will be it. I promise. Unless . . ."

"Unless what?"

"Unless you change your mind"

"I'm not. I can't."

"OK. But at least do me one favor. Well, two actually."

"What's that?"

"First. I need a little inspiration. Promise me that if—no, when—I make the Senior Tour, you'll spend the weekend with me at my first tournament."

"Ha," Laura said. "I'll be—what?—forty-six by then. You wouldn't be seen with me."

"Not in tide time. Anyway, will you promise me that?"

"That's silly. I can't make a promise like that."

"Well at least say you'll consider it."

"OK, I'll consider it if you'll do what I asked you—about not contacting me."

"I'll try."

"Good," she said. "And the second favor?"

Neal put his hand on her shoulder and said, "Go with me to Bird Island tonight. Just one more time. And drink a glass of that Asti I've got chilling on the boat there. And look at the stars and the moon. And look at me as if I mean something to you. And let me look at you the same way. Because you do mean something to me Laura and I think I mean something to you. And then let me look at you directly in your eyes and stroke your hair and kiss you and you kiss me and we'll make love and we'll pretend that we're the only two people on this planet. For just tonight, just you and me. The King and Queen of Bird Island. Just one more night. It would mean a lot to me, Laura."

She thought for a second and said, "You practiced that, didn't you?"

"About an hour."

"It was good."

"Thanks. So you gonna go or not?"

"Only if you'll ask me again — and just like that."

CHAPTER THIRTY-TWO

Friday, July 30

Man, Neal, you knocked the hell outta that ball." It was Mark, a young assistant pro at Lion's Paw Neal had met a few weeks earlier and was now his partner in a hastily arranged match with a twosome from Virginia.

"High rollers," Mark had described them by phone Wednesday night. "And they're good. But if we stitch, I think we can hang. Your back OK?"

"Never better. Been getting some pretty good therapy."

Neal liked Lion's Paw. In fact, if it had tees and greens, Neal liked most any golf course. And on this Friday morning, this his last day of sabbatical, his last day at Sunset, he felt good. He thought to hell with the money. If they lost, they lost.

To hell with the newspaper. He'd just go back and do his thing and whatever would be would be. And Laura. He had no regrets. Who would? So what if it was over. So what if he couldn't spend the rest of his life with her. He'd had this. This summer. It would do. It would have to—for the next seven years at least.

So for about four and a half hours, he forgot about all else and just played golf. Later, when he thought about it, he considered that chip-in birdie on number one the key.

"Quite possibly," he told himself later, "that ball could have missed the pin and I'd have a nasty little four-footer left for par that I could have blown."

But the ball didn't miss the pin. It caught it solid, climbed it a bit and dropped straight down for a three. When one of the Virginians missed a twelve-footer for birdie, he and Mark were one up and on their way.

It was on hole number five Mark made his comment.

"I blistered that bitch," Neal conceded. With the wind at his back, the drive covered at least 285 yards. Probably 292 he figured as he checked the yardage book. A soft eight-iron left the ball six feet from the cup and he sank the putt to go three under after five.

Later that day, on the drive back to Raleigh with the top down, he recounted the round in his head. It was as if he was in the press tent after his first round on the Senior Tour in seven years, detailing the round for the media as he had often heard pros do:

"Number one, par four, 417 yards, shoved the drive in the right rough but managed to get a six-iron on the fringe from about 182 out. Chipped in for a birdie.

"Two, par five, 517, hit a good drive, but pulled a one-iron in that trap about fifty yards from the green, hit a sand wedge out, missed an eighteen-footer for birdie. Misread it.

"Three, par three, 204, hit a four-iron hole high, thirteen feet away. Almost missed the putt, curled it in the right lip.

"Four, par four 428. Pretty tough hole. But hit a good drive, five-iron to the front of the green, but the pin was back. Two putted from about fifty feet.

"Five, par four, 415, hit a killer drive to take off the dogleg. Eight-iron to about six feet, made the putt.

"Six, par three, 228, had a little wind behind us. Hit a two-iron, left it out. Chipped up from the fringe and made a four-footer for par.

"Seven, par four, 402, hit a lousy drive, almost put it in the lake on the left side, got a seven-iron on the green, two-putt.

"Eight, par five, 520, hit a big drive and put a three-wood on the green. Two-putt birdie from about thirty-five feet.

"Nine, par four, 386, hit a weak drive in the trap on the right side of the fairway, but had a good lie. Got it about twenty feet away with an eight-iron and two putted."

Neal couldn't recall a better front nine. Had he ever been four-under at the turn? Maybe so, but never on a course this good. They were playing it back. The front was 3,517 yards. Every bit of it. But the ground was fairly hard. He got some good roll on his drives.

His career best was a sixty-five, but it was on a par-seventy-one course. He'd shot thirty-three, thirty-two that day, about four years ago. Not bad for someone who didn't even play golf until his junior year in college, Neal thought.

"I didn't exactly grow up in a country-club family," he figured he would one day explain to the sportswriters. It was after his divorce he got serious about the game. With no wife or kids at home, combined with a job that consisted of a lot of night work, Neal managed to play practically every day the weather allowed.

"Number ten, that tricked-up par four, 400 yards. Two-iron off the tee, kept it in play and put a five-iron about eighteen feet away, missed the putt. Should have made that one.

"Eleven, par three, 202, hit a four to about sixteen feet and made the putt.

"Twelve, par four, 383, busted the drive but hit a pitching wedge fat and two-putted from forty feet.

"Thirteen, par five, 527, had the wind behind us. Busted the drive, should have been on in two, but pulled a three-wood in the left bunker. Blasted out to eight feet and made the putt to go six under.

"Fourteen, par four, 418, dogleg left, hit a great drive, but just dogged a seven-iron, chipped up to about five feet and saved par.

"Fifteen, tough par four, 445, busted the drive but was in the right rough about 190 out. Hit a scalded four to the left fringe and two-putted.

"Sixteen, short par four, 384 dogleg right, decent drive, nine-iron to twelve feet, made the putt to go seven under."

It was at that point in the round Neal was confident he'd finish with no worse than a sixty-five, with only the easiest par three and a not-so-tough par five to go.

"Seventeen, par three, 185, hit my worst shot of the day, a five-iron that almost went in the water on the right. I don't know how it stayed out. Didn't have much green to work with, but managed to get it up and stop in about thirteen feet past and made a lucky putt. Luck counts, too."

And then came the last hole — one he would never forget.

"Eighteen, par five 542, blistered the drive, was about 240 to the middle of the green. Pin on the back. I was pretty pumped. Hit a one-iron."

"You laying up?" Mark had asked when he saw Neal with an iron.

"Hell, no," Neal replied.

It was as if it was the last shot of Neal's summer. He tried to recall what he was thinking as he lined up the shot and finally figured he wasn't thinking.

"Whew, you smoked that," Mark said as he and Neal watched the low shot soar toward the green, taking a big hop on the front. "That could be tight. Hell, could be in."

"I really hit the one-iron well. Ball must have hit the pin. I thought it was going to be long. Did anybody see it hit the pin?"

"Yes," a reporter replies. "It hit the pin. Almost went in."

"Anyway, tapped in for an eagle from, gee, I guess three-and-a-half inches," he continues. "Nine-under, sixty-three. Obviously I'm quite pleased with the round and will be happy to answer any questions. Yes?"

"How does it feel to have this kind of round your first time out on the Senior Tour? You're currently the leader in the clubhouse by six shots."

"That's why I'm out here. To try to win golf tournaments. What can I say."

At the back of the press tent, Neal spies Laura, who's spending the week with him at the tournament. She blows him a little kiss. She may be seven years older but looks just as good as ever to me, Neal thinks. Maybe better.

"Gentlemen, if that's all your questions, I need to get back to my room and rest for tomorrow," Neal tells the press.

"You plan to keep your same routine?" a reporter asks.

"Most definitely. I plan to do tonight just what I did last night and tomorrow morning just what I did this morning. It worked for me."

"One last question — after you tapped in for the eagle, it looked like you kissed the ball and said something to the sky. What did you say?"

"I said, 'Thank you, Kindred Spirit.' "

"What's that mean?"

"It's a beach thing. You wouldn't understand."

Neal exited the interstate about thirty miles from Raleigh. Some fantasy, he thought. But probably the real thing — the last six weeks — was better than any fantasy even he could cook up. It was around six-thirty in the afternoon. He stopped at a convenience store, got gas, bought some chips and a Pepsi. He considered going by the office and hanging around the newsroom until the press ran. The next day, he figured, he'd go to the newspaper and start catching up — but only after an early morning walk. He really was in the habit. Then later maybe hit some balls at CCC or even play nine holes. He had promised he'd work the desk Saturday night for Lou, who was on vacation until Tuesday. He'd need to be there by four. So he decided against going to the office that night. He just went home to his condo. Saw one of the neighbors when he was unpacking his car and they chatted a bit. He was sorry to hear about Mr. Myerson's stroke. The Myersons lived just two units down. They were nice people.

Once inside, the first thing he did was tape the picture of Laura on the mirror over his dresser in the bedroom. He really appreciated her giving it to him. He made a note to buy a frame. Later he would perform an all-too-familiar routine: sort through his mail, clean his golf clubs in the kitchen sink, thaw a steak, cook it on the grill and eat it alone in front of the TV.

WEEK SEVEN

CHAPTER THIRTY-THREE

Saturday, July 31

As instructed, Laura walked toward Bird Island around six-thirty in the morning.

"Oh, and one last favor," Neal had said Thursday night just before they said good-bye.

"Will you let up on the favors?"

"This one's not too tough. Saturday morning, if the weather's OK, walk to Bird Island. Around our usual time. Around six-thirty or so."

"Why?"

"Because I'm going to get up and walk around the condo complex and see if we can connect telepathically."

"Will you get real?"

"Come on, Laura. It's worth a shot. You never know."

"You're so full of it, as usual. But yes, I'll walk. I probably would anyway. I walked on the beach in the mornings before I met you and I'll keep doing it after you're gone."

And now he was gone. Laura felt lonely on the beach. But it could be worse, she thought. She would adjust. Adjust to not seeing Neal. Adjust to living with what she had done.

Adjust. She needed to adjust. Today, she would start adjusting. She even considered going to church Sunday. Not church. The oceanfront worship service held each Sunday morning at Sunset by the fishing pier. She really ought to get up and at least take the children. Had they ever gone this long without going to church? Had she? Maybe, but not often.

"I've got too much free-floating anxiety," she finally said to herself. "Need to find something to focus it on. That's it. The children. I'll worry about the children. No, that's dumb. But what? Why not just quit worrying? What good will it do?"

She walked fast. Fast enough to break a sweat. When she got to Bird Island, she looked instinctively at the dunes. At once she felt guilt. Then she was OK with it. Then guilt. But big deal. It was over now. Over. But over and over again, she knew, she would think about it. What had possessed her to do it? she would ask herself. What had possessed her to end it? She almost could imagine herself living with Neal. But then again, she couldn't. And why wasn't Jay coming down this weekend? Too busy, he had said. But he'll probably figure out a way to get to that damn boat, she thought.

Calm down now, she thought. This is crazy. You can't undo what you've done. Look ahead. Be in control. Think about tennis. The lessons with the children were coming along. They would play every day for the rest of their final week at Sunset, she thought. If they wanted to. She didn't want to force it. But they seemed to be loving it.

It was at about that time, just as she crossed back through the inlet, that she noticed the airplane. Nothing unusual — it was just one of those little planes that often patrolled the beaches towing an advertising banner. Airborne billboards, a cost-efficient means of getting a message to the tourists, long banners with block letters, usually promoting a restaurant, amusement park or T-shirt shop — $8.99 ALL YOU CAN EAT or T-SHIRTS 2 FOR $10.

But something about this plane struck her as unusual. And then, as it approached her from the east, it hit her. What was an advertising plane doing buzzing the beach before seven in the morning? Not much of an audience at that time. She couldn't remember having seen one on any of her other morning walks. Must be practicing.

As the plane approached, its engine noise clashing with the drumming of the surf, she looked up to check the message. At first she couldn't make it out. And when she finally did, she could only manage a double take. Finally, the words in plain view, she sat on the beach and watched it fly past.

The message was brief, intended for a select audience. It simply read: GOOD MORNING STARSHINE.

CHAPTER THIRTY-FOUR

Tuesday, August 3

T HE LAST WEEK WAS moving fast, it seemed to Laura. In just a few days they'd be back in Farmington. And in less than four weeks, the children back in school.

Around ten in the morning, just as they were getting ready to go to the beach, the phone rang.

"You make me sick," the voice on the other end said when Laura answered the phone. It was Noell.

"What are you talking about?"

"You. I can hear your tan and here I am sitting in my office with a suit and hose on, white as a ghost. And it's August. I need to get out in the sun."

"What are you saying?"

"I'm saying I'd like to come visit you."

"You're kidding."

"I'm serious. Is it OK?"

"Of course."

"Good. Because actually I'm not at the office And I'm wearing a pair of shorts and a T-shirt and I've got my bags packed. You know how presumptive I am."

"So when will you be here?"

"How long does it take?"

"About three hours. If you don't stop."

"Great. I'll see you in two."

Noell didn't make it in two hours, but it was close.

"I could have made it in two if it hadn't been for that damn state trooper stopping me and then I got to the bridge just as they were opening it," she told Laura that afternoon as they settled into chairs on the beach, Noell's cooler between them. The children had joined in a volleyball game down the way.

"You mean you got another speeding ticket," Laura said. "Haven't you heard of cruise control?"

"I don't like something being in control of me. Too confining. But just for your information, no, I didn't get another speeding ticket."

"Did you use that crying routine again?"

"No! I used a new one. I used position power. When he found out I'd been hired as an assistant to the state attorney general in Raleigh, he let me slide with a warning."

"How can you lie like that?"

There was a long silence. Noell looked away and bit her fingernails. Finally she turned and looked at Laura. "I wasn't lying. That's why I came down here. To tell you."

"That's too far to commute. Don't tell me y'all are moving to Raleigh. What's Jim going to do?"

"No, I'm moving to Raleigh, Laura. Jim's not. We've separated. We signed the papers yesterday. He's staying at his parents' house until I find a place in Raleigh."

"I am not believing this," Laura said.

"Believe it, girlfriend."

She and Jim had done an excellent job of keeping their troubled marriage quiet, Noell explained. They'd been contemplating the separation for nearly a year. But it all fell into place in the last few weeks when Noell landed a job she really wanted and found a young attorney, a Farmington native, to take her practice.

"Fred Pollock's son, Nick," Noell said. "He's been practicing in Kinston for about a year and he's just gotten married. He'll do well. Everybody in town knows the Pollocks."

The job, she explained, was a lucky break.

"The new attorney general used to teach at Campbell. He taught a couple of my courses in law school and remembered me."

"I don't doubt that," Laura said.

"It's a pretty good job. And I don't start until the first of September, so I've got plenty of time to find somewhere decent to live. I guess I'll just rent at first."

But Noell seemed reluctant to discuss the reason for the separation.

"Why, Noell?" Laura finally asked, figuring that if Noell thought it was none of her business, she could tell her so.

"I don't know, Laura. A lot of reasons. Some good, some not-so-good, I guess."

"If you don't want to talk about it, don't feel compelled," Laura said.

"I do. I really do want to talk to you about it. But I can't right now."

"That's O—"

"Because I just drank two beers in about ten minutes and I've really got to pee."

Laura laughed. "Help yourself," she said, motioning toward the ocean.

"I hate peeing in the ocean," Noell said.

"Yeah, but it's a long walk back to the house just for that."

"Is our sportswriter friend still here? Maybe I could go to his house."

"No, he's long gone," Laura said calmly. "Somebody else is staying in that house now. What's so bad about peeing in the ocean? Everybody does it."

"You really think so?" Noell said.

"No," Laura said. "All these people sit out here for hours on end drinking soft drinks or beer and holding it. Of course everybody does it. I've even learned to do it."

"Actually I don't want to get my hair wet."

"Like you've got to put your head underwater to go?"

"Don't think that I'm going to just walk out there and stand in waist-deep water for about forty-five seconds and then come back out. Everybody will know. But if I go out there and swim around a little bit, then they may just think I wanted to go swimming."

"Noell, are you nuts? This doesn't sound like you. Whatta you care if somebody knows you're peeing in the ocean?"

"I'm just a big bundle of contradictions, aren't I?"

"Well, yeah, but who isn't," Laura said.

"I don't know. I think maybe I am going nuts. I mean, this whole damn thing is not as simple as it sounds. You've never run out on your husband before and you've never gotten a divorce before and you've never faced the prospects of being thirty-seven years old and going home to an empty apartment and shit, I can't believe this is happening to me."

She looked as if she might cry. Laura didn't think she'd ever seen Noell cry.

"I'm sorry," Laura said. "If there's anything I can do for you—"

"There is one thing," Noell said. "Go with me."

"To Raleigh?"

"No, the ocean. I don't want to do it by myself. Don't you have to go, too?"

"Sorta."

"But don't stand too close to me."

"No problem."

They walked toward the water.

"I know you think I'm crazy," Noell said.

"I don't think you're crazy."

"Well then you're wrong, Laura. You're wrong."

AS THE AFTERNOON WORE on, Noell's mood improved, helped in no small part by many more beers.

"Gotta pee again," Noell once said with a laugh. "And this time I'm going by myself. And I'm not even going to get my hair wet. I don't care what everybody thinks."

"That's it, girl," Laura said. "Throw caution to the sea."

The women played with the children. Acted like children. Laughed. Played. Picked on each other. Supported each other. They even had a chicken fight in the ocean, Meagan on Laura's shoulders, Jacob on Noell's. They floated over waves. A crab pinched Noell's toe once and she screamed. Then Laura screamed. Then Meagan and Jacob screamed. Had it not been for the threat of a thunderstorm around five-thirty—

as well as an empty cooler — they might have stayed on the beach until dark. Once back at the house, just before the storm came, Noell took a nap.

"I've been getting about two hours of sleep a night lately," she said. "I hope you don't mind."

"Not at all," Laura said.

"This has been very therapeutic," she said.

"I'm glad we could help."

"Not y'all. The beer."

Laura sat on the back porch by herself. Bonnie was cooking dinner and insisted she didn't need any help. With company in the house, she was going all out.

"Don't be silly," she had said when Noell offered to take the Babsons out for dinner.

Jacob was playing with the Game Boy on the couch. Meagan was doing something in her room.

The storm was rough at first but soon subsided to a steady shower. Laura watched the raindrops strike the dock behind the cottage. Low tide had been around three that afternoon. The marsh was beginning to fill again.

Bonnie soon joined her on the porch, a glass of wine in hand — some expensive stuff Noell had brought.

"Rather dry, but it's OK," Bonnie said.

Laura decided she should tell Bonnie about Noell and Jim.

"Oh, my," Bonnie said. "Oh, my my my."

"Do you mind if I ask her to stay the rest of the week?" Laura asked.

"Of course not. I like Noell. I'm going to miss her."

"Me, too," Laura said, though she tried not to think about it. Her best friend was leaving. But she shouldn't think of herself at a time like this. She had other friends in Farmington. Anna, Carol, Lindsay. And Pam Aycock. Thinking back, she should have invited Pam and her children to the beach. But she hadn't.

"You know, I never really cared for that Beaman boy," Bonnie said. "Never really cared for the Beamans. As a matter of fact—and I probably wouldn't be saying this if it wasn't for this wine—but I've never really cared much for living in Farmington. Do you?"

"It's OK," Laura said, not sure what to say.

"I just might buy me a house down here and just stay down here most of the time. Not all the time. Not in the winter, of course. But about half the time. Y'all could come stay with me in the summer and during vacations. And Frances likes it here. She could stay with me some. And the girls would probably come here. They don't like coming to Farmington. I don't blame them. But they would probably like it here. And I could stay by myself some. I get around pretty well for a woman my age. Who knows? I might even find a man down here."

"Sounds like a winner to me," Laura said.

"Oh, I'm just being silly. Let me go inside and finish dinner. Imagine that. Me with a house at the beach. Me not living in Farmington. For heaven's sakes. It's just silly."

"I don't think it's silly," Laura said.

"Oh, it's silly. Jay wouldn't hear of it."

NOELL SLEPT THROUGH DINNER. By eleven, Laura decided to turn in. She was just about to write Noell a note and tell her to help herself to the leftovers in the refrigerator when she heard her friend walk in.

"Good gosh," Laura said. "Eating at Red Lobster tonight, are we?"

"I am in pain," Noell said slowly.

She was clad only in a white T-shirt and a pair of panties. Her face, arms and legs were about the color of a stoplight, Laura thought.

"Didn't you use sunscreen?" Laura asked.

"I was trying to catch up with you. I'm cooked. Oh, god I'm in pain."

"Come over here in the light and let me see," Laura said, grimacing once she did.

"At least this will give me something to get my mind off everything else," Noell said.

Being a doctor's wife did have some advantages, Laura thought. Jay had given her thorough instructions on how to treat every known beach ailment from sunburn to jellyfish stings to shellfish poisoning. She went to her bedroom and emerged with a large duffel bag.

"The medicine kit," she told Laura.

"Damn almighty," Noell said. "I haven't seen this much dope since I went to a Grateful Dead concert at Duke. Any Quaaludes in there? They might help."

"Probably. There's no telling what's in here."

She found some pills for pain. And some hydrocortisone cream and some Benadryl spray.

"You should eat something with these pills," Laura said.

"Just open that bottle of wine I brought. I'll wash 'em down with that."

"No. You can't drink anything with these. I could just see that headline in the Farmington paper now: 'Local Attorney ODs at Babson Beach Retreat.' "

Noell ate but only a small amount. Then took the pills.

"Tell Bonnie it was great," she said.

"I will. Now go take off your shirt and lie on the bed and I'll put this cream and spray on your back," Laura said.

"Hey, this could get interesting," Noell said.

"Will you shut up? And if you tell anybody about this—"

"It'll be just between us boys."

As Laura was applying the cream, Noell asked her, "Do you think I'm a terrible person?"

"No."

"Yes, you do."

"I do not."

"You should."

"You're not a terrible person, Noell. You're a wonderful person. I think a lot of you."

"But that was a pretty terrible thing I did, huh? That fling with old fart-face Dan Harvey."

"Is that what this is all about?" Laura asked.

"Among other things."

"I thought you said y'all had put it behind you."

"I lied. Jim never put it behind. He never let it down. 'Where are you going? When will you be home? Who are you going with? Who was that who called?' It just got to be too much."

"I thought you said he hadn't been faithful either."

"I don't know. I have my suspicions, that's all. But he always denied it. But I really think in his mind it's OK for him and not OK for me. Does that make any sense? And then there's that damn thing about children. It's not my fault I've got bum ovaries. Blame my mom or blame my dad or my great-great ancestors but don't blame me."

"It's nobody's fault," Laura said.

"But it really bothered Jim. He really wants children."

"You could have adopted."

"Oh, hell no. He wants one with 'Beaman blood running through its veins.' I'm gonna shut up. I'm getting depressed again. You think Jay would write me a prescription for Prozac?"

"I doubt it. But look, Noell, you'll be OK. I know you. You'll be all right."

"But I shouldn't have done it," Noell said glumly.

"Done what?"

"That thing with Dan. I should have known better. Shown more restraint. Used a little common sense. I know you wouldn't have done something like that."

Laura thought for a minute. She wanted to say something. Started to, then stopped when Noell slammed her fist on the bed and yelled, "I'm sorry I fucked up. How many goddam times did I say it to him? How many goddam ways? I'm sorry I didn't live up to his goddam expectations. But I just didn't. I didn't know that was my goddam job."

Laura stroked Noell's hair. "It's OK, Noell," she said. "It's OK. Really."

After Noell gained her composure, Laura said, "I had an affair once."

"You're shitting me."

"No, I'm not. I did. I'm not very proud of it, but I did."

"You gonna tell me who?" she asked, trying to force a smile.

"No."

"C'mon."

"No," Laura said. "You don't even know him. It was a long time ago. A long, long time ago."

"Did you tell Jay?"

"Of course not."

"You think you ever will."

"No. And if you ever tell—"

"I would never—"

"All I was going to say was: If you ever tell anybody, I will deny it. Till the day I die."

Laura had finished with the cream. Noell slipped on her shirt and gingerly sat up on the bed.

"You know, Laura, some people will tell you that the key to a good relationship is complete honesty. But I think the key just might be almost complete honesty tempered with just the right amount of dishonesty."

"You may be right," Laura said with a chuckle.

"Makes sense, doesn't it. After all, we all make mistakes, don't we?"

"Yes. Yes, we do."

"No point in letting them ruin your life, huh?"

"That's for sure," Laura said. "And I'd like to think that both of us have a lot of life in front of us."

Chapter Thirty-Five

Wednesday, August 4

Laura didn't know why she had put it off. Some couldn't have done that. But for her it was easy, even natural. She had lived a life of putting off things she wanted to do in favor of doing what others wanted to do—for the most part, she thought, until a few times this summer at least.

She had wanted to go to the Bird Island mailbox since Friday, but other things had come up. She'd been with the children all weekend. And now Noell. But it worked out on this cloudy afternoon that Noell, Bonnie, Meagan and Jacob were caught up in a game of Monopoly around three o'clock. It had rained on and off all day, which was a blessing for Noell.

"I really need to go do something," Laura said. "Take about an hour or so. If y'all don't mind."

"Heavens no," Bonnie said.

"Where are you going?" Noell asked.

"Just something I need to do. OK?"

"No problem."

She thought about walking to the mailbox, but it would take so long. She didn't want to get caught in a shower on foot. She decided to drive to Julie's Sweet Shop, rent a bike and go for it. Ten bucks, what the heck.

The ride was a pleasant one, a southeast breeze zoomed her down the beach, the bike wheels' thick treads flinging damp sand on her. It won't be easy coming back, she thought. But she was in shape. She knew she could handle it.

She made it through the inlet easily, the tide was just right. And at last she reached the place. The bench beside the mailbox was deserted. She flipped through the steno pads and finally found it. Neal's had to be the worst handwriting in the bunch, she thought. But still she could make out the words:

July 29

Dear Kindred Spirit,

I've been thinking a lot about you, your name that is. It would be a great name for a quarterback, I think. But in looking through my dictionary—I'm a writer by profession; we're into the dictionary deal—I found a lot of definitions for both your first and last name. Let's take the first name first. Kindred: As I remember, it's things such as related by blood, like, similar, one with which one has an affinity. As for spirit: soul, a supernatural being, a person's emotional or moral nature, state of mind, personality.

To be honest, it all kind of left me confused. Now I know what Kindred Spirit means to a lot of people who visit Bird Island. I can tell that by reading through the letters. Some think you're like God. Others think you're this pervasive feeling of decent mankind that will save this island from the perils of development. All that's great with me. But to tell you the truth, I don't think God has a mailbox on Bird Island. I could be wrong—I have been before. But I just don't think so. And I also think (sorry, pal) one day this place will be developed. They'll build a bridge from Sunset to Bird, bury a bunch of damn septic tanks in the ground, pave a few roads and build six-(hell, probably seven-) figure homes. If I could stop it by chaining myself to a sand dune or something, maybe I would do it. But I've got other stuff to do. Still, maybe there are enough dune-huggers around here that will at least stave it off. Nevertheless, just in case you are God, I want you to know I'm making a very generous donation to the Bird Island Preservation Society.

So, what's this all about? I'm not even sure now. But I guess what I'm trying to say is that the term "Kindred Spirit," according to the definitions at least, can mean a lot of different things to different people. Nothing wrong with that as I see it. So here's what it means to me:

I think sometimes you just connect with some people. It's an intangible thing. My profession deals with athletic competition. I've seen it many times. People connecting with other people to achieve something beyond what any of the individuals ever dreamed possible. National championship trophies, Super Bowl rings, Stanley Cups and the like. Or maybe just a winning season when all us experts were predicting the pits. But if you ask any of them about it, it's not the trophies, rings and cups they remember. It's the feelings they shared that were important.

This summer I had such an experience. I connected with someone. At Sunset Beach and on Bird Island, too. (Hope you didn't mind.) Never, ever, have I connected with someone like that before. We had a certain affinity. A certain shared state of mind. But there were complications. Many complications. But take my word on this: until I quit breathing, until I quit living, I'll be hoping. And I want her to know that if there's something I can do to make it happen, I'll do it. She doesn't think so, but I would. All she's got to do is tell me.

But even if we never connect again, and maybe we won't, I want her to know that for a time there we were of Kindred Spirit — at least my definition of it. We will always have that.

NN

Hard to top that, Laura thought. After all, he is a writer, even if he is just a sportswriter. But after a time she wrote:

August 4

Dear Kindred Spirit,

I did something this summer I can only describe as terribly wonderful or wonderfully terrible. I'm not sure. At this point, I'm not sure I know the difference. There's so much I could say, but I'm afraid it would all be inadequate in light of what has already been said. So I'll just say this: I also "connected" with someone this summer. If there were some relatively painless way for all involved, we still would be today. But I can't see it. I can't see a path to that. All good things must end, right? At least that's what they say. I for one always hoped they were wrong, but I guess they're right.

But I will, nonetheless, fondly remember the time when, as my friend sort of said, we were the Spirit.

LB

CHAPTER THIRTY-SIX

Thursday, August 5

NOELL LEFT AROUND NOON. Much to do, she said. The sunburn turned out not to be so bad.

"I think I've got a good base now," she said as Laura walked her to the car. "Maybe I'll lay out or go to a tanning bed before I start work. Get a good tan. I want to be looking good that first day. Might even show up the first day without hose. That would be a hoot."

"I think I would wear hose in the attorney general's office," Laura said.

"But that would be a good way, right off the bat, of showing my creativeness and independence."

"I think I would wear hose," Laura said.

"OK, mama. I will."

Laura hugged her friend.

"You're crying!" Noell said. "Don't do this to me."

"I'm sorry," Laura said. "I'm just going to miss you."

They hugged again.

"You better come see me," Noell said. "And often. As soon as I find a place you and the kids will have to come up and spend the weekend. We'll go shopping and to the museums, a concert, whatever. And bring Doc. But only if you have to."

"That'll give him a chance to go to the sailboat."

"Oh, the boat," Noell said. "We hadn't even talked about that. I've never even seen it. I guess we really screwed that up for y'all."

"It's OK."

"Jim's going to offer to let Jay buy his half."

"Whatever. I don't care," Laura said. "They can do whatever."

"I think you should go ahead and tell Jay about the separation. I'm sure Jim hasn't. I don't think he's told anybody but his parents."

"I will."

After Noell left, Laura went inside the cottage. She felt restless. Bonnie had gone shopping. The children went with some neighbors to see a movie in Myrtle Beach. It was cloudy and had rained on and off all morning. The forecast was for more of the same. She didn't feel good about her children being with people she hardly knew. The Russells from Tennessee. They were on their second week, and they seemed like nice people. Jacob and Meagan had hit it off well with their children. It had been a blessing. The children were just fine with them. Why did she always worry so much? About everything at that.

She sat down in the den and turned on the TV, only to turn it off again a few seconds later. She picked up a magazine and thumbed through the pages. Two more days and they would be at home. And when was Jay coming down? They hadn't talked since Monday and he had been vague.

He did say he'd close the office early Friday and get down as soon as he could. Help pack up, clean up and haul them all home on Saturday. Knowing him it would probably be midnight Friday before he got here, Laura thought — after she and Bonnie had already done all the packing and cleaning.

Suddenly Laura slammed the magazine down on the floor and headed for the telephone. She dialed Jay's office. It was twelve-twenty-two. They should have the morning patients about cleared out. The office closed from twelve-thirty to two each afternoon for lunch. Then the second shift came. The last appointment time was five-thirty. But like all doctors' offices, the schedule always ran an hour or so behind, sometimes two. No one was turned away. Forty bucks here, fifty there, Medicare here, Medicaid there. They just kept coming and he kept treating them.

"Connie, this is Laura. Is Jay available?"

"He's with a patient, Mrs. Babson. Can I have him call you?"

"I'll hold. Tell him it's important."

"Is something wrong?"

"I just need to talk with him as soon as possible."

She's a nosy little snot, Laura thought. I've never liked her.

Jay finally came on the line in about five minutes. "What's wrong?" were his first words. "Something with Mom? Or the kids?"

"No, Jay, I just need to talk to you."

"About what?"

Laura was nervous. But she was going to do it. "I want to know when you're going to get your goddam ass down here."

"What in the world is wrong with you?" he yelled.

"I'm sorry. But we've got to check out by nine-thirty Saturday morning and there's a lot of packing and cleaning to do and I want to know if you're going to be down here tomorrow afternoon to help or if you're going to get here at midnight and let me and Bonnie do it all."

"I'll be there as soon as I can," he said with indignation. "I'm trying to make a—"

"But the real thing is Noell's been down here," Laura said as if she didn't hear Jay, "and she's told me something that I'm really upset about and I need to talk to you about it."

Had Laura seen Jay's face at that very moment, she would have seen the blood drain from it. Oh, shit! he thought.

"What did she tell you?" he asked sheepishly.

"I'll talk to you about it when you get down here. I don't want to talk about it on the phone. Hell, Connie's probably listening in anyway. Are you there, Connie?"

Laura thought she heard a click on the line. But she wasn't sure.

Jay was in a panic. Damn, I can't believe this has happened, he thought. How did Noell find out about this? What if Jim told her? Maybe Darrell told? Damn.

"Look, just calm down," Jay said frantically. "Calm down. We'll work this out. I've got about three more in the waiting room, I think. I'll have Connie reschedule the afternoon and tomorrow — send them to Tu or something. I ought to be out of here in thirty minutes or so. I'll run by the house and get some clothes. Then I ought to be there by five. Is that OK?"

Am I dreaming? Laura thought. The man is actually going to close the office and come down here? I don't believe it.

"That would be good," Laura said.

"Great. I'll see you soon," Jay said. "And Laura. I love you. I really do. We'll talk about this. There's a logical explanation."

"Good," she said.

When Laura hung up the phone, she felt disoriented.

"It worked," she said aloud. "I don't believe this. It worked. I took control. I spoke my mind. And it worked. I don't believe it. Something must be wrong."

"DADDY'S HERE," MEAGAN YELLED around five. I still don't believe it, Laura thought.

But Jay was there. He brought his suitcase in. Hugged his kids, his mother and his wife.

"This is a pleasant surprise," Bonnie said. "I couldn't believe it when Laura said you were coming today."

"Glad I could work it out. Didn't want y'all to have to do all the packing and cleaning. Plus I missed y'all."

He went to the bedroom to change into some shorts. Laura followed.

"Maybe we should go for a walk," he said.

"That'll be fine," she said.

They left the Laughing Gull and walked to 40th, Laura's familiar route. They walked in silence for a time. The sun had finally come out, warming up the wet pavement, small clouds of steam floated about their feet. It was humid and Jay was sweating. It's hot, but it isn't all that hot, Laura thought.

"I'm glad you came down," she finally said. "I'm sorry I was so harsh on the phone. I was just upset. That's all."

"Look," Jay said, though he wasn't looking at her. "I can explain this whole thing."

It was an explanation he'd rehearsed over and over on the long drive to the beach.

"I don't know what Noell told you," Jay said, "but nothing happened. Nothing."

What in the hell is he talking about? Laura thought.

"It was dumb. I know I shouldn't have done it. But nothing happened. Nothing."

Laura thought for a second. "Why don't you just tell me the whole story, Jay. And start at the beginning, please"

"OK. I'm going to tell you the real story. I don't know what Noell—"

"I know you don't. I just want you to tell me."

"I guess I just got carried away with the sailing or something or the excitement of the boat. I don't know. I've looked forward to getting that boat."

"So tell me."

"Anyway, after y'all left that day, we had a really good sail."

"The day after camp was over."

"Yeah, right. And we were coming in and Darrell and Jim started talking about going out for dinner to this place down there that had a band and I said I couldn't. That I had to get to the hospital. And they kept on and on and—"

"And on!" Laura said. "Just tell me."

"Anyway, I didn't really want to go, but it was like they'd think I was like . . . I don't know . . . henpecked or something."

"Henpecked? You? Me?"

"I don't know. Henpecked or something."

"You mean pussy-whipped," Laura said. "You didn't want them to think you were pussy-whipped."

"Laura!" he said in astonishment.

"Go on. Tell me."

"Anyway, so we went out."

"And?"

"And I drank more than I should have. A lot more. I don't know when I've been so drunk. Not since college. You remember that time when I was in med school and they had that keg party —"

"Don't change the subject, Jay. What happened?"

"Well, I was real drunk."

"I understand that. What happened?"

"Nothing. I told you that. I wasn't so drunk that I don't distinctly remember that nothing happened."

"So nothing happened?"

"Not really. I'll admit I did dance with her a few times."

I'm not believing this, Laura thought.

"I hardly remember them coming back to the boat with us. That's the truth."

I'm really not believing this, Laura thought.

"But nothing happened. I didn't even know they had spent the night until the next morning. Honest. I woke up and saw this damn woman beside me and my head was pounding and I was like —"

"I'm definitely really not believing this," Laura said. "You mean to tell me you slept with a woman on our boat?"

"I didn't sleep with her," he said. "She just slept beside me, I guess. I don't know. Sometimes I think maybe Darrell set it all up or something. Or maybe he and Jim. What did Noell tell you?"

"Nothing."

"Whatta you mean?"

"She didn't tell me anything about that. She told me she and Jim are getting a divorce."

"A divorce. Over this?"

"No, Jay. Not over this. I swear, the way you jump to conclusions I'm surprised you can diagnose a common cold. Noell doesn't even know about that night in Oriental. Or if she does, she didn't tell me."

"So who told you?" he asked.

"Don't you understand? You did."

"What?"

"I didn't know anything about this wild night on the boat. What I was so upset about was the Noell and Jim are splitting up. Noell's moving to Raleigh. She's already got a job up there. In the attorney general's office."

"Now I'm not believing this," Jay said.

"Let's walk on the beach," she said. By this time they were at the beach access. They walked across it in silence, broken only when Jay spoke to everyone he met.

"Hi," someone said.

"Fine and you?" he replied.

Once they were on the beach, Laura directed him east.

"But it looks more deserted that way —"

"I said that way," she said, pointing to the pier.

Finally Laura brought the conversation back around.

"So the only reason you told me was because you thought Noell told me," she said. "Is that it?"

"No. I was going to tell you. Really I was. The next time I saw you."

"If you had wanted to tell me, you could have come down here that next day. Or the next day. Or the next. It's not like you couldn't find me. And what did you do last weekend? Go out dancing again?"

"No. I worked all weekend. Really. Look, Laura, I'm so sorry. This thing has worried the hell out of me. I was going to tell you. I just didn't know how. But I'm glad I have. I know you're mad and I don't blame you. But I'll make it up to you. You've got to believe I would never do anything, not intentionally, to jeopardize our marriage. I mean, you and the kids are everything to me."

"Everything to you?" Laura said. "Jay, we're nothing to you."

"That's not true."

"Jay, if we were everything to you, you would have been down here this summer with us. If we were everything to you, you'd come home at a decent hour each night. If we were everything to you, you'd hire a doctor and spend a little bit of time with us. If we were everything to you, you wouldn't have gone out that night in Oriental with the guys because either we would have been on the boat with you or you would have been here with us. So don't stand there and say we're everything to you."

"I know, but work, Laura, that's a different thing. I know I shouldn't have done that in Oriental. That was dumb. I know. But work, Laura, I mean, I don't have a choice there."

Should I say it? Laura thought. When would there be a better time? Never. Get it out. He's on the defensive here.

"Get real, Jay," she said. "If you never worked another day in your life you'd never run out of your father's money."

He was stunned. "How do you know how much money my father has?"

"I don't think he has any now, unless he managed to take some with him."

"I didn't mean that. How do you know? Noell tell you?"

"No. Estates are public records. I went to the courthouse and looked it up one day."

"You did what?"

"Well, it seemed you weren't going to tell me. I think I have a right to know, especially when my children are involved."

"Why didn't you ask me?" Jay said.

"Why should I have to ask? Why didn't you tell me?"

"I don't know."

"I think you do."

Jay stopped walking and put his head down.

"Your father—he told you not to tell me, didn't he?" Laura said, wondering if she was going a little too far.

Jay looked away and wouldn't speak.

"And he told you not to hire another doctor, too, didn't he?"

Still no answer. Silence means consent, Laura thought.

"Wow," Laura said. "What a legacy: Keep your wife in the dark and keep your practice to yourself, son. Don't trust anybody. Don't ever trust anybody, especially not a woman. Was it something like that? Jay, at the risk of my life here, let me just mention something."

"What?"

"Your father's dead. And at times I think our marriage isn't too far behind."

She turned and walked the other way, back toward 40th Street.

"Laura, wait. What are you saying? I'm really sorry, but I really don't think this one night, this one mistake should—I mean, I've never been unfaithful to you."

"Jay, I don't give a damn about that one night in Oriental. Big deal. You got drunk and made an ass of yourself. Who hasn't done that?"

"So what are you talking about?" he asked.

"Jay, evidently your idea of being faithful and mine are a little different. I'm supposed to be honored that you've never run out on me when you won't even take the time of day to act—not say—but act like I mean something to you."

"I don't know what you're saying, Laura. It's like I just don't understand you anymore."

"I'd say you've got that just about right. If you don't understand the importance of things like birthdays and a night out on the town once in a while with your wife, you most certainly do not understand me. But maybe you could if you tried. Jay, all of this could have been avoided. All of it. I'm not saying it's all your fault. It's mine, too. But it all could have been avoided."

"All of what?" he asked.

"All of this damned unpleasantness, Jay," she said. "We could have avoided it—should have avoided it."

They walked on in silence until they reached the 40th Street access where Laura asked, "You ready to head back to the cottage?"

"If you wouldn't mind, I'd like to walk on the beach some more. By myself. If that's all right."

"Sure. That'll be fine. I'll be at the house."

Once on the walkway, she stopped at the spot where Neal had waited for her those many mornings. Neal, she thought. How could she have done that? And after she had, how could she have let him go? But she had done that, too. And now look what was left in its wake.

She watched Jay walk down the beach toward Bird Island. He looked like someone she didn't know. About the only thing they had in common right now, she thought, was a last name, an address and two children. But it didn't have to be that way. She stared off in the distance at the huge mound of sand that was Bird Island. She could see it plainly.

She'd get through this, she thought. Somehow she'd get through this. Maybe she should tell him about Neal. Maybe in time she would. But why? Just to make her feel better and him worse? Absolve her guilt and rub his face in it. No, she wouldn't tell him. And no, she wasn't going to feel guilty about it. It just happened—there was no undoing that.

What a bizarre day this turned out to be, she thought. But it wasn't all bad, was it? No, not at all. In many ways it was a good day; in many ways it was a start. Not much of one, perhaps, but at least a start. She'd see to that. And an end as well. She'd already seen to that.

After she turned and headed toward the street, Laura paused, looked again toward Bird Island and said with a slight smile, "Thank you, Kindred Spirit."

CHAPTER THIRTY-SEVEN

Saturday, August 7

LAURA RETURNED FROM HER walk, the final walk of the summer, about seven-thirty in the morning. In two hours or less, they'd leave the Laughing Gull, their home for the last seven weeks. Jay was just getting up. He'd been very cooperative, the tension between them still evident but steadily waning.

"I'll start loading the cars as soon as I get something to eat," he said.

"What can I fix you?" Laura asked.

"I'll just get some cereal or something," he said.

By eight the children were up. Bonnie had left the day before to visit Frances again. She'd come home to Farmington Sunday.

"You go. We'll take care of all the cleaning," Laura had told her. "It's the least we can do."

As they were getting the cottage organized, Jay observed, "We need to try to get to the bridge before ten. That should put us at that McDonald's on I-40 around lunchtime. We can stop there and then we'll be back home early in the afternoon."

"Jay, I was thinking," Laura said, "that maybe we could go to Southport and take the ferry over to Fort Fisher. The kids would enjoy that."

"Isn't that out of the way?"

"Sure. And maybe stop at the aquarium there. I've heard it's pretty good. Then maybe have lunch in Wilmington at some place decent. And if the weather's good, maybe even tour the battleship. Jacob's been wanting to do that."

"I don't know, Laura. Aren't you ready to get on home?" Jay asked.

"Not really," she said.

"Oh."

"Just kidding. But maybe it will do us all good to take the long way home for once. Just the four of us. We'll still be back before dark."

To her surprise, Jay didn't argue. And he even kept his composure when, around nine as he was loading the cars, it rained again.

"You're soaked," Laura said when he came in the house.

"I won't melt," he calmly replied. "But I don't know if we should take the ferry if it's raining. But I'll let you lead the way. You decide."

By nine-twenty they had left the cottage and driven to the real estate office to drop off the keys. By the time they reached the bridge, the sun made another appearance. Maybe they'd take the ferry after all, Laura thought. But either way, she'd decide.

The line of traffic waiting to exit the island was a long one, as always was the case on Saturday mornings in the summer—vacation over for many, just starting for others. From the rearview mirror of the Suburban, Laura could see Jay and Jacob behind her, seated in the Mazda. She thought about the day she snapped. Almost snapped. It seemed silly now.

It would be high tide soon, Laura deduced from watching the cars ahead go over the bridge. The floating portion of the bridge, the wooden planks in the middle, was flanked by large sheets of metal that were hinged at each end, connecting to the fixed portions of the bridge. At low tide, the middle of the bridge was below the level of the causeway. Cars went down the metal sheet, then onto the wooden planks, then back up the metal connector on the other side. At high tide, the bridge formed a large hump. Somewhere between, it was level. A simple functional design, it served its purpose well.

Laura watched as the water flowed steadily back into the marsh on either side of the road, the tidal creeks having taken shape again, as they did twice a day. The same thing again and again, day after day. Every twenty-four hours and fifty-one minutes, she remembered, the moon would circle the earth, the seas in tow. Two high tides and two low tides. The pontoon bridge at Sunset Beach would rise and it would fall, the bridge tenders watching the cars come and go. And on the hour, they would open the bridge, allowing the boats to make their way. Over and over it would happen. No matter what.

Sure, Laura thought, they could knock down that old bridge and build a new one, probably would one day. And they could put houses on Bird Island, probably would do that, too. After all, people — not moons and tides — were in charge of those decisions. And we people will continue to commit our indiscretions and fall victim to our frailties, all the while showing callousness where kindness is needed. In that regard, we're as reliable as the tides it seemed. And after all, she reasoned, weren't humans and their feeble attempts at relationships just a bit trivial compared to things of real constancy. We put too much ego into it, too much pride. And never enough caring, never enough effort.

But that didn't mean she couldn't try, try just a little harder. If she chose to. And maybe she would. But would he? Maybe so.

As that bridge rose and fell, Laura presumed, some people would be happy, others sad. Some would do right, others would screw up. And all would grow older — some learning a thing or two along the way, others not.

Meagan interrupted her. Laura had almost forgotten she was in the car with her.

"Mom," she said, "what are you thinking about?"

"Oh, nothing . . . but look!" Laura said, pointing at the marsh on Meagan's side. "An egret. Isn't it lovely?"

"Sure is," Meagan said. "You know, I wrote a poem about an egret. Did I read it to you?"

"No, I don't think so, but I'd love to hear it." She had enjoyed Meagan's poetry this summer — most of it at least.

Meagan searched through a notebook she called not her journal but rather her "journey," found the poem and began to read:

> The Regret of the Egret
> By Meagan Babson
> One glorious sunrise on Sunset,

"Did you get that part?" Meagan asked. "Sunrise on Sunset?"

"Yes, I got that part. Very clever. Now start over."

"OK," she said.

> The Regret of the Egret
>
> By Meagan Babson
>
> One glorious sunrise on Sunset,
>
> I met a quite talkative Egret.
>
> I asked if he had a regret;
>
> He said none that he couldn't forget.

"Very good," Laura said. "No . . . excellent." She put her right hand on the top of Meagan's head, leaned over, pulled her close, kissed her forehead and said, "I love you."

"I love you, too, Mom."

As the traffic crept forward, they admired the waterway, the mid-morning sunlight glancing off its flat surface.

"It's so calm now," Meagan said.

"Storm's over," Laura observed quietly.

"Mom?"

"Yes."

"Are you crying?"

Laura wiped a tear from her cheek. "I guess I am—just a little."

"I'm kind of sad, too. I'm gonna miss the beach."

"Me, too."

"Do you think we'll ever go to Sunset again?"

"Sunset," she said, pausing a moment. "I doubt it."

"You're kidding, right?"

"Right," Laura said with a smile. "I'm kidding."

"I thought so."

Just then Laura again glanced in her rearview mirror and saw Jay and Jacob talking. Something funny must have been said—or done. They were both laughing. Jay finally looked her way. She waved and he waved back. It was good to see him smiling for a change.

At last the light was green in their direction. Laura maneuvered the Suburban onto the fixed portion of the bridge as she had done so many times that summer. After climbing the metal sheet, it rumbled over the wooden planks. She heard the familiar muffled noise that sounded like distant thunder, though it was always just beneath her. They passed the bridge tender's station, descended the metal sheet on the other side and at last reached the road.

Safe passage to the mainland, safe passage to home.

EPILOGUE

Saturday, December 18

NEAL NEVER WAS SURE why he had asked for the assignment that day. Not that it was unusual for him to cover a North Carolina Tar Heels basketball game. But this one didn't promise to be much of a contest—the highly ranked Heels playing host to a hapless bunch who probably would be collecting autographs after the game.

The game lived up to all his expectations. Midway through the first half, Carolina led by more than twenty. The afternoon crowd in the massive Dean E. Smith Student Activity Center—the "Dean Dome"—numbered about 13,000, leaving more than 8,000 seats empty. The students were away for the holiday break. With still ten minutes left in the first half, the opponents' head coach called his second time-out of the game, following a steal and thunderous dunk by one of UNC's many superstars.

Neal was sitting at the press table at the west end of the court, by this time totally bored. He was taking a few notes when the crowd suddenly let out one of its biggest cheers of the day. At the other end of the court, through one of the archways leading back to the dressing rooms, a familiar figure emerged. But rather than dressed in red and white—the colors of UNC's arch-rival N.C. State—this Santa Claus wore a Carolina Blue suit trimmed in white fur.

Neal chuckled as the crowd roared. He glanced above Santa to the scoreboard to note the time. "Maybe I'll interview that guy," he mumbled.

It was just then he saw her—or at least thought he did. Had to be her. Her husband and kids, too. They were seated under one of the scoreboards in the corner of the lower deck. Pretty good seats, Neal thought. Old Doc must have paid dearly for them. At an earlier game that season he had noted the names of Dr. and Mrs. Jacob Willard Babson Sr. on the arena's fancy donor roster at the main entrance. The rights to purchase tickets passed only by will.

Neal had wondered all through the football season if he would have a chance meeting with Laura at a Carolina game in Kenan Stadium. He had never asked where their seats were. He once spent an entire quarter surveying the crowd through binoculars, but trying to find even Laura in a crowd of more than 50,000 was hopeless.

Neal got the attention of Elliot, who was making ample use of a photo pass. "E, let me borrow a camera with a long lens. Longest you got," Neal said.

Elliot complied, bringing Neal a Nikon with a 300MM lens. Neal framed the Babsons in the viewfinder. Jay was in the aisle seat. Then Jacob, followed by Laura and Megan. He continued to keep an eye on them, losing track of the game.

It was with just under nine minutes left in the first half, with the Tar Heels shooting a free throw at the basket nearest Neal, that he saw Laura get up, move past Jay and start up the steps to the portal that led to the concourse. Neal quickly got up from his press seat and went up the nearest aisle. He was nearly out of breath when he reached the top, looking intently to his right. He saw Laura enter the restroom outside section 124.

Neal considered forgetting about it but instead walked down the nearly deserted concourse and leaned against the wall outside the women's room. A huge picture of the 1974-75 Tar Heels hung above his head. That had been Phil Ford's freshman season, Neal remembered. Carolina beat State in the finals of the ACC Tournament. He had covered it, had written a damn good story on Ford.

Though Laura was in the restroom for only a minute, Neal felt as if she would never emerge. He could feel sweat dripping down his left side. He hoped his hair was in place. He cupped his hand in front of his mouth and exhaled, checking his breath.

Just then she walked out, no more than ten feet away. She turned left toward the concession stand, unzipping the leather purse she carried on her left shoulder.

"Merry Christmas, Starshine," Neal said.

Laura stopped and looked over her shoulder as Neal approached.

"Merry Christmas to you," she replied calmly.

"How are you?"

"Good. And you?"

"Still not as good as you, but I'm working on it."

Laura wore a white knitted turtleneck sweater decorated with various Christmas scenes. And a short, black pleated wool skirt, black tights and flat black suede shoes that had holly leaves stitched about the top. Her hair, still shoulder-length, was darker, her skin fairer than the last time Neal had seen her. Her hair was pushed behind one ear, exposing a gold starfish earring.

Neal had seen the earrings in the jewelry store in Raleigh one day while looking for a new money clip. He wrapped the earrings and mailed them, without a note, to Laura Babson, Farmington, NC. He didn't know the address but figured correctly that in Farmington it wouldn't make much difference.

"I got the earrings. Thanks," she said. "You shouldn't have."

"How did you know they were from me?"

"I wonder," she said. "It's not every day I get earrings in the mail. Plus I recognized that sloppy handwriting."

"I'm glad you're wearing them."

"I've only got a minute," she said. "Kids want popcorn."

Inside the arena, the crowd cheered another Carolina score. So many things they could say, they both thought. But why try in a minute? But why not?

"You look great, Laura," he said. "Really great."

"You, too. I've never seen you in a tie before. Or long pants for that matter."

"Never seen you with hose on. You look good. But a bathing suit does seem to suit you better."

"Only you would think so."

"So how's life in the metropolis of Farmington?" Neal asked. "I guess your husband finally got a day off."

"Things are pretty good, actually. Jay and I have really had it out a few times over certain philosophical differences. A few times there I thought I was going to have to go live with you."

"You'd be welcomed with open arms," he said.

"But it's getting better. It's getting there. Plus, Jay hired some consultant to assess his practice and the guy convinced him he'd make more money if he hired not only one doctor, but two. One started the week after Thanksgiving. Another's on the way. I think it's going to work out."

"I hope it does, Laura."

"Me, too."

"And I'm sure your kids are keeping you busy."

"Very. And, oh, I almost forgot: I got a part-time job."

"You're kidding."

"No. Believe it or not, I coached the girls tennis team at ole Farmington High this fall."

"So how'd that come about?" he asked, not sure if he should tell her he'd already heard about her job from another source.

"It's a long story and one of the biggest scandals in town. The former coach, this young guy who taught at the high school, apparently had a few private lessons over the summer with the number three player. Just as the season was starting, they found out she was pregnant. He was quickly exiled from the county, of course, even though some locals said the girl was all to blame. You know how that is. Anyway, the principal was in a bind and he knew I had played tennis and next thing I knew I said yes. He's even asked me to coach the boys' team this spring. But that one's still in doubt. Word is some of the school board members have 'expressed concern' about a so-called 'attractive female' coaching the boys, if you know what I mean. I sent word back that I would make sure they wore condoms if things got out of hand."

"Good for you," Neal said.

"It's really been fun—even though we had a pretty lousy team. Meagan was my assistant. She plays all the time now. By the end of the season I think she could have been in the top six. But gosh, Neal, here I am just talking about me. What's up with you? I've actually been reading your columns. And I saw the book in a bookstore. I bought it."

Not much, he reported. Trying to make the transition from football season to basketball. He was making a feeble attempt at another book. And his golf game was steady, maybe even improving a little, which it seldom did this time of year. "Our little agreement has been a constant source of inspiration," he said.

"I told you I was only considering it," she said.

"That's enough inspiration for me."

"Of course, I figured you already had a new flame," Laura said teasingly.

"Well, sort of," he replied. "Funny I should see you. Guess you hadn't heard. Or have you?"

"Actually, yes. I just wanted to see if you'd fess up to it."

"So Noell told you?"

"She's never been one to keep secrets."

"I should have figured as much," he said. "You never told her about us, did you?"

"Are you kidding? And you won't either if you know what's good for you."

"Oh, I promise. Not a word," he said. "But I did want you to know this wasn't really my idea. I mean, she called me first."

"Hey, I got no problem with it," she said.

"It's nothing really serious at this point. We've only been out a couple of times. I mean, if there's any way you might change—"

"No, my letter still stands, I assume you read it."

"Yeah. I went the Sunday after you left. Couldn't wait for Labor Day. It was well said. Maybe you should be a writer."

"I don't know about that. But I will say I'm maybe a little envious but also excited about you and Noell. I think it's a match made in . . . well, somewhere interesting. But one word of advice: Even if she's dumb enough to ask, don't tell her she's number twenty-three."

"I've already thought of that," Neal said. "I'm just going to tell her she's my first Noell."

Laura winced. "Only you," she said, shaking her head.

"Just kidding," he said.

"I know," she said. "But really, Neal, I hopes it works out. Maybe we'll run into you two at Sunset next summer."

"So y'all are going back?"

"Oh, sure."

"Unfortunately for me, I'm left out. Elliot told me today he just sold the house. I told him I didn't want to hear about it. All I know is he thinks he got a helluva price."

"He certainly did," Laura said. "But I think it's worth it."

"You mean—"

"Bonnie. I showed it to her before we left. She was hooked. It took some scheming, but we finally convinced Jay she needed to diversify her portfolio with tangible assets. We just closed last week. I haven't even had the chance to tell Noell."

"Sonuvabitch," Neal said, shaking his head. "The king is dead."

"Long live the queen?" she asked.

He nodded and laughed. "Long live the queen."

"And it's so weird," Laura said. "It's like that house has suddenly become some big rallying point for our family. We're planning to spend New Year's there and even Jay's sisters and my parents say they're coming. Of course, I'll believe it when I see it."

"Maybe there's something to that kindred stuff after all," Neal said.

"Who knows? But with that many kindreds around, I'm just going to be ready to flex."

"Good idea," he said.

"But Neal, stick with Noell—that is if it's best for you two," she said. "Maybe y'all could even stay with us at the beach next year. Who knows?"

"Hey, if she puts up with me until next summer, we'll be there."

They looked away from each other in silence for a moment. "This has been nice," she said. "But I've really got to go."

"But before you go, Laura, please, I've got to know."

"Why?" she asked, knowing what he meant.

"It's like that movie: 'I gots to know.' Come on, tell me the truth. I deserve it, I think. And for once, a serious answer out of you would be appreciated. For just a second there, maybe just an instant, maybe for several weeks and maybe even now — it doesn't make any difference — but at some point, did you love me?"

Laura looked away from him. And then back. She took a deep breath and said, "Yes."

"I thought so."

"You knew so."

"Yeah, but I just wanted to hear you say it."

It was at that moment they actually looked directly at each other for the first time in the conversation. Neal felt his throat tighten. He thought he detected a tear in her right eye. She carried the Coke in one hand, the popcorn in the other. She took a quick step forward and kissed him on the cheek.

"Take care of yourself, Governor," she said.

"And you, Starshine," he replied numbly, realizing that indeed there were tears in her eyes — and now his as well.

Neal crossed his arms, leaned against the wall and watched her turn — turn and walk that walk, down the concourse toward the entrance to section 121. He could smell her perfume over the arena's more familiar aromas of pizza, popcorn and floor wax. The pleated skirt swayed gently above her knees. Neal stared at the hem, losing himself in it. He imagined her on the beach—on Bird Island—walking away from him. The dream. That damn dream. Was he living it? He could feel the currents pulling him through Mad Inlet, out to sea. He could taste the salt water. Yes, he must be drowning. But in what . . . love . . . lust . . . self-pity?

Then it hit him: No, she had not left him for dead. In so many ways, she had rescued him. For here he was, still breathing, still hoping. But what about her? Would she be OK? God, he hoped so, though he couldn't be sure.

Inside the arena the crowd roared again, jolting him from the trance. Twice, just before Laura turned to make her way back through the portal to her family, it looked to Neal as if she might stop—stop, turn and look his way. Both times he considered calling her name but didn't.

©Keith Barnes

About The Author

TRIP PURCELL IS A North Carolina writer whose work has appeared in numerous magazines and newspapers, including the *Durham Morning Herald*, where he was an arts and entertainment reporter, and *The Wilson Daily Times*, where he was news editor. He has a bachelor's degree in sociology from Barton College and a master's in journalism from the University of North Carolina at Chapel Hill, where he taught undergraduate writing courses. *Sunset Beach* is his first novel.